Written
On A Rock

First printing, May, 2008
ISBN Number 978-0-9799950-4-0

Front and back cover photos supplied by Martha Phillips. The front cover photo depicts The Georgia Guidestones. Information about this real-life landmark appears on pages 23-25 and 154.

Cover design by ThomasMax (Lee Clevenger and R. Preston Ward)

Published by:

ThomasMax Publishing
P.O. Box 250054
Atlanta, GA 30325
404-794-6588
www.thomasmax.com

Written
On A Rock

To: Nina's Friend — JoAn,
Hope you enjoy this
mystery — history - romance !
Martha Phillips

Martha Phillips

ThomasMax

Your Publisher
For The 21st Century

A Word from the Publisher

You hold in your hand the winning entry from the 2007 ThomasMax "You Are Published" contest held annually in conjunction with the Southeastern Writers Association's conference and workshop. *Written On A Rock* is the second annual winner. In 2006, the first year of the contest, the "book deal" was awarded to Randall Arnold of Watkinsville, Georgia, for *The Resemblance.*

This book also won the "best novel" award at the 2007 SWA Conference, judged by Lou Aronica, President of The Fiction Studio, one of the instructors at the conference.

If you are a writer, chances are that you would enjoy SWA's annual conference and workshop, held in June of each year. Our venue for more than three decades has been beautiful St. Simons Island in coastal Georgia, located near Brunswick, roughly halfway between Savannah and Jacksonville. Those who attend the conference and meet eligibility requirements may enter the ThomasMax contest (along with a host of other contests). The ThomasMax winner receives a book contract and 25 free copies of the book; the author pays nothing unless ordering additional copies.

We invite you to check out our website at www.thomasmax.com and the SWA website at www.southeasternwriters.com.

Acknowledgments

A bushel of thanks goes to family and friends who encouraged my creativeness, and to Ed for reading two drafts and giving me much needed direction, to Elizabeth who read the first awful draft and gave me great editing suggestions and her mother whose positive comment helped me make the decision to work on the next draft.

Thanks to my readers: Loraine and Nina, for continuing to encourage me to publish and to my Canadian Connections of Encouragement, Diane and Mel, whose praise built my self-esteem and enabled me to push on toward publishing. Big batches of thanks to Sharon who spent hours with editing and helping with general clean up *and* encouragement, Linda who kept me straight on song titles and facts, Sandra who did a fantastic job of helping me with the time line and Tonya who found those sneaky little typos on the *almost* final draft.

To my water aerobics class at the Athens YMCA who endured the birth and growth of many of my characters, yet allowed me to continue exercising with them and helped me control the stress in my life, I thank you.

For weekly encouragement I thank the members of the Oconee Cultural Arts Foundation's Writers' Group, especially Pat, who gave me a copy of the Southeastern Writers Association's newsletter announcing their annual conference.

Many thanks to the Southeastern Writers Association for allowing me to attend their 32nd Annual Conference where I received much needed knowledge and to Lou, the Advanced Fiction Instructor who gave this novel first prize status and gave me fabulous words of encouragement – thank you forever. To Lee and others at ThomasMax for offering a publishing prize at the conference and choosing this novel for the "You Are Published" award, I thank you for the award, the assistance you continue to give and the opportunity to be published.

My everlasting love and thanks go to Phillip, who lights up my life and keeps me balanced, and to Weaver who creates botanical gardens for my enjoyment and reads my stuff without getting ill (sick or irritable). My love forever to Eric, whose light I will always remember.

Not one person listed above is responsible for any errors found in this book. I accomplished those all on my own and apologize for each and every one of them. To all my future readers, I send my sincere thanks.

... *M. P.*

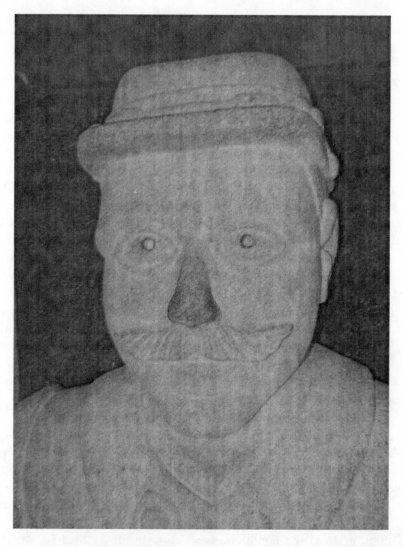

"Dutchy" is a statue of a Confederate soldier, the first granite statue made in Elberton. His checkered history is legendary in the area. Details about Dutchy can be found on pages 21-22 and 142-143. (Photo by Martha Phillips).

This work of fiction is dedicated to non-fiction victims of abuse.
May those who did not survive rest in peace.
May the survivors find a way to live in peace.

Chapter One

"Eyes of Time"

A blanket of history enveloped the town with a thickness Dee had hardly penetrated during the nine months she had been a resident. As she drove down Tate Street, turned on to North Oliver, and made her way toward the public square, she thought, "Each time I venture out I see something that makes me want to go digging into this town's past." She couldn't remember a time when she wasn't interested in history. Today made more sense to Dee if she was cognizant of yesterday's events and details of the past. Living in Elberton and daily learning more about the town and its people and their life styles made her more determined than ever to be a part of the vibrant community.

She loved everything about her adopted town . . . except now and then she would experience strange sensations, anxieties that seemed to come and go with neither pattern nor logic. As she looked to her right at the Elbert County Courthouse she thought about how Elberton, like so many small southern towns, held family secrets as well as facts that were well known. She understood how the citizens felt attached to the rich history it represented. But she didn't understand why she felt a personal attachment.

The strange sensations of familiarity definitely had something to do with living in Elberton. Prior to moving here she had never experienced such weird feelings. And there was also that same vague dream. She shrugged it off, navigated her way around the town's square and reached over to answer her cell phone. She saw her parents' phone number on the display.

"Hi, Mom."

"Hi, Love. How did you know it was me and not your dad?"

"I was sure Dad would be on the golf course by now."

"You know him well. I didn't get an answer at the apartment and decided to call you on your cell phone to ask if all is well with you. Where are you headed so early on a Saturday morning?"

"Would you believe an estate sale?"

"No! Not my daughter who hates shopping. What brought this on?"

"Emmy. She's already there and is certain there's something at the sale I really need. Want me to look for anything for you?"

"I can't think of a thing. We got rid of so much when we moved into this house and we still don't have room for another thing."

"If I see something I think you can't live without, I'll call you."

"Then you're okay?"

"I'm fine, Mom. Thanks for calling. Tell Dad 'hello' for me."

"I will. See you soon, Love. Bye."

"Bye, Mom." Dee wanted to tell her mother about the weird vague dreams but decided to wait. She had already told Emmy, her roommate, about them but had not summoned the courage to share them with anyone else.

She was lost in thought as she turned left on Georgia Highway 72. She realized the locals would never have referred to the road as Highway 72. They would have said, "Turning onto the Calhoun Falls Highway." She glanced at her odometer. The place should be about three and a half miles on the left past the turnoff. A few miles down the road she saw the remains of what once was a wooden-rail fence. About half a mile down the road the dilapidated fence was interrupted by a drive with a huge sign that read "Estate Sale By Elbert Auctions." The date and times were also listed, and she knew she was in the right place. She turned to the left even though she saw no signs of life; only a part of the roof and a chimney showed a house on the hill.

Her car meandered up the drive that had once been smooth sheets of concrete. However, the concrete had long ago cracked and broken. The holes had been filled with gravel, making her small beige Honda bounce and threaten to stop as she managed to go forward on what was left of the pitted driveway. As she slowed to a crawl to accommodate the rough ride she was able to see the landscape of the once well-kept lawn that introduced the old plantation house she knew was on the hill.

A strange streak of light to her left made her turn her head in that direction only to see a patch of land that had been idle for years where points of green shoots barely showed the new growth of grass and weeds above last year's pale dead straw. The background looked like a forest of hardwoods and pines outlined with green scrubby plants and bare vines waiting for its new growth to claim this year's space. The foliage had been creeping and adding to its territory for years. The trees grew back so far

Dee couldn't see where they stopped. A chill ran up her spine as she looked at the overgrown green space. *There it was again, that feeling of anxiousness for no apparent reason.* She realized the flash of light she had just experienced was more than strange; it was like a message sent in a split second and should mean something to her. What? She didn't know or understand what it meant. She made herself look away. Maybe she had imagined it.

The right side of the drive had escaped the vine tentacles, and trees were scarce at the bottom of the terrace, but it still looked rough and bumpy with last year's dead grass and weeds. The occasional volunteer tree or shrub poked through the tight grass and weed roots to compete for the heat and light of the sun. Amazingly, the jonquil bulbs had prospered and the field was dotted with patches of yellow and green, shining in the bright morning sunlight. Dee thought about asking permission to pick a few on her way out. They would bring the fresh look and smell of spring into their small apartment. The next terrace contained more pines and hardwoods hiding the house and its surroundings.

The drive curved slightly and Dee's vision did a quick sweep up the driveway. She got her first glimpse of the stately house at the top of the hill. With its old brick veneer and large two-story-high columns spaced across a porch that stretched from one side of the house to the other and wrapped halfway around the sides, the house possessed a majesty that only wealth and privilege could have accomplished. Pure neglect covered the house like a dark cloud with its paint-chipped wooden trim, broken and missing shutters, and roofing tiles curled or missing. Some metal rain spouts lay on the ground; others barely hung from the edge of the roofline, threatening to fall with the first puff of wind. Even so, it was clear that the original intent of the builder had been to create a showplace.

Crepe myrtle trees lined each side of the drive, their naked tan limbs lifting to the sky with abandonment, attesting that pruning shears had not been used for years. Soon small reddish-green leaves would appear on the now-barren branches. Some crepe myrtle trees had not survived the years and left empty spaces here and there.

Numerous cars parked near the house verified her late arrival. As she made her way up the drive, she saw Sophie, Emmy's old Volkswagen convertible. It was easy to spot Sophie, an antique painted white with a tan cloth top. The most distinguishing feature was Emmy's hand-painted eyelashes and eyeliner above Sophie's front headlights. Emmy loved the car because it reminded her of the "Herbie" movies of the 60's and 70's and she hardly ever talked about her car without talking about the movie.

Her family had a thing about cars. Most of their cars had names. Her mom's car was labeled "Big Mabel." Big Mabel was a huge white Lincoln Town Car and very appropriate for Mrs. Jackson, who needed plenty of space to accommodate her shopping sprees. Emmy had inherited her mom's shopping genes and had convinced Dee there would be treasures galore at this estate sale.

The Dunsman family hadn't lived in the house for years. Emmy didn't know where they were or if any of the descendants would be at the house today. According to Emmy, at one time the Dunsman family and two or three other families owned all the granite industry in Elberton, unlike today with numerous granite businesses scattered throughout the county.

The cars were parked helter-skelter with no order at all. Dee was forced to park quite a way down the drive. That suited Dee fine. It was a perfect early spring morning for getting a little exercise. In just a few weeks school would be out for summer vacation, and Dee looked forward to taking long walks and not having to do lesson plans. Most of all she was looking forward to waking without an alarm.

Dee got out of the car, stretched her tall, slender body and smoothed her dark shoulder-length hair. Her eyebrows and eyelashes matched her dark hair and highlighted her light complexion. Maybe Emmy was right and she just might find a real treasure today. Emmy had spent the night at her parents' home with the understanding she would meet Dee at the estate sale. Dee heard Emmy's hearty laugh as she looked up to see her roommate coming down the steps of the big house, her breasts bouncing with each step.

Emmy's petite frame was the opposite of Dee's tall slenderness. Emmy's sensual heart-shaped lips could tease without saying a word. Her naturally curly, short strawberry-blonde hair was worn as if the wind had just whipped through it. The freckles scattered across her nose and cheeks became more noticeable as she approached Dee.

Emmy was as creative as Dee was pragmatic. They had met at the University of Georgia when Emmy was a junior and Dee was a sophomore. They had several classes together and became good friends after their first conversation. The theory about opposites attracting certainly applied to their friendship.

Growing up in Atlanta, Dee had been absolutely taken with Emmy's small town stories. Elberton was approximately an hour's drive from Athens, home of the University of Georgia, and Dee had made that drive with Emmy several times. Emmy finished college first and returned to

Elberton to teach Language Art Classes at EMS, Elberton Middle School.

Dee graduated the following year and had applied for teaching jobs in Georgia including Cobb, Fulton and Clayton Counties. While waiting for an answer she received a call from Emmy. Dee recalled Emmy's excitement, so much so that Dee had to calm her down to get the facts. By the end of the conversation Dee not only knew about the opening for a Georgia history teacher at EMS, she found out Emmy had already talked with the school superintendent, a friend of her dad's. Dee was partial to Elberton long before she became a resident.

As Dee walked toward Emmy she wondered for the thousandth time why Emmy had chosen Language Arts, or what Emmy's mother called "Reading and Writing," instead of Visual Arts. Emmy had a flair that was definitely artsy. However, she seemed delighted to be involved in the process of developing a new curriculum for the Language Arts Program at the middle school. Emmy was well endowed with creative genes as well as shopping genes.

"Caught you!" said Emmy, "Daydreaming again! You sure had that faraway look."

Dee laughed, knowing she was prone to daydreaming.

"And just how many treasures have you laid aside?" Dee asked, noticing Emmy was empty handed.

"I have a stash on the porch. I can't wait for you to see it."

They talked as they walked to the front of the house and up the steps. "Are the books placed together, or do I have to go through the whole place to see them?" Dee questioned.

"Most of them are on shelves on the back porch. However, there are some scattered in other rooms."

They reached the top step at the same time and Emmy tugged on Dee's sleeve and pulled her to the right. "Come this way. I want you to see the hand-crocheted bedspread I found."

They wound their way around two large armoires and two trunks to get to the end of the porch. Just as Emmy described, there in the front corner of the porch near the outside edge was a small stash of Emmy's finds. Dee wondered how long Emmy had been there and if she had looked through the entire house. Emmy proceeded to separate the bedspread from the other items.

"You did see the stains, Emmy?"

"Sure. But my Granny Nida can get a stain out of anything. Besides, I expect that to be a bargaining point. It should be discounted quite a bit with those stains."

Dee laughed and remembered the many times men had mistakenly placed Emmy in the "dumb blonde" category. Emmy enjoyed playing the part and often said or did silly things to encourage the illusion. She never boasted about her great SAT scores or the fact that she placed in the top of her graduation class at the University of Georgia.

"While you find more treasures to haggle over I'm going around back to try and find something historical. I hope to find some old history books to use in class next year. I'm in somewhat of a dilemma for next year's curriculum. I'm sure glad I have all summer to work on it," Dee explained.

"Delores Dupree," Emmy admonished, "This is supposed to be a fun thing. You are making work out of it. Repeat after me. This is Saturday. I do not work on Saturday."

Dee laughed, "I know. I know. But, I can't let an opportunity get past me regarding history books. Maybe I'll find some good Elbert County history. You grew up here. You already know more from osmosis than I'll pick up if I live here the rest of my life. I promise I'll buy something frivolous today."

"That's the spirit."

"Want to meet back at the front steps when you're finished?" Dee asked.

"Or I'll find you if I finish first. I've been here since seven-fifteen and have pretty much gone through the downstairs. I don't know if they have anything upstairs. From the bedroom furniture I've seen, it looks as though they've pulled everything from upstairs and placed it downstairs and outside on the porches.'

"Okay," Dee agreed. She looked at her watch and made a mental note that Emmy had an hour's head start. Maybe she should have given her longer. Dee had no doubt she would be the one having to hunt Emmy.

Dee decided not to go down the steps and around the house because of the weeds and clutter. She stepped through the front door and had to wait a few seconds until her eyes adjusted to the dark room. Lights were on, but the sunlight from outside had been so much brighter. As her eyes adjusted to lower light, she realized she was in a large foyer. A chain from high above held a long, elegant chandelier.

There were stairs on both sides with a long landing at the top dividing the wings that led to the upstairs bedrooms. Three large stained-glass windows banked the outside wall of the second-floor landing, their prisms sending spots of color to the nooks and crannies in the downstairs foyer. As she took a few steps forward, leaving the foyer behind, she found herself in a large circular area that appeared to be a sitting room with an extremely high ceiling.

Furniture, large and small, was stacked along the walls, leaving very little of the frayed and torn wallpaper showing. Loads of family memorabilia could be seen stacked around the room. Dee wondered if there were family members alive. If so, why would anyone walk away from so many family heirlooms? The chandelier in this room made the foyer chandelier look miniature. It was a huge replica of the one in the foyer and hung from the high ceiling. A large round table below the chandelier was piled high with odds and ends. Dee could imagine this room at its best with a magnificently large flower arrangement in the center of the table. "Wow, what a showplace this was," she thought.

As she skirted around the furniture and a few treasure hunters, she made her way through to the breakfast room toward the back of the house. She saw the formal dining room off to the right as she made her way. From the breakfast room she opened the door to the closed-in back porch and saw the shelving to the right. There were plenty of books, but she wondered if she would have the patience to go through them or be able to handle the amount of dust collected on the shelves and the books.

The shelving looked as though it had been moved from the house intact with all the books on the shelves. She pulled a faded copy of *Georgia History — The American Revolution* and an autobiography written in the early 1900s about an Elbert County Negro who survived the Peon system of slavery titled *The New Slavery in the South*. She placed them on a nearby table to pick up later. She looked at the other side of the porch and saw makeshift tables with boxes and baskets of stuff. It looked as if the tables held mostly junk and had been thrown into the containers without anyone organizing or even sifting through it.

Dee picked up a flashlight from a cardboard box. Batteries were obviously in the flashlight; otherwise it would not have been so heavy. She pushed the button to see if it worked. No luck. She concluded that it had probably not been used for years. She moved a couple of grease rags and saw what looked like an eyeglasses case. She picked it up and blew the dust away. With a frown, she opened the case and for some reason felt as if she were trespassing. She had never thought of glasses as being particularly personal. She could see the top part of the black frame. She pushed her purse strap over her shoulder to free both hands, pulled the spectacles out and was surprised to see them intact . . . dusty, but in good condition. As she held the glasses the strange anxious feeling came creeping back in and the phrase "eyes of time" echoed in her head as though someone from far away had said those three words.

Dee placed the glasses back in the case and placed the case back in the box with the screwdrivers and other junk. She noticed a pair of sunglasses with one lens out. It occurred to Dee that both pairs of glasses seemed out of place in a box with tools and greasy rags. She had wasted enough time with this junk. She walked back to the bookshelves, determined to focus on titles and look at most of the books regardless of the dust. Within a few minutes she added several books to the stack she had left earlier on a table.

She had no intention of buying more than the books until she remembered her promise to Emmy that she would buy something frivolous. She wandered back to the table with the cardboard box and picked up the glasses and case. Dee thought, "What could be more frivolous than these?"

Emmy surprised Dee when she showed up ready to go. Dee was trying to balance several books, the glasses and her purse. Emmy had already paid for her purchases and locked them in Sophie for safekeeping. Emmy helped her carry her booty and showed Dee where and to whom she should pay. Everything was a bargain. Only one book cost more than a dollar, but it was worth it. It was about Elbert County and had pictures along with a synopsis of each picture. *History!* Dee was sure it would give her at least part of the background she was seeking. The glasses cost a quarter. Dee drove home and placed her estate-sale purchases in the utility room behind the kitchen near the back door. Emmy was excited about her stash and headed toward her parents' house to show her mom.

Dee spent the following Saturday with her parents in Marietta and arrived back at the Elberton apartment about ten-thirty in the evening. The girls' duplex apartment was small and they made every effort to keep it organized, yet comfortable. The kitchen was in the middle at the back of the apartment. The dining space and living area were in front of the kitchen. Emmy's and Dee's bedrooms and baths were across from each other, divided by the living room. Emmy shared the expenses and spent most weeknights in the apartment. However, Emmy spent many nights at her parents' home and always let Dee know when she would be staying with her parents.

Dee was assaulted by the strong smell of wine as she walked into the apartment. She was headed toward her room when she saw Emmy propped on the sofa like the Queen of Sheba with a "go to Hell" look that made Dee wonder if she should go on to her room or stop and talk with Emmy. She decided on the latter course. "Emmy, are you okay?"

Emmy slurred some of her s's in reply, "Why would you assk sssuch a dumb assss question?"

Dee would have laughed, but she knew Emmy well enough not to laugh when she had single handedly finished off three fourths of a bottle of Chardonnay. Emmy seldom had more than one glass of wine. She was holding her left foot up to the light as she looked at the inside of her ankle.

"What's wrong with your foot?"

"Nothing. Jusssst thinking."

"Maybe right now is not a good time to think. What's on your mind?"

"Ssee thiss?" Emmy said holding her foot up to Dee for inspection.

"Yes."

"Well, I want it off." She touched her cold wine glass to the small red and black tattoo on the inside of her ankle. Dee knew about the small butterfly outlined in black with red initials F & M inside. The ampersand was the body of the butterfly with the initials in the wings. The F was for Fred and the M stood for Em (the name Fred, her former sweetie, always called Emmy).

"Oh, Emmy, don't worry. It's so small no one sees it anyhow. Your mother still doesn't know you have it and it's been there for years."

"I don't care about that. I jusssst don't want anything on or around me that remindsss me of Fred Rafferty."

"I wonder what Fred is doing these days." When Dee first met Emmy she was living with a roommate in a two-bedroom apartment off Baxter Street in Athens. Fred had just moved in with them. All their friends knew they were crazy about each other but weren't allowed to ever say Fred lived there. Emmy didn't want her parents to know; therefore, she and her roommate screened all the telephone calls. Fred let the answering machine record the calls, and when Mr. or Mrs. Jackson came around Fred was just a friend of both girls or purposely absent. Just before Emmy graduated they broke up. Fred said he wasn't ready to commit for a lifetime. Emmy pretended it didn't matter. Dee remembered how hard it was for Emmy to hide the hurt, especially when the news got around that Fred had gotten into another relationship immediately after breaking up with Emmy. Emmy returned to Elberton and Fred stayed in Athens to complete the three years left in the six-year program with the landscape architect school.

Emmy put the wine glass up to the tattoo as though she could give the butterfly a drink. She let a few drops flow on to the butterfly and tried to lick the wine off. She couldn't get her ankle to her lips. The wine dripped on the carpet and coffee table. "Ssshit," she said. "It'sss never coming off."

Emmy was funny when she wasn't drinking and could be even more entertaining after a glass of wine. When she was happy she would share her infectious hearty laugh and would have everyone else laughing with her. Tonight was not one of those times.

"Come on, Emmy," Dee said as she took the glass of wine from Emmy's hand and placed it on the coffee table. "I think you've had enough. Even with all the yoga you do, a contortionist you are not."

Emmy was docile as Dee led her to her bedroom and pulled the covers back. Emmy climbed in without argument and Dee pulled the covers over her without trying to get Emmy to change from her T-shirt and sweat shorts. Just before turning out the light, Dee looked back toward the bed. Emmy was already sound asleep. Dee returned to the living room. She placed the almost-empty bottle of wine in the fridge, poured out what was left in the glass into the sink, wiped the wet ring caused from the wine glass left on the coffee table and headed toward her room.

As an only child, Dee found it odd to do things like putting Emmy to bed. She had never had to share with a sister. She knew Emmy would do the same for her. In fact, she had, last year when they went with a couple of other girls on a trip to the Sugar Bowl game in New Orleans. They hooked up with several other UGA students and Dee spent a lot of time with a guy named Jerry.

They started on Bourbon Street in The Quarter, drinking Hurricanes and wandering the streets from one party to another before crashing early the next morning with two more girls in the room reserved for the weekend. Later that day at the game, she didn't feel wonderful but she made it through and they partied again that evening. On Sunday, she and Jerry took a boat ride on the Natchez imbibing Bailey's Irish Crème with coffee. By the time she returned to the hotel, she barely made it to the bathroom to throw up. Jerry was not impressed and left her with Emmy, who had been on her way out with the others.

Emmy stayed with Dee and handed her a cold wet washcloth and held her hair back away from her face while she emptied everything she had swallowed the last twenty-four hours into the toilet.

The long ride home on Monday was made mostly in the rain and Dee was totally miserable. She was thankful the others did the driving while she lounged on the backseat nursing a headache and sore throat. Long ago her Aunt Connie had told her to stay healthy when drinking alcohol she should take extra vitamin C because the alcohol zapped it. Dee didn't have the vitamin and by the time they arrived back in Athens she was sick.

The next week she had to wait in line at the UGA Health Center, along with many other students whose health had suffered from the New Orleans trip. It took a round of antibiotics and several days of rest to get back to normal.

Dee learned a valuable lesson on that trip. Liquor made her sick and she vowed to stick with the occasional glass of wine and stay away from the hard stuff. She left the memories of the trip behind as her mind drifted to the glasses she purchased at the estate sale. In her mind's eye, she saw haunting dark eyes beneath thick lashes peering through the clear glass lenses. She shivered.

Chapter Two

"Calm Down, Heart"

It was several weekends later that Dee had time for the books she had purchased at the estate sale. She pulled the box from the utility room to the kitchen. Once she got the box near the kitchen table she took several books out in order to lighten the box enough to pick it up from the floor and place it in a chair. As she took each book out, she pushed the glasses case to the side. Her interest was in the books. The glasses were truly a frivolous purchase. However, she couldn't complain about the price.

Dee took an old rag from the utility room and sprayed it with furniture polish. She wasn't sure furniture polish was right for dusting the books. She knew she didn't want to use water or anything that would damage the books and cause more deterioration. As she walked back into the kitchen, she looked into the box; the glasses were the only thing remaining there. Using her foot she pushed the box aside and sat down, intent on dusting every book before she carried all of them into the living room.

It took three trips to get the dusted books to the living room coffee table. She sorted them according to subject and lined them on the bottom shelves at each end. The coffee table was long with doors in the middle for storage space and open space at each end beyond the doors. She filled up the space on both ends.

The spines of some books faced the outside toward the wall that held the television and stereo system. The remaining books — those she wanted to read first — were stacked with their spines facing the sofa within easy reach for later reading. "Summer!" Dee thought. She was hoping to have plenty of time for reading during summer vacation. She couldn't resist opening a small book about the two granite statues that had been made for the town square to honor Confederate soldiers.

The first statue, Dutchy, had been such a disappointment to the locals he hadn't lasted long. They pulled him down and buried him. She read about the building, called a shed, where the statues were cut and shaped from a huge piece of granite. She learned that granite sheds usually had metal roofs and siding and were cold in the winter and hot in the summer. The second statue, Dutchy's replacement, looked more like the tall, skinny Confederate soldiers depicted in the history books.

After reading the history of the statues, she went to the kitchen and picked up the box. The glasses case moved. She took the case out and placed it on the kitchen table. She took the empty box into the utility room, broke it down and placed it in the recycle box.

She reached up and grabbed a bottle of glass cleaner off the shelf and headed toward the kitchen. She sat down at the kitchen table and reached for the glasses case. She pulled the spectacles out of the case and cleaned each lens with the bluish fluid and a paper towel. The lenses were housed in a black plastic frame with a silver triangle at each outside top corner. Both side arms had something printed on the ends that fit behind the ears. Without having a magnifying glass, Dee thought she could read "5 1/2 LIBERTY U.S.A." on both.

Dee also used the glass cleaner on the glasses case. The clean case showed rust-colored flowers enclosed within double gray lines in a scalloped design. The background was off-white. The case had a small tear to the right of the snap and Dee could not get the stains off the bottom of the case. The right corner had a black stain that would not come off. The same rust-colored stain was below the snap. She put the glasses on and realized they had to be prescription. Both lenses were not the same; however, it was clear to Dee that the owner more than likely had to have used them for reading at all times — they were that strong. The lenses were not as thick as Coke-bottle glass, but certainly strong.

Dee wondered where she had heard the term "Coke-bottle glasses." She probably had heard it in middle school. Children could be cruel when using the thickness of the bottom of a Coke bottle to describe a classmate's eyeglasses. They also used words like "four eyes."

More and more as she handled the glasses, Dee wondered about the owner. She opened the case again. The inside was a faded white with additional stains. "How did I miss this?" she thought, surprised to see the name *Mollie A. Tremane*. The name was faded but written on the top edge of the inside of the case. The name was more than likely written with an ink pen. Some of the letters were not solid. Mollie A. might have been Mollie H. Below Mollie's name, the optometrist's name and address were clearly stamped in black. It was much smaller than the hand-printed name above, but Dee could still read "Dr. W. A. ADDISON" on the first line with "ELBERTON, GA" on the second line.

"Mollie Tremane. Mollie Tremane. That name means something to me," she said out loud without realizing it.

"Hey, Dee." Emmy said as she opened the front door. "Caught you again, didn't I? I think you spend too much time alone. Maybe that's why you talk to yourself."

"I do not," Dee said defensively. "At least I don't think I do."

"Take it from me, you do. What's all the cleaning stuff about?"

"I'm just cleaning up the dusty books I bought at the estate sale," Dee explained. "What did you do with your stuff?"

"Sophie. I had to leave it all in the car. I went to Mom's and she wouldn't let me in with it." Emmy frowned. "She said she had enough junk. Do you think I can get away with washing the crocheted bedspread in the washer?"

"No. I think it might fall apart. It's so old. Plus, it would never get its shape back. You will probably have to hand-wash it."

"Or, I may have to go back to plan A and take this to Granny Nida. Like I said, she can get a stain out of anything. I might ruin it left on my own." Emmy picked up the glasses and said, "Cool."

"You are looking at my frivolous purchase from the estate sale. The glasses cleaned up really well. The case is not in great shape. But, look at this inside." Dee opened the case and pulled back the top in order for Emmy to see the faded print inside.

"Looks like M-O-L-L-I-E. What's this in the middle?"

"I think it's an A or maybe an H. I can't tell. I believe the last name is Tremane. What do you think?" Dee questioned.

"Yep. I think it's T-R-E-M-A-N-E. The doctor's name is clear. But, I don't know a Dr. Addison in Elberton. We can ask Mom about him."

Emmy sat down, still holding the glasses. She put them on. "Wow. Somebody really needed these. The left lens is thicker than the right. Did you notice?"

"I noticed they were different. But, they both are quite strong," Dee agreed. "Does that name mean anything to you?"

"Nope." Emmy said as she handed the glasses to Dee. "I almost forgot. I came back to invite you for dinner tonight. Dan is home. Mom is cooking lasagna. She knows how much you love it. Okay?"

Dee asked Emmy if Dan was home for just the weekend. Her mind pictured Emmy's good-looking older brother and hoped he would be in town for more than a few days even though she knew he was in a relationship and wasn't interested in her. He was tall with reddish dark hair and beautiful blue-green eyes. A few years ago he graduated from Georgia Tech with an Architectural Engineering degree. Dee first met him at Emmy's UGA graduation and saw him a couple of times at their parents' house in the last year.

"I think he plans to drive back to Atlanta tomorrow afternoon, but I'm not sure. I think he kinda likes you, Dee."

"I doubt that," Dee retorted. "I thought he was involved with someone."

"No, he and Sheri broke up several months ago. Well, anyway, he sure didn't object when Mom suggested you come to dinner. He had a big smile on his face."

Emmy headed outside to get her box from the estate sale. She came back in quickly with her bundled-up bedspread and other items and headed to her room. She turned just enough for Dee to catch her parting words, "I'll be ready in about thirty minutes," obviously taking it for granted Dee had agreed.

Dee headed to her room to change into something that didn't smell like glass cleaner and furniture polish. She changed from jeans into clean Capri pants with a matching top. She combed her thick dark hair back, twisted it and clamped a large combed hair clip on top to hold it in place. She pulled a few strands loose at each temple and used the curling iron to create spiral curls. She dotted her cheeks and nose with a light makeup and spread it out, hoping to give the illusion of no makeup at all. After applying a small amount of green eye shadow she said to herself, "That's enough." She slipped into a comfortable pair of sandals and left her room thinking she did not want to overdo it and make Emmy's family think she was trying to impress Dan. Not that she was interested in impressing Emmy's brother. Or so she told herself.

Dee and Emmy drove across town and parked in the back. The concrete driveway had been extended between the house and garage where Mrs. Jackson parked Mabel and Mr. Jackson had a large workshop. They pulled in behind a small Ford Escort belonging to Emmy's Granny Nida, a frail lady with white hair so thin her pink scalp showed in several places. Bent slightly from osteoporosis, she was slowly getting out of her car. Her light blue ankle-length pants matched the morning glories on her cotton blouse and highlighted her white hair. She carefully placed her SAS white lace-up shoes on the concrete and stood in place for a few seconds to get her balance. At eighty-three years of age she continued to drive and had no idea that every one in town watched for her sage-green car in order to get out of her way. Onida Smith had lived at the local senior citizens home, Elsburg Towers, for the last twelve years.

The numerous wrinkles in her face rearranged themselves as she smiled mischievously. Her Georgia accent was heavy as she addressed her granddaughter, "Emmy Lou, didn't know you'd be here, Honey. When you gonna settle down and give me those great-grandchildren you promised?" Her light blue-green eyes sparkled behind thick light framed glasses.

Emmy took her grandmother's arm. "Granny Nida, I never promised you great-grandchildren."

Granny Nida stopped walking and looked up at Emmy. "The day you were born you looked at me with a look that promised me great-grandchildren. Now don't go denying it now after these many years. Yore mama did her part, now you gotta do yore's." Granny Nida took a step forward.

Emmy shook her head and knew it would do no good to argue. She held the back door open for her grandmother to enter. "Granny Nida, remember Dee?"

Granny Nida stopped again. She found it difficult to walk and talk at the same time. "I shore do. Dee Dee, yore as pretty as ever. You girls want to hear a joke?"

"Is it a dirty joke or a funny joke?" Emmy asked, knowing her grandmother had the propensity to slip in an off-color joke here and there.

"A joke doesn't have to be dirty to be funny, but *I haven't heard one.*"

Dee smiled. Granny Nida had a reputation to keep up and she was doing a good job of it today.

Emmy looked at her grandmother's glasses and saw what might have been lotion smeared on the bottom edges of her wire-rimmed glasses. "Granny Nida, what's that under your eyes and on your glasses?" Emmy asked.

"That's my cure for the bags under my eyes. I'm gonna look ten years younger."

"But what is it?" Emmy asked again.

Granny Nida leaned toward Emmy and whispered, "It's Preparation H."

"Why would you do that? Isn't that for treating hemorrhoids?"

"Shhhhhhh. Don't tell yore mama. She'll git on her high horse and git all upset. Some time ago I read that Preparation H could shrink baggy skin like it shrinks hemorrhoids and I'm gonna get rid of these bags under my eyes. And, if it works real good I'm gonna use it on a lot of other places." She took her right arm away from Emmy's supporting arm, held up her left arm, pinched the loose skin under the upper arm, wiggled it and said,

"If it works on the baggy eyes, this flab is next."

"Well Granny Nida, you be careful. If you get that stuff in your eyes it could affect your eyesight." Emmy helped her grandmother take another step into the house.

As soon as they walked through the back door and into the den, Granny Nida cornered Dan and asked him if he had any new jokes to share. Emmy and Dee headed to the kitchen to help Mrs. Jackson put dinner on the table. Dee caught a glimpse of Dan, who waved to her before turning his attention to his grandmother. She heard his distinctive laugh, a male version of Emmy's hearty laugh. "No, Granny Nida. Can't think of one."

"Well, Danny Boy, maybe next time. By the way, did you hear 'bout that terrible wreck in Athens last week?"

"I don't think so."

"You didn't hear 'bout three couples being killed when their van turned over?"

"No."

"The driver survived, but the three couples died and went to Heaven. When they got there, they met St. Peter at the Big Gate and when the first couple asked to go in, St. Peter said, 'You both spent all yore time collecting material things, including houses, land and jewelry. Why, Mr. Wilson, you even married a woman named Pearl.' St. Peter turned them away. When the second couple stepped up, St. Peter said, 'The two of you focused yore entire lives on partying and drinking. Mr. Jones, you even married a woman named Brandy.' St. Peter shook his head as he turned them away. The third couple took one step forward when the man looked at his wife, took her by the elbow, turned her 'round and said, 'Come on Fanny, we don't stand a chance.'" Granny Nida laughed as if she had just heard the joke instead of telling it.

Dan laughed too, as his mother admonished him from the kitchen, "Dan, you know Mom is incorrigible. Don't encourage her."

After dinner, Emmy and Dee helped Mrs. Jackson take the food and dishes from the dining room to the kitchen. It was obvious from one look at Mrs. Jackson from whom her children inherited the red tint in their hair. Mrs. Jackson's hair had turned a red-brown as she had aged, but the basic color was there with a few gray hairs here and there. Emmy and her mom were about the same height, both shorter than Dee. Mrs. Jackson carried some extra weight even though Dee did not consider her fat. She remembered Mrs. Jackson saying once, "I am not fat. I am pleasantly plump." Mrs. Jackson and Emmy shared most of the same facial features, light green eyes as well as the name Emily even though the younger woman had been known all her life as Emmy.

Emily Jackson had been a stay-at-home mom until Emmy entered high school; then she started working part time in a downtown jewelry store. She loved meeting the public; Mr. Jackson teased her and was known to say her jewelry bill was more than her salary. She was good-natured about it and would say it didn't matter, look at all the nice people she got to meet.

Ronald Jackson's personality was reflected in Dan's serious nature. He was not quite as tall as Dan's six feet, two inches, and wore his brown-and-gray hair short in the crew cut military fashion. He had a ruddy complexion, a thick neck and a hump on his nose, which had been broken some years back in a high school football game and again in a fight. He had a reputation as a fighter in his younger days. His eyes were light blue and glowed with pride when he talked about his children. He obviously adored both Emmy and Dan. He owned the same hardware store his daddy had started. It was located on the town square, not far from the jewelry store where his wife worked. He had worked with his father through high school and continued to manage the store after his father's death. Years ago he accepted he would never be wealthy, but the hardware business had kept them financially stable.

Granny Nida left as soon as dinner was finished. She had to be back at Elsburg Towers before dark. Her daughter walked out with her to be sure she was on her way. She had a habit of lingering if she could corner one of them to tell just one more joke. Mrs. Jackson returned to the kitchen after seeing her mother off. She looked at Dee and said, "Mom's a mess. I believe she's getting worse as she gets older. They say if a woman lives long enough she will say and do things just like her mother. Imagine what I'm in for."

She laughed, "I'm not really worried. I can't remember jokes now. And, if I try, I tell the punch line first and mess it up. Why should I expect to get better at it when I'm older? Mom may forget to take her medicine, but she never forgets a joke."

Mrs. Jackson continued, "And, if she reads it, she believes it. When Dan was about five years old Ron and my dad took him to see the horses. Mom and Dad still had their horse farm near Bowman when the kids were little. The pasture they walked through to get to the barn had not been mowed and the weeds were as high as Dan was tall. When they came back in Dan had little red bumps all over his shoulders, stomach and arms. Mom had read about a cure for chigger bites in some magazine: to keep chigger bites from itching, paint them with fingernail polish. It supposedly smothered the little mites and killed them. So Mom found her red nail polish and painted all the bites. Dan looked pitiful when Ron brought him home. Ron explained what happened and I understood. After all, I grew up in her house." She paused as she placed the empty lasagna casserole dish in the sink.

She went on to tell Dee that when she bathed Dan and got him ready for bed that night he felt warm. She took his temperature and sure enough he had a slight fever. After checking him out, she discovered he had chicken pox. *Her mother had painted all his chicken pox with red nail polish.* She had been expecting Dan to come down with them because he had been exposed several times in his kindergarten class. "My red polka-dotted little boy looked weird for a few days, but he didn't itch. I guess it wasn't a bad thing. He never had any scars from the chicken pox either. As I said, Mom's a mess and she's got something going on now. I cleaned her glasses shortly after she came in and she became all secretive when I questioned her about what was on them." Emily Jackson smiled as she shook her head.

Dee laughed as she put a couple of tea glasses beside the sink. She decided she would let Emmy tell her mother about Granny Nida's Preparation H project.

Dan came in and quietly told his mother that he wanted to take Dee to see something and asked if she could do without Dee for the rest of the cleanup.

"Sure," Mrs. Jackson replied in a conspiratorial manner and a big smile.

Dan walked over to Dee, placed his hand under her elbow and said, "I've come to rescue you from kitchen duty." He maneuvered her out the back door almost before she knew he had said anything.

"Daniel, stop. What are you talking about?"

"I have something to show you. From the conversation at dinner I got the impression you don't know much about Elberton. I want to educate you," Dan said, knowing he would get a rise from that comment.

"You want to educate me? Just because you are older, much older, doesn't mean you know more," she retorted.

He had managed to keep her moving toward his green Cherokee Jeep and opened the passenger door for her. "Okay, if I don't show you something you are going to love to see or something you've never seen before, do you agree to come to Atlanta one weekend and go to dinner with me?"

"And what will you do for me if I have seen what it is you have in mind? Or, what if I don't really give a heck and don't love it at all? What do I get?" she continued his silly game.

"Whatever you want," he replied.

Not having a comeback, Dee shrugged and said nothing until she was seated in the Jeep.

"Besides, you haven't even gotten acquainted with Freddie."

"Who is Freddie and why would I want to meet him?"

Dan moved around to the driver's side and continued the conversation as he got in and fastened his seat belt. "You just met Freddie when you put yourself on that seat, my dear." Dan spoke in an exaggerated fashion, lifting his eyebrows up and down.

"Oh, I should have known. It's your car."

"Or, I would say my truck. Guys call SUVs trucks and girls call them cars. You know, it's that Venus and Mars thing. Freddie is Freddie because it's the name of a stuffed green frog I had when I was a wee lad. You did notice my truck is green. Right?" Dan couldn't resist teasing her.

"Actually, the SUV thing is a right-brain, left-brain thing," she said with confidence. "I should have known about Freddie. Your whole family has a thing about naming their cars. I don't get it."

"You'll get used to it. Don't worry. Come to think of it, Dad hasn't named his truck. I'll have to talk with him about that. Can't have a Jackson with a vehicle that's nameless, now can we?"

Dee laughed. She would probably never get used to named cars, and almost anything the Jacksons said or did could easily be related to movies. Movies and cars. How could she complain? It wasn't like they were vices. They were fun.

Dan backed out of his parents' driveway onto South Oliver Street and headed toward town. After passing the old Elbert Theatre, he continued through town. The public square was on the right and remained the hub for Elberton businesses, even though many businesses had come and gone, retail stores and family-run restaurants were plentiful. He could see his dad's hardware store on the far side of the square across the street from the pizzeria.

With Memorial Day rapidly approaching, Dee looked with special interest at the tall granite memorial in the middle of the square commemorating the Confederacy. The granite soldier was tall and thin as if he had been frozen in time and still hungry. He stood with his long, narrow rifle beside him and a battered wide-brimmed hat on his head. It reminded Dee of one of the books she had purchased at the estate sale . . .

a story about how Elberton got started in the granite business. The first Confederate statue was made for the sole purpose of being erected on the Public Square. This monument was not the original.

"Dee, you have a weird look. It's kind of sad." Dan sounded concerned.

"I'm fine. I was just thinking about the memorial — there." She pointed to the tall monument to the right. "Do you know the story of the first one?"

"Vaguely." Dan didn't remember much about a first or a second one. "You've been here just a few months and you already know?"

"Only because I just read about it from a book I found at an estate sale."

"Didn't the first monument have a weird name?"

"Yes. He acquired the name 'Dutchy' not long after he was erected. The locals didn't like him very much."

"I used to know all that. What happened to him?"

"The ladies of the Confederate Memorial Association negotiated his creation with a foreigner who had moved to the states and lived somewhere up north and knew how to carve a monument. Somehow in the translation of what was required, he didn't understand what a Confederate soldier in uniform looked like. I think he came from the Pennsylvania Dutch community, and that might have influenced his perception. The ladies sponsored the statue to honor those from Elbert County who fought for the Confederate cause. Dutchy was completed and erected in 1898. He was not tall, thin or hungry-looking as the current one. The survivors of the war as well as others felt that Dutchy did not in any way resemble those he was supposed to be honoring. He was short and dumpy looking with a cap on his head."

Dee continued, "Two years later, they — I don't know who — roped and pulled Dutchy down in the middle of the night. I think he lost his legs in the process. The next morning Dutchy was found and a huge hole was dug right there on the square for his burial. I suppose they thought he was too heavy to haul away. I'm not sure if his legs were buried with him or not.

"Dutchy was the first granite statue made in Elberton. After him, an Italian saw the potential for the use of Elberton granite for more than headstones. He purchased or leased the shed for his business and created granite memorials and statues in the same plant where Dutchy was made. After that the granite industry grew all around Elberton and Elbert County. Dutchy didn't get to see most of it. He stayed buried for eighty-two years.

The Elberton Granite Association had Dutchy dug up and pressure washed in 1982. It's easy to remember the year, since he was pulled down in 1900. He cleaned up well, no tell-tell signs of being buried in the Georgia red clay for years. Since his resurrection, I understand Dutchy can be found in the museum along with information about his infamous life as Elberton's first memorial statue."

Dan waited for her to finish and said, "I forgot you're a history teacher."

"Oops. Sorry. I didn't mean to go into my teacher mode," Dee apologized. "However, I love the story."

"You might want to talk with Dad. I'm almost certain he was on the square, along with hundreds of other people, the day they dug him up. He could tell you about the legs."

Dan reached over and took her hand in his as he passed the town square, keeping his eyes straight ahead as if this small gesture was insignificant. Her heart skipped a beat as his fingers closed around her left hand. She smiled and made no effort to move her hand from his. They traveled several miles in silence enjoying their time together and not questioning the past or the future.

He had released her hand by the time they passed Elmhurst Cemetery headed out of town. Across from the cemetery a small park boasted several large monuments honoring those who lost their lives protecting America's freedom. Dee thought about all the deaths represented in that small area and how many families had been affected by war. She knew she had been blessed and had not had to deal with many deaths in her life. Her grandparents died years ago and were the closest deaths with which she had dealt.

Dee's curiosity was building regarding their destination. She decided to break the silence. "How long are you staying in town?"

"Just through lunch tomorrow." He verified what Emmy had already told Dee. "Mom has something she wants me to help her with in the morning. I'll leave shortly after. Why, want me to stay longer?"

"Oh, no. I have to work tomorrow anyway. I'll be at school pretty much all day."

"I have vacation time coming up. Want to spend some time together?" he said hopefully.

"What do you have in mind?" She wondered if he expected Emmy to join them. "Emmy and I will be finished with school in a couple of weeks."

"Did I say Emmy?"

"No. I included Emmy. It wouldn't seem right to leave her out."

"Well, maybe she would be interested in what I have in mind. I thought we could drive over to Abbeville, South Carolina. There's a neat little bed-and-breakfast on the square; it's the Belmont Inn that offers a theater package that's fun. The play takes place just across the street from the Inn. You're into history; the package includes a tour of one of the historical homes. What do you think?"

"Sounds like fun. Do you take all your girlfriends there for a rendezvous? Or, . . ."

He interrupted her, "You don't have a very high opinion of me. Do you?"

"Well, I . . .,"

Again, he interrupted, "Mom and Dad took us there for a children's play years ago and I understand they are still in business. Probably under different management. I saw a write-up not long ago in the travel section of the *Atlanta Journal and Constitution*."

"I'm sorry and I apologize. I suppose I will have to take you out of the category I've placed most guys in these days," she said with sincerity. "The play package thing sounds like something I would enjoy. I've not been to a play since I left Athens."

"I'll call and find out if they have anything coming up this summer. Maybe there will be something of interest for both of us." Reluctantly he added, "I guess Emmy could come, too."

Dee felt better. She could keep it casual with Emmy along. She had not been around him enough to form an opinion about a permanent relationship. She wondered if he would make a good friend or great lover or both and decided to wait and see what happened. July seemed a long time away.

They stayed north on Highway 77 and passed through Clarke's Junction. Dee wondered again about Dan's destination.

Dan slowed the car about seven miles out of Elberton. She looked at him and he pointed to her right. This was it. She was surprised to see several huge granite slabs standing on the hill. They looked awesome and out of place. Dee felt sure the space had once been part of the nearby pasture where cows grazed. "Stonehenge," she whispered. It definitely was the most interesting sight she had seen since moving to Elberton. She vaguely remembered them being mentioned in a conversation at some time in the past and couldn't believe she had not pursued information about them.

"No." he corrected, "These are The Georgia Guidestones but some people call them America's Stonehenge."

"Out here in the middle of nowhere?"

"You got it." He pulled onto the side road leading to the parking spaces. Dee had not taken her eyes off the stone panels. When Dan finished parking, Dee's side of the car was just yards away from the stones.

She hopped out of the car almost before it stopped. The slabs of stone looked large from the road. Up close they were even more impressive.

"What's inscribed on the stones?"

"I'll explain all that. For now, let's just watch the sun going down." It was a nice evening. The weather was perfect and almost no traffic traveled the road. "It's a better view in the summer and winter. The stones are arranged in such a way the light shows at an amazing angle during the summer and winter sunrises and sunsets. On the center, or Gnomen Stone, an eye-level oblique hole was drilled in such a way the North Star is always visible." Dan walked around to the side of the stone to show her the opening.

He continued, "Another cut, again in the center stone there," He pointed to a slot, "forms a window, which aligns with the position of the rising sun at the summer and winter solstices and at the equinox so the pattern indicates noontime. How's that for history?"

"They're amazing now without an equinox. You're amazing." Dee declared. "Tell me more. To whom do they belong?"

"I guess they don't belong to anyone. Or, at least no one knows who is responsible. The person or persons responsible chose to not be known. A Mr. R.C. Christian commissioned them on behalf of an out-of-state group. The people who worked with him were sure it was not his real name. The land is probably in his name."

"Are they old?"

"You mean the stones or the sponsors?" he teased.

"The stones, silly."

"Nothing like Stonehenge. It was late '79 or early '80s when they were finished; however, I understand the project had been in the works for years."

"Is there a purpose? There are obviously etchings on the stones. What do they mean?"

"Each stone is done in a different language," Dan was beginning to wonder if he could remember all the details and it was too dark to read the words on the stones. He had seen them years ago. He kept forgetting that Dee was a history teacher. At least he had finally caught her attention.

The sun was going down. "Let's come out again sometime when we have more daylight. It's getting dark fast."

"Promise?" Dee tried to get a commitment. If she had to, she could find her way back without him. Somehow that thought made her feel lonely.

"Sure. You asked the purpose. When we come back you will be able to read the message, 'LET THESE BE GUIDESTONES TO AN AGE OF REASON.' The words ask that now and in the future we all consider the world's population in several ways including balancing with nature and limiting the population, rule with reason, protect all people with laws that are fair to all, seeking harmony with each other and God. Well, I don't think the word was God. It was something like 'a greater being' or 'infinite being.' And nature. That was used a lot, like balancing nature, taking care of nature, leaving room for nature and that kind of stuff. I'm sure they meant environmental issues. Someone or several people felt they were important enough to write them in stone."

"Is there a book about the Guidestones?" Dee knew she had to have additional information.

"I'm sure you can get specific and accurate information from the museum. Maybe they have a brochure."

"The museum where Dutchy is. Right?"

"Yes."

"I passed it many times and always meant to stop, now I have two reasons to stop by — Dutchy and the Guidestones." She grinned at but did not verbalize the thought that a rock band might use such a name and made a mental note regarding a visit to the museum.

The sun had set, the darkness broken only by occasional lights from cars headed toward Elberton or to Nuberg, the small town a few miles ahead. Dan turned the car around and drove a few yards to the main highway. He waited for a car to go by and pulled onto the road toward Elberton.

Dee was well aware of Dan's close presence as they drove back to his parents' house. He had truly made an impression on her and she hoped to get to know him better.

"Penny for your thoughts," he said.

"A penny's too much," she countered. There was no way she would let him know what she had been thinking. She was thinking back to when she had first met him at Emmy's graduation. She had seen him coming up the steps where she was sitting with Mr. and Mrs. Jackson.

She recognized him from pictures at the Jackson's house and Emmy's pictures at the apartment. The UGA stadium was busy that day. It was a beautiful day and the sun glinted on his red hair, making it look far redder than it actually was. His short, thick and naturally curly hair enhanced his handsome features.

She watched as he stepped in front of several people in their row, to her left, making his way toward his parents. She did not realize how closely she watched his progress until their eyes met and he held her gaze for a few seconds with his blue-green eyes. She was mesmerized by his every move and embarrassed to be caught so blatantly staring at him. His tall muscular body created a shadow that fell over her as she scooted to her left in order for him to get by. The buzz from conversations taking place all around them made it difficult for Dee to be heard so she stood up, leaned toward Dan, and introduced herself as Emmy's friend.

He responded with a smile and said, "It's a pleasure to finally meet you Dee. Emmy sings your praises all the time."

As he made his way past Dee and his mother to sit beside his father on Dee's far right, Dee heard his mom ask, "Where's Sheri?"

"Her brother is graduating from North Carolina State and they've all gone there for a few days."

That brought Dee back to reality. She knew he was involved in a relationship. "Calm down heart," she thought. "This guy is not for you." She sat down and thought about Dan's high school yearbook she and Emmy had perused some time ago at Emmy's parents' house. The book listed Dan as a high school senior. He had been a classroom officer, on the football team, the debating team and several other extra curricular activities. One picture showed Dan with the homecoming queen. The caption below stated *Dashing Dan*. She couldn't help but agree. He had to have dashed around to be involved in so many activities. He was dashing in other ways, with a sex appeal that made Dee blush when she thought about the way his muscles moved under his lightweight shirt and tight jeans. She made herself not look at him or think about him. She started looking for Emmy. The graduation class was filing into the stadium and some graduates were already near their designated seating area.

Now, as then, she was thinking about herself as a little girl who had said she would "grow up, get married and have red-headed children." She wasn't about to broach that subject with Daniel Jackson.

When Dan drove into the driveway at his parents' house, he looked at Dee, "Think you could put me on your calendar in the next few weeks? Next weekend, I have to be out of town. But, the next Saturday is April 10, and Easter is the 11th, and I plan to come back home. Will you be here that weekend?"

She knew her smile left no doubt in his mind that she wanted to spend time with him. "I'd love to spend time with you. I plan to go to Mom and Dad's, but I could drive to Marietta on Sunday morning."

He knew she was cutting short her weekend with her parents, but was delighted she could spend some time with him.

Easter weekend couldn't come fast enough for Dee. Emmy spent Friday night with her parents and wasn't in the apartment Saturday morning when Dee decided to enjoy a yoga session. She and Emmy had taken classes at the Athens YMCA and purchased a DVD for beginners after she moved to Elberton. It had a.m. and p.m. programs and Dee found it more practical to do them as one session; otherwise, she would end up never getting back to the missed one. She and Emmy had never gotten beyond the beginners' stage. It was enough of a workout. They always used the space behind the sofa, which separated the living area from the small entry into the apartment and used the large rug at the front door as padding when exercising. Dee placed her yoga mat on the rug, leaving room for Emmy to walk around her if she came in while Dee was exercising.

Dee was about halfway through the yoga DVD, following the instructor's directions for a dog pose and was on all fours stretching up through her arms and lifting her pelvis in the air when she heard Emmy at the door. Dee's backside was facing the door. Emmy opened the door and was talking with Dan as they entered the apartment. Dee saw them as she looked beside her left leg. Emmy laughed.

Dee knew her face was red. Not only was she upside down with all the blood flowing to her head, she was mortified that Dan walked in, not face to face, but face to butt. She didn't move. She couldn't talk. She just "dog posed" until she heard Emmy make a comment about her "cheeks in the air." Dan laughed as he bent down and said hello. He had her laughing as she bent her legs, turned around and sat, hugging her knees to her chest. He offered to help her up. She took his hand and he pulled her up and into his arms. His hug felt warm and cozy.

After getting over the initial embarrassment of the yoga dog-pose, Dan and Dee spent most of Saturday together and had their first real date on Saturday evening. He chose to take her to Athens for dinner at Rafferty's on the Atlanta Highway and a movie at the Carmike Theater. They mostly talked about their jobs and hobbies, keeping the conversation casual. Dee knew she had always set high standards for the men in her life, and she was excited to feel that Dan was fitting perfectly in so many ways. She wasn't especially happy that he traveled a lot with his job, but she was impressed that he took his responsibilities seriously. When they arrived back in Elberton late that night, she was floating. He kissed her goodnight at the door — a kiss that felt just right — not too demanding, but memorable. Her hand caressed the back of his head as she thought, "This is *the* red-headed man. I just know it."

The next day, on Easter Sunday, she drove to Marietta to join her parents for lunch. After speaking to her dad, she joined her mother in the kitchen. She knew she was smiling more then usual and her mother's question confirmed it. She placed her arm around Dee's shoulders, "What's the silly grin about? Dee, you look like you're about to burst."

"Remember the red-headed man I'm suppose to marry when I grow up?"

It was Anna Marie's time to smile. "I sure do. You were quite adamant about it for years."

"I think I've found him, Mom."

"Sam," Anna Marie called from the kitchen, "you'd better come hear this."

Sam joined them. "What's this all about?"

"Your daughter has something to share with us. Did you notice Dee was smiling like a Cheshire cat when she came in?"

"I thought she was happy, that's all."

"Okay, Dee. Tell your dad about the red-headed man in your life."

Dee told them about how she had been interested in him from the first time she met him, but he was in a relationship at the time. She went on to tell them about how he and the girl broke up, the time she had spent with him since then and the plans they had made for future dates and trips, including the trip to the bed-and-breakfast in South Carolina.

Her parents expressed some concern. Wasn't it a little premature to make such a decision since she hadn't spent much time with him?

Dee smiled and told them Emmy had been invited and planned to travel with them on the South Carolina trip. She didn't elaborate about how she felt in her heart about Dan.

Sam placed his arm around Dee's shoulders and gave her a squeeze. "Actually, I'm glad if it works out that Dan is the red-headed man you've talked about. The Jacksons are such a nice family, I'm sure Dan is a fine young man."

Mr. Jackson, Emmy and Dan planned a surprise birthday party on

Sunday, April 25, for Mrs. Jackson's birthday even though her birthday was Monday the 26th. They purposely didn't tell Granny Nida until Saturday. They were sure she couldn't keep the secret for long; they weren't really sure she could keep it for one day. However, they wanted her to participate and she did need some lead-time just to be ready.

Dee was excited because Dan came to Elberton on Friday evening. They spent time alone on Friday evening, went shopping with Emmy on Saturday to buy supplies and food for Sunday's birthday party, and managed a few hours alone on Saturday evening. Each time they were together, their casual interest became much more personal. Dee loved everything about him and she felt his interest was way beyond casual before the weekend was over.

Concern kicked in when Dee discovered that Dan's work required him to be out of town most of May. She felt their romance had blossomed and feared he didn't have the same strong feelings for her — until he called. Each time he called all the insecurities faded away.

He made up for it on Memorial Day weekend and she was included in all the Jackson family activities. At first she felt strange being Dan's girlfriend instead of just Emmy's friend and roommate. His family had accepted them as a couple and Emmy let Dee know she would be in late on Saturday evening — ensuring Dee and Dan had some time alone. Dee cooked a light dinner for them and they enjoyed the much-needed privacy.

Dee knew she was purposely keeping Mollie out of the picture . . . for a while.

Chapter Three

"The Puzzles Increased"

Mollie was an enigma. That was the last thought Dee had before
going to sleep. Mollie's glasses had been on her dresser for some time and
each time she saw them she wondered why the name, Mollie Tremane,
seemed so familiar. The phrase "eyes of time" would again float through
her thoughts leaving her with the haunting feeling that the glasses held
some importance. The feeling and the words slipped away as quickly as
they appeared.

It was the first week in June. School was out and Dee had finished all
her end-of-the-year work. "Free! Now I can plan that vacation to San
Francisco for which I've been saving, spend time with my folks and, who
knows, maybe spend more time with a certain red head. Maybe he would
like to go to San Francisco. Ummmmmm." She smiled as she thought of
him. When he couldn't be with her, he called her. Dee could hardly
believe she was so looking forward to the bed-and-breakfast trip. She
wouldn't admit to herself or to anyone else how excited she was.

Dee woke up before Emmy, enjoyed a short session of yoga and was
in the process of enjoying a hot cup of Earl Grey tea and eating a bagel
with cream cheese when Emmy came in.

"Good morning," Dee greeted the petite blond as Emmy stumbled
into the kitchen half asleep.

"Morning," was all Emmy could get out that early in the morning.

"You won't believe it, Emmy. My subconscious must have worked on
the Mollie Tremane thing all night. This morning I woke up and
remembered where I heard the name," Dee said excitedly.

"How can you be so perky so early in the morning? You aren't
always up so early."

"Don't you want to know what I remembered?" Dee could hardly
wait to share her discovery.

"Okay."

"Remember last fall when I was trying to find a way to get my class
interested in Elbert County's history? I assigned each student to cover a

period of time. They had to look up something in the newspaper from several decades involving a person or persons and they had to complete the story either to the end or to the current status. Remember?"

"Not really," Emmy wouldn't commit to anything before she was completely awake.

"Oh, well. Anyhow, Marie Willsen did an article on a girl who was missing. I remember it well because the report was extremely short and I gave it back to her to complete. She had only the fact that a girl was missing back in the early '60's. She said that's all she found. I told her she had to find out about the girl's family and if they still lived in Elberton and if not, where. Her second report wasn't much better; however, she had added that the girl's parents are buried in the Elmhurst Cemetery and their obituaries were about a year apart. I think they died in the 1980's.

"Emmy," Dee made Emmy look directly at her to be sure she was paying attention, "I'm almost certain the girl who was missing was Mollie Tremane and I believe she had siblings."

"So?"

"Why do you think her glasses were at the Dunsman house?" Dee asked.

"Maybe she was a friend of someone in the Dunsman family. How should I know?"

"I graded Marie's paper and gave it back to her. I wish I had made a copy. I think I'll do a little investigating on my own." Dee decided to include a trip to the local newspaper, *The Elberton Sun*, in today's schedule.

Later that day Dee stopped by the newspaper office located on the public square and inquired about how to look up obituaries from the eighties. The receptionist, an older woman with a nice smile, sent her to an office in the corner of the building where a young man was hard at work at his computer, his back to Dee as she entered the room. "Excuse me," she said quietly to keep from startling him. He turned around. "I'm sorry to bother you; however, I need to know how to look up information that would have appeared in *The Elberton Sun* about twenty years ago and possibly some articles from the sixties."

"We might have something here from the eighties. I'm sure we don't have copies from the sixties. You can find all the old and the newer information at the main library at the University of Georgia. They have it on microfilm," the young man offered.

"I've spent some time there researching papers when I was a student. Are the newspaper copies in the basement, too?"

"They are and they also have printers and copiers. You can get copies without taking so many notes."

"Thanks. You've been most helpful." Dee said. As she was backing out of his office, she envied his workplace. It was on the corner of the public square with windows facing the square and the side street. Since it was almost noon, she walked across the side street to have lunch at the restaurant on the opposite corner from the newspaper office.

She contemplated riding to Athens and spending the afternoon looking for the articles. After remembering how long it could take to go through scads of microfilm she decided to make it an all-day affair and drive over the next day. She also wondered where Marie Willsen had gotten her information. Surely, she had not gone to Athens and gone through microfilm. Maybe she had been unfair with the grade she had given. She made a mental note to ensure the next class would list their source or sources of information.

The next morning she got an early start. Even though it was early June, a cool front had moved in overnight and the summer day had started clear with just enough coolness to feel good. She drove by the museum on College Avenue and remembered her promise to herself to visit "Dutchy" and pick up information on the Guidestones. She didn't have time today, which was just as well. When she saw the sign in front of the museum she realized the museum would not be opened for a while. The hours for the public were posted: Monday – Sunday 2:00 – 5:00 p.m. and closed during the winter months. She would have to keep that in mind.

Dee had never been so aware of granite businesses as she was on the trip to Athens. They were plentiful. She passed a granite company sign to the right just after crossing the Madison County line. As she drove past Tiny Town, she realized the granite industry had spread to neighboring counties long ago.

Seeing the small towns around Elberton made her realize how many job opportunities had been created since the first stone soldier was chiseled from the gray granite. She had always referred to Elberton as a small town and laughed as she thought of the oxymoron, "Elberton is a large small town." Each quarry required people with specialized skills to cut and remove granite from the earth; truck drivers were hired to move the heavy rock from the quarries to the sheds; each shed employed numerous skilled laborers to cut and finish the rock; each quarry and shed required an office staff with secretaries, bookkeepers, marketing and sales personnel, and finally, additional trucks and drivers were needed to deliver the finished product. It was no wonder Elberton had grown as the industry's need for employees increased year after year.

She still had to drive through the next three "C" towns as she called them — Carlton, Comer and Colbert. By the time she got past the "C" towns to Hull she was almost to Loop 10, which would take her to North Avenue. Getting to campus could be a puzzle. Only because she had been a student did she know the route she wanted to take. She was lucky and found a parking space next to the main library. She also knew that would never have happened without this being summer vacation.

Dee chose several boxes of microfilm and sat at the machine prepared to be there for a while. She decided to take the newspapers starting with 1989 and work backwards. *The Elberton Sun* was a weekly publication. It would be easier than having to look through daily publications. She was certain the Tremanes had died before 1990. She placed the spool in and started the process of scanning page after page. She soon realized she needed to go straight to the obituaries. Otherwise, she would be looking at microfilm for weeks.

She found nothing in the 1988 and 1989 papers regarding the Tremanes; however, she found an obituary in January 1988 for Mrs. Marcine Taylor Dunsman, preceded in death by Michael Dunsman, Sr., her husband. She decided to make copies of any reference to the Dunsmans as well as the Tremanes. She looked at her watch, saw that it was almost noon and felt discouraged. "I'll scan 1987," she told herself, "then, I'll go to lunch."

A few minutes later she was looking at Frank James Tremane's obituary. He was born August 2, 1924 and died January 11, 1987. The article was brief and without any frills. It stated that his wife, Opal Jankins Tremane, had preceded him in death. He had a surviving son, Frank Albert Tremane, a daughter-in-law and three grandsons, all of Easley, South Carolina. Mr. Tremane was a member of the Broadcast Baptist Church and had worked for the local granite industry as a polisher and a cutter. Burial was in the Elmhurst Cemetery with the Holmes Funeral Home in charge of arrangements. Services were scheduled for January 13, 1987 at 2:00 p.m. at the Broadcast Baptist Church. Mollie was not mentioned.

Why was Mollie not mentioned? Dee left the library with the question haunting her. She finally concluded that the family did not know how to list her. No one knew for sure if she had preceded him in death. They could not have listed her as living somewhere. What a hard decision for a family to make. She decided she did not need to go through any other spools for the 1980's. She felt sure she could find Mrs. Tremane's obituary; but it wouldn't tell her more than Mr. Tremane's.

The puzzles increased each time she found another piece. Her thoughts about the obituary stayed with her as she walked through the University Columns on North Campus headed toward "The Grill," her favorite place to eat on College Square. She knew she could eat quickly and get back to the library to look through the 1960 newspaper articles.

Unsure of the years with which she was dealing, this time she chose the microfilms from 1959 and 1960. She started with January 1959 and went through September without finding anything of interest except a few articles with photographs in the Business Section where Mr. Michael Dunsman, Sr., had been mentioned in connection with the fast-growing granite industry. He wore dark glasses in each picture. The Dunsmans had also been mentioned in the community news regarding social events and travel with an article describing Beatrice Dunsman's graduation from a school in Virginia. The newspaper ran a picture of Michael Dunsman the second week of October. He was in his football uniform and the headlines read, "Dunsman Scores Again!" It praised him for making the play that won the football game for Elbert High School. It was the final game for the regular season and placed the team in the playoffs. Dee looked closely at him. He looked familiar. As she had done with Frank James Tremane's obituary, she made a copy.

She continued with the microfilm through the end of 1959. She inserted 1960 and scanned January through April without anything of interest. The third week of May carried the story for which Dee had searched. At the bottom of the front page was a picture of Mollie with a header, "Missing Girl." It went on to say, "Mollie Tremane, a sophomore at Elbert High School, has been missing since last weekend." Even though the picture was in black and white, she recognized the eyes. They seemed to look through the lenses without the same intensity Dee saw in her mind when she first purchased the glasses. A shy smile was reflected in her eyes. She wore a dark vest and a white shirt with a collar. Her hair was cut just below her ears and turned under in a pageboy style with short bangs pushed to the right side of her forehead. The written description listed her as medium height, black hair, olive complexion and green eyes. She left Saturday afternoon to help an elderly neighbor. The neighbor confirmed her arrival and departure. She left the neighbor's house at approximately 3:00 p.m. Saturday and had not been seen or heard from since. Chief Jim Taylor had asked for anyone knowing about Mollie's disappearance to please come forward. The article included a phone number for the police station.

Dee wondered if the paper carried other articles about Mollie, such as, any efforts made to try and find her. Two weeks later an article stated that the Chief of Police, Jim Taylor, was continuing the search for Mollie and, at the request of her parents, had asked two local divers to check the quarries in Elberton and the surrounding areas. The article went on to explain how some young people had been using the quarries with standing water as a place to swim, ignoring the "no trespassing" signs. The search had been made with no results. Mollie Tremane was still missing.

Mollie's picture was, again, in the paper the following week with Chief Taylor requesting any information regarding her disappearance. After reading each article Dee made copies. She continued through the end of 1960 and was disappointed to find no other articles related to Mollie. She found one of Michael Dunsman, III, with a headline, "College Bound," showing him at the driver's side of a large dark Cadillac packed and ready to leave for college. His grandfather was handing him the keys to the car. The article mentioned the car had been a graduation gift in June. She copied the article and placed it in her folder.

She was exhausted. She gathered her purse and the file with the copies and drove back to Elberton. She had not lived there long enough to call Elberton home. Atlanta was home. Sadness consumed her. Questions kept coming. Did Mollie know the Dunsman family? Had she been friends with them and left her glasses at their house?

The first thing Dee did when she got home was to shower and put on pajamas. She was too tired to go out and realized a session of yoga was much needed. She didn't bother changing from her pajamas as she started the DVD. She turned the volume on low and faced the TV, felt her mind and body listening to the instructor as she anticipated the next pose and began to relax. The meditation at the end of the p.m. session always made her feel peaceful.

Afterwards, she made a sandwich, watched a movie on TV and went to bed early. Emmy had left a message saying she would be staying with friends and would see her the next day. Dan had called and left a message for her to call him on his cell phone. She got his voice mail and left a message that she was returning his call and hoped all was well with him. They had played telephone tag for several days. She longed to see him again, but his job kept him out of town a great deal of the time.

The following morning Dee had nothing on her schedule. Sleep had eluded her for almost the entire night. When she did doze off she had the recurring dream of a song and a car. Both were always vague. Her body had finally succumbed to sleep about six a.m. Later, she heard Sophie in the drive. Emmy would be coming in soon. She looked at the clock radio on the table beside her bed and was shocked to see it was already ten-thirty. She felt like a zombie and was sure she looked like one, too.

After forcing herself out of bed, she splashed her face with water and felt refreshed. Not wonderful, but refreshed. She walked through the living room to the kitchen and was surprised not to see Emmy. She wondered if Emmy had gone straight to her room. She and Emmy used "Do Not Disturb" signs when they wanted privacy. She walked back through the living room to Emmy's door and knocked since the sign was not hanging on the doorknob.

Emmy's muffled voice came through, "Come in."

"You look worse than I feel. What's wrong?" Dee was concerned. Emmy was almost always in a good mood — after she was fully awake.

"I stopped by Mom's this morning and she and I had a disagreement," Emmy said with a frown.

"It can't be that bad. What was it?"

"Dee, you know Mom and I agree on almost everything . . . everything except religion. She is really pissed off that I want to change churches. Remember how much I enjoyed the Episcopal Church in Athens? You know. The one on campus. Mom acted like the Episcopalians weren't connected to the Christian faith. Yet, they believe in the Bible almost the same way as the Methodists and Presbyterians. Just a little more tolerant about individual choices. And I am all for individual choices."

"I remember how much you enjoyed the church on campus," Dee replied.

"I think Mom thought I would just pick up where I left off when I moved back — the same little girl with no changes. I have changed. She's disappointed and I hate disappointing her. It's not like I've become an atheist. She accused me of being a 'Doubting Thomas' when I told her the Bible was written years after Jesus lived and nowhere did I see a quote stating, *'I am Jesus Christ and I approve this message.'* You know, like all those political messages on the radio and television. She said she didn't send me to college to lose my religion. That's when she stopped talking. When Mom stops talking, trouble follows. I got out quickly."

Dee was not sure what to say next.

"Well, I have changed," Emmy repeated. "I think for myself now. I'm not going to accept a faith because every generation before me accepted it. I have to believe for myself. I'm not sure what I believe in. But I hope to find out. It probably won't be what she wants. I hope she will respect my right to make my own decisions. Come to think about it, I have the right to be an atheist if I want to be." She looked at Dee and added, "Not that I am one. I believe in God and I believe God loves us all, even me."

Dee felt secure with her spirituality and considered herself more spiritual than religious. Two years ago she had an experience that had changed her life. She questioned God about life and why some people had to suffer more than others and why there were so many religions and churches. She didn't get the answer she expected but she did receive a peace within herself that she felt came straight from God and that it was all right that people had choices. Like Emmy, she felt that God loved everybody. She didn't want to sound "preachy." She told Emmy that she needed to talk to her mother about what a good job she had done in making Emmy independent and able to think for herself and that different isn't always bad — maybe unfamiliar, but not wrong.

"I'll talk with her again today. Maybe she will be more open. I'll try not be so defensive . . . unlike this morning," Emmy planned ahead. "How was Athens yesterday? Any luck?"

"It took all day, but I got it." Dee walked over to the coffee table in the living room and picked up the folder. They both went to the kitchen. Dee asked, "Feel like looking at these?"

"Sure. It'll get my mind off other things," Emmy agreed.

Dee sat beside Emmy and opened the folder. The copy on top was a newspaper article with a picture of a young man in his football uniform and holding his helmet under his arm. Emmy picked it up to get a better look and said, "This reminds me of someone."

Dee countered, "I thought the same thing."

"I got it," Emmy said, "He looks like the guy who starred in that movie, 'The Prince of Tides,' except younger and meaner."

"I don't think that's it for me." Dee sounded puzzled. "But, maybe it is. That may be why he seemed familiar to me too."

"Look. This one of Mollie favors Natalie Wood. Remember the actress whose death was questionable when she fell off the boat she and her husband, Robert Wagner, owned? I think it was Robert Wagner. My mom's favorite movie is 'Splendor in the Grass.' It's ancient. Natalie Wood was very young and the movie was somewhat controversial for the times. Actually, my mom loves any movie Natalie Wood was in. What are you up to today?" Emmy asked Dee as she thumbed through the other articles.

"Not much. I'm going to coast today. How about you?"

"I think I'll take a day off also. The confrontation with Mom zapped my energy. Let's put on some easy listening music and relax."

"That I would love," Dee sighed.

Emmy went to the living room, picked up the remote and found the music she sought on a satellite music channel. The quiet haunting voice of Enya came floating through the air singing *Only Time*. All Enya's music was soothing including her song *Wild Child*. It was a good song, but not wild, perfect music for relaxing. She walked back into the kitchen and got a bottle of cold water from the refrigerator and a snack from the pantry.

Dee finished her breakfast and went to the living room sofa. She started out sitting upright, but quickly slid down into the soft cushions as she listened to the phrase *"you cannot change what's over but only where you go"* from Enya's song, *Pilgrim*.

The dream that was always vague became very real as the music changed to a different time, *"Sixteen candles make a lovely . . . '* *A red convertible with a tan top was slowing down. Mollie walked faster.*

Emmy heard Dee whimper and groan. "Dee. Wake up! Wake up! You're having a bad dream." Dee continued to make frightening noises. Emmy shook her and forced her to wake. Dee looked up and Emmy saw fear in her eyes.

Chapter Four

"Clara"

It was the second week in June when Dee called her mother's sister, Connie. Dee didn't hear the phone ring after she dialed the number. All she heard was "hello." Connie's second "hello" came quickly after and almost didn't give Dee time to respond. Just as Connie was taking the phone from her ear she heard a frantic, "Aunt Connie. Don't hang up. It's me, Dee."

"Dee, Honey, I thought no one was there."

"I dialed your number and you answered before it rang. I hesitated because I expected a ring instead of a hello."

"I'm so glad you called. You have been on my mind for the last couple of days. Are you all right?" Connie sounded concerned.

"Oh, I'm fine, thanks. I was thinking about coming to see you. Are you busy this weekend? It's been a long time since you and I had a chance to visit."

"Too long, Dee. What time on Saturday? I'm having breakfast with a friend. Well, really, it's brunch at ten o'clock. I'll be home by noon. Or, if you like, you can go with me. Annie wouldn't mind. Come spend Friday night."

"Thanks, but I have plans for Friday evening. Knowing how difficult it is for me to get started some mornings, I think noonish should work well for me."

"That will be great, but I can't help wondering if you are really okay. You sound serious about something. You aren't worried about me, are you?"

Connie wondered if Dee thought she was lonely. It probably had more to do with the feelings Connie had been having about Dee. Connie had been receiving visions of Dee in turmoil. One vision had been quite clear showing Dee tossing and turning while trying to sleep. All the visions had involved a fear factor. Connie knew something significant was happening in Dee's life and the vibes were not good ones. She would have called Dee soon, if Dee had not made the first move.

"No, I'm not worried about you," Dee assured her aunt. "There are a couple of things. First, I do want to see you and second, I'm working on some research and hope you can help me." Dee didn't know what help, if any, Aunt Connie could be.

"I can't imagine how I can help a school teacher with research. Don't worry, Honey. I'll enjoy seeing you regardless. Any chance of you staying over till Sunday?"

"Yes. Yes, I'd love that. You and I can do brunch on Sunday. On me. Okay?" Dee offered.

"Sure, Love. I am so excited and can hardly wait to see you. How is your mom?"

"Sorry, Aunt Connie. I don't really know. You probably have talked with her since I have. I called her several days ago and got the answering machine. Then, Mom called me when I was out. So, no real news from Marietta."

"It's been about two weeks for me. Let's call her this weekend when you are here," Connie offered. "Won't she be surprised?"

"Thanks. You're wonderful. See you Saturday. Love ya."

"Love you too. Bye now."

Connie hung up the phone. With a thoughtful look on her face she wondered what Dee was up to. Dee usually planned her visits way ahead, being the most organized person in the family. Dee's mom was impulsive, often scatterbrained, and said what she thought regardless of the consequences. "Oh, well," Connie thought. "Dee will be a pleasant change regardless of this research thing."

Dee spent the next couple of days catching up on laundry and cleaning her side of the apartment. She left some time for reading and was delighted with her choices from the estate sale. The more she learned about Elberton, the more she liked it. She had lived in Atlanta and Athens, but Elberton was different and she was enjoying that difference. She realized she loved teaching. The past year had been a learning experience for her as well as her students. She loved middle school students. They were so eager to learn and were far more competitive than the memories she had from her middle-school years. The students who excelled in everything were especially fun to watch. Her first year was in the newly built school, creating new experiences for the students as well as herself.

When Saturday came Dee was happy she had told Aunt Connie she would be there around noon instead of earlier. She exited off I-85 just long enough to eat a turkey sandwich at Arby's. Since she had given Aunt Connie a vague arrival time, she used her cell phone to call and let her know she should be there by twelve-thirty if she didn't run into stop and go traffic on I-85. Normally, she would have called her mom and dad while she was on the road. However, she did want to surprise them from Aunt Connie's place. Dee started moving toward the right-hand lane at the Shallowford Road exit, preparing to exit at Clairmont Road. Connie lived in Decatur, not far from the business district.

She pulled into the drive at twelve-twenty-five p.m. Aunt Connie must have been waiting anxiously since she appeared on the front porch before Dee could get her overnight bag from the car.

"Need some help?"

"Thanks, but I can handle it. I didn't bring much."

Dee received a big hug. Connie held the door open for her as she entered the small house. The house was perfect for her aunt and Dee always felt at home here. Dee walked with her aunt to the guest bedroom where she placed her small bag on the bed.

"Have you had lunch?" her aunt asked thoughtfully.

"Yes. I stopped on my way in."

"Okay. Let's go outside. It's not too hot in the shade and I need to sit and relax for a while." They walked through the living room. A drop-leaf table was below double windows to the right of French doors leading to the patio. The table displayed a collection of family pictures. Dee stopped to pick up a picture of Aunt Connie with her three sisters.

"This is new. When was this taken?"

"About six months ago. The four of us went to lunch at a place near your mom's." Connie's comments made Dee think about her folks' move to Marietta two years ago. They had lived near Midtown in Atlanta most of Dee's life and Marietta didn't feel like home to her. They had moved to a smaller house. Her dad hoped to retire and sell his portion of an interior lighting business to his partner in two or three years. Their downsizing would help make retirement financially feasible.

"This is a great picture. It's amazing how four sisters can be so different," Dee observed.

"True, but it's obvious your mom is the youngest."

The picture showed each sister with one to four fingers in the air. Aunt Becky held up one finger, Aunt Connie showed two, Aunt Pat held up three and her mom held up four. Dee laughed, "Whose idea was it to show the order of births?" Dee had forgotten that Aunt Connie was left-handed until she noticed all the women, except Aunt Connie, had their right hands raised.

"Your mom's, of course. She always wants everybody to know she's the baby."

The picture clearly showed how Dee favored her dad's side of the family. The Reynolds Girls, as they liked to be called, were all shorties compared to Dee and her dad. Dee and her father were tall with thick black hair and green eyes with flecks of brown. The Girls shared a light complexion, freckles and eyes of blue. Past that, they didn't look like sisters. Except for Aunt Becky, they had managed to keep off the extra pounds many women gain in the forties. Dee's mom, Anna Marie, was about five feet six inches tall. Rebecca, Connie and Patricia were three or four inches shorter.

Anna Marie's hair, naturally darker than the others, showed some gray. Dee was unsure about the natural color of the others, who had used color for years. Dee wondered if they were all white haired beneath the dye. They were all dressed casually, each with her own style. Aunt Connie's style usually included a throwback to the sixties. Aunt Becky was married to Uncle Boyd; Aunt Connie had never married and Aunt Pat was in the process of divorcing Uncle Charlie. Or, Uncle Charlie was in the process of divorcing Aunt Pat. He had threatened to leave every time he didn't get his way about something.

Even though she had inherited the color of her eyes from her dad, she had inherited how she used her eyes from her mom's side. The Girls had reputations of putting their spouses and children into place with just one look. They teased Dee, accusing her of taking *the look* to another level. From the time she was a little girl she used *the look* to let her cousins know they had done something to displease her. It was known as the "if-looks-could-kill-you'd-be-dead" look. Her cousins had shortened it to "The Look." She displayed it infrequently; however, when she did, the receiving person had no doubt about her feelings.

Aunt Connie had beautiful brown hair with highlights, both from bottles. Her thin lips were always poised for a broad smile. Her most striking feature was her deep crystal-blue eyes. Dee often thought they were the kind of eyes that could see straight into the soul. Aunt Connie always wore loose-fitting bright-colored clothes and sandals. Her outfits often included belts, both cloth and metal, that would buckle to the side with one end hanging low. She often stated, "Comfort is of the essence."

She had worked for years at a ticket office for Delta Airlines. She retired early and was in the process of creating a second career in songwriting. A year ago she had sent a demo to Nashville and had some success. The song made the bottom of the top-ten chart in country music with a crossover into pop. Her second song was being pitched in Nashville, and Connie hoped to hear any day that it had been accepted. She had written a slew of songs, but it was a tough, competitive business, the process was slow, and more songs were turned down than accepted. Luckily she didn't depend on it for grocery money, even though she had to live frugally.

She also had a small income that covered her travel and meal expenses involved with an unusual job she chose to keep to herself. She led her family to believe she had mostly lost her psychic visions. She worked occasionally under a pseudonym with the Georgia Bureau of Investigation to find murderers when traditional methods had failed. She never charged more than her expenses and her efforts were purely altruistic in nature. Her psychic abilities gave her an outlet to serve others when her bank account did not allow charitable contributions.

Dee placed the picture back on the table and followed Connie to the patio where two glasses of sweet iced tea were waiting. "Ummmmm. Thanks. I need this," Dee said, delighted. She was even more pleased when she took a drink and discovered a peach flavor. "What a surprise. I haven't had peach-flavored tea in years. I forgot how good it is."

She and Connie settled into lounge chairs in the shade and enjoyed sipping tea in the quiet peace that surrounded them. They both knew once the conversation started, they would be busy. It was always that way with them. They knew each other well and shared many of their deepest feelings with each other. They talked about Dee's job and Connie's hobbies for almost an hour before Connie asked, "What's bothering you, Sweetie? I got the impression you were on a mission when you called me the other day."

"I don't want to upset you. This subject may be taboo, but I just have to talk with someone about this. At one of our family gatherings years ago, I remember Aunt Pat teasing you and calling you 'Clara.' The other sisters gave her that 'you-shut-up look' and she did. I asked Mom about it later and she explained that you sometimes had visions when you were very young. Visions not seen by others. I'm curious about how you handled it."

"I did get stuck with 'Clara' for a while. Some kid at school called me that, shortened from clairvoyant. I predicted something that really happened. I forget what. Becky beat him up. One thing about my sisters and me — we can say anything in the world about each other, but Heaven help the person who says something against one of us. They'll have Hell to pay.

"But I handled it then and I handle it now. The visions are different than they were when I was younger. If I receive a threatening vision, I try to act on it. However, most people don't want to deal with it, so I pick and choose my battles. Oh, and when I was younger, the visions weren't near as bad as the reaction I received when I tried to talk about them. Mom and Dad did their best to help me, but they didn't understand. They sent me to doctors and finally to a psychiatrist. She listened and helped me accept the fact of the visions, but didn't have much help as far as dealing with them or the people who made fun of me for having them. Why do you ask?"

Before Dee could answer, Connie blurted, "Oh my God! It's personal. You're asking for yourself, aren't you?"

"Yes."

"Recently or for years?"

"Just recently. I'm sure nothing like this has happened before."

"Does your mom know?"

"No, I haven't had a chance to tell her," Dee explained.

"Want to tell me about them?" Connie's voice conveyed compassion.

"Yes, I do. It started when I moved to Elberton. I kept hearing a particular song and the sound of a car engine slowing — over and over. At first they were vague and I thought I was having the same dream. Then, last week they became realistic and the fear intensified. I felt the same fear as the person in the vision. Is that weird or just the way it works?"

"That's the way it works. Something must have triggered the visions when you moved. Moving can be traumatic. However, if you've never had visions before, it must surely be something local. Tell me about them."

Dee started with the short visions of hearing the "Sixteen Candles" song and the sound of the red convertible's engine slowing. The extreme fear in the visions and Mollie's disappearance led Dee to believe she had been killed. Connie didn't interrupt.

When Dee finished, Connie said, "Poor baby. You really did get dumped on." She realized how negative that sounded and tried to correct it, "I'm sorry. That was a poor choice of words. Obviously, Mollie Tremane is trying to share with you, not dump on you. Do you have the articles?"

"They're in the bedroom. I'll get them." Dee got up and stretched.

"While you do that, I'll put a quiche in the oven. It takes almost an hour for it to cook. I hope quiche and a salad will suffice for dinner tonight." Connie held the door for Dee.

"Sounds great. Thanks for listening."

Connie hugged Dee. "We aren't finished, yet. I'll meet you back on the patio. The quiche is ready to go in. I like an early dinner. Hope that suits you."

"It suits me fine," Dee agreed. Her sandwich at lunch was long gone.

Within minutes, Dee had the folder with the newspaper articles laid out on the patio table. Connie found her walking around the small back yard. The variety of plants and colors were amazing with one corner especially interesting. Connie had arranged an unusual topiary. She obviously had spent a great deal of time creating such an array. The shrubs were shaped in circles and squares. "Very unusual," Dee thought — both the shrubs and her Aunt Connie.

"My garden is small, but suits me just right." Connie joined Dee in her tour of the garden.

"This is beautiful. You must spend a great deal of time out here."

"This is where I feel closest to my maker. I get my best spiritual fix out here," Connie said.

"The newspaper articles are on the table. Take a look. Maybe you can help me with this."

"Honey, I'll try. But, I have to say I think this is going to be your deal. It's not that I don't want to help you. It's that if Mollie has somehow tuned into your psyche, she may not want to or be able to share with me."

"That's okay. If I could just get some guidance, I would be grateful. Anything at all. I don't know where to go with this. I have some ideas. For instance, I've been thinking about contacting her brother who lives in South Carolina. But I don't know if it's a good idea. It may be a huge mistake," Dee countered.

They stepped onto the patio. "Let's take a look." Connie spread the articles on the table and silently perused one. "Sit down over there." Connie pointed to the chair across the table as she sat down.

"Remind me, Sweetie, if I forget when the quiche should be ready to come out." Connie looked at the picture of Mollie in the first article about her disappearance, then flipped through the other articles. "Something is missing from all this. There has to be something to tie all this together with you. There has to be a connection with you and Mollie. How did you initially know about her? And, why did you make copies of the Dunsman family articles?"

"I learned about Mollie from a story one of my students researched, initially. However, the real stuff started happening after the glasses. Aunt

Connie, I forgot to tell you about the estate sale. I bought Mollie's glasses at the Dunsman estate sale back in the spring and felt that somehow that family interacted with Mollie's. I don't know how."

"Okay. That makes sense. What doesn't make sense is that you were having partial visions before the student's paper and before you bought the glasses. There must be another connection." A puzzled wrinkle creased her brow, then quickly dissipated.

"It's time for the quiche. Let's eat." As Connie stood to go inside, she continued, "Let's look at all you have. Visions where Mollie is terrified. You only know she disappeared. You know Mollie is the person to whom the glasses belonged. What are the questions?"

"I'd like to know how the glasses got into the Dunsmans' belongings. The lenses are so thick it makes me believe Mollie would have worn them all the time. She would not have just left them somewhere unless she got new ones. If the families were friends, that might make sense even though it wouldn't change anything. Assuming the visions are true, the driver of the red convertible caused Mollie to be terrified and is the culprit. That still doesn't answer how they got into the Dunsman house," Dee added.

"How about Mollie's brother? Has anyone in the family verified that she never reappeared?" Connie wondered.

"No. He's the one in South Carolina I haven't gotten in touch with. What do you think?"

"There is the outside chance that eventually Mollie showed up somewhere since 1960. If anyone knows, it would be her family. The obituary didn't mention Mollie. She might have been left out of it because she had been cruel enough to hurt her family by running away. Did you say she has only one brother?" Connie was feeling unsure about a lot of things.

"There was only one son listed in the father's obituary."

"I believe you should at least try and talk with him. He can shed some light about the family's interaction with Mollie after her disappearance, if there was any. Do you want me to go with you?"

"That's a generous offer, Aunt Connie. I think I'll go alone. If I chicken out, I'll call you. I agree. Frank Tremane just may hold the keys to all the closed doors."

"I doubt he has all the answers, but he is a starting place."

"Aunt Connie, I can't help but wonder why I am having the visions. If the visions are real and Mollie died, it would have been more than forty years ago. Wouldn't she have shown someone else all this before now? I can't imagine why me and why now?" Dee was truly perplexed.

"I wondered that earlier. I was not sure you had gotten that far. Obviously, the glasses acted as a catalyst in some way. However, you were getting readings of some sort before the glasses and before the school project."

"They were vague before the glasses," Dee agreed.

"Let's mull over this again in the morning. Maybe we will be given some direction. I think the quiche is ready, or about ready. Let's eat and then watch a good movie to get our minds off this and, hopefully, have a good night's sleep."

By the time Connie made each of them a small salad to go with the dinner and Dee set the table, the quiche was ready. The peach tea they enjoyed earlier was gone and Connie served ice water with the meal.

Cleanup didn't take long and they were out of the kitchen soon after finishing their meal. Connie had rented *"Oh Brother, Where Art Thou."* She had not seen it and hoped Dee had not. Dee had seen it; however, it was such an entertaining movie she was happy to watch it again. For the remainder of the evening they laughed and had a good time.

Sleep was erratic for both of them. Dee did not have visions or dreams of Mollie. She woke up twice thinking about the next step, but the night was not a total loss. Connie didn't fair so well. She was truly concerned about Dee and could find no good answers to her dilemma. She had a difficult time going back to sleep after waking.

They both slept their best between six and nine a.m. Dee heard Connie moving around and forced herself to get out of bed.

"Good morning. I don't have to ask. I know you didn't sleep well or you would have been up already," Connie said, greeting Dee as she walked into the kitchen.

"Good morning. I usually am perkier than this in the morning, much to my roommate's chagrin. It takes Emmy a while to join the living." Dee replied and smiled, thinking of Emmy.

"Speaking of Emmy, you haven't told me much about her good-looking brother. Tell me more," Connie begged. "I heard through the grapevine, Anna Marie's of course, that you have more than a casual interest in him. Did I hear right?"

"You did," Dee confided. "He has such a wonderful smile and a laugh to remember. You know, one of those hearty laughs you hear when you walk into a room and know he's there." Dan was a much happier subject than the visions. She updated Connie and told her about the trip to The

Guidestones and how Dan seemed to be making sure they would be spending time together. She told her about the date they had Easter weekend, his mom's birthday party and the upcoming trip to Abbeville. She said, "Even when he's traveling, he calls me often. He's so thoughtful."

"Whoa. I can hear it in your voice and see it in your eyes. Honey, I believe you've fallen pretty hard for him already."

Dee didn't try to deny it.

They called Dee's mom and talked about things in general. Dee didn't want to discuss the visions on the telephone. She would tell both parents the next time she was with them.

They discussed where to go for brunch. Connie suggested Everybody's Pizza near the Emory University Campus. Dee agreed, and since her car was parked behind Connie's, she drove. They started from downtown Decatur, turned onto North Decatur Road, passed the Emory Law School and arrived at Everybody's Pizza just ahead of the lunch crowd. Dee adored thin-crust pizza and was especially delighted when she found she could take off the vinaigrette and add tomato sauce and artichoke hearts to the cheese pizza on the menu. She and Connie ordered separate salads and shared the pizza. They took their time with the meal and purposely talked about anything except visions. Dee grabbed the ticket from the waiter and gave him her credit card before Connie had a chance to renege on the agreement of who would pay for brunch.

Time slipped by quickly and soon it was time for Dee to think about driving back to Elberton. She drove back to Connie's place and retrieved her overnight bag.

"Remember, you promised to call if you feel uncomfortable seeing Mollie's brother alone," Connie reminded Dee.

"I will. I think a visit with him will determine the next step," Dee sounded hopeful.

They exchanged hugs and Dee started for home. The trip was uneventful and she chose to make it without the noise of the radio or a CD. She spent most of the trip going over the conversation she had with Dan two nights before. He called her from Florida where he and several friends from work had gone for a long weekend of fishing — a trip that had been planned for more than a year. They talked past midnight and it took her a while after that to settle into sleep.

Dan had a way of making her feel so good about herself. She smiled almost all the way home. Near the end of the trip she thought about how they had learned so much about each other and talked about almost everything . . . except Mollie. She frowned as she thought about the visions. He seemed so open about any topic that came up. She hated keeping her visions a secret, but she just wasn't ready to tell him about them. Because she was so drawn to him physically, she had a hard time backing off when their relationship headed toward intimacy. But she wasn't willing to make that commitment until she saw his reaction to the visions. He had been very patient with her so far and had not made her feel guilty for not pursuing a physical relationship. She wondered how long he would remain so understanding.

Chapter Five

"Leave Us Be"

Dee looked on the Internet to find Frank Tremane's address. She used MapQuest to get the directions to his house; however, she had no idea how she was going to approach him. She thought about using the pretext of following through on some of her students' stories about Elberton. She thought about pretending to be someone other than Dee Dupree. Meeting face to face seemed important, yet quite scary.

She decided to take a chance and drive to Easley without calling first. It was the third week in June, and she hoped he and his family were not on vacation. If they were not at home she would stay overnight at a hotel nearby and go by their house the next day. She planned to do some shopping for school supplies in Anderson on her way to Easley or on the trip back. Either way, it would not be a total loss.

She felt she would have a better chance of finding them at home on a weeknight. She decided against Wednesday in case they were at church. "Thursday will be good and I can stay over till Friday if necessary," she told herself.

It was a bright, sunny day when she left Elberton in mid-afternoon. The signs were easy to follow from Anderson to Easley. She drove through Easley toward Pickens. Just past Mill's Hill, Inc., she saw a brick mailbox on the right. A small placard on top read Tremane. She took a deep breath and turned into the drive. The house was several yards from the road, leaving space for a well-kept lawn. There weren't many shrubs near the road; however, near the house showed signs that planning and thought had been put into the planting and care of the flowers and trees. A separate drive led to a small shop behind the house. A sign beside the drive read, "Tremane Brick Masonry Company." She noticed an area in the back with a brick barbecue pit and a small brick wall surrounding a brick patio.

A new silver Mazda was parked in the carport with an older blue GMC pickup truck behind it. Dee pulled in behind the truck. She was still debating as to the best approach. She decided to play it as it came. As she walked past the truck, she saw the temporary dealer tag on the Mazda. She walked to the front door, realizing they would know immediately a stranger had come to see them. She was certain their friends and family used the back door in the carport. She was tempted to do so herself and would have if it had not felt so dishonest.

She heard talk inside; was it the television or a conversation the Tremanes were having? She rang the doorbell; it took several minutes before a man in his fifties with thick black hair pulled back into a short ponytail answered the door and waited for her to say something. Tall and slender, he had thin lips, a tan complexion and slight graying around the temples. His dusty navy-blue work clothes made Dee wonder if he had just gotten home. His eyes were brown. Dee guessed he had Italian ancestry.

"Mr. Tremane?" Dee sounded terrified.

"I'm Frank Tremane."

Dee stood a little taller. "Mr. Tremane, I'm from Elberton and I've been doing some research on your family. Would you have time to talk with me?"

"I can't see how my family could be of any interest to you."

"I want to show you something," Dee said as she reached into her purse for the glasses case. "Does this mean anything to you?" She handed him the case.

He didn't take the case. He shook his head and said, "No, not a thing."

Dee continued to hold the case out to him, opened the case and took the glasses out. Frank Tremane looked bewildered. Dee put them on and watched his expression turn to a look of remembrance.

"Where . . ." he stumbled on his words and looked as if he had been hit in the stomach. His voice intensified. "Who did you say you are?"

"Frank," a woman called from inside as she approached the front door. "What's wrong?" She pushed him aside to get a look at Dee. Dee was silent. Mrs. Tremane stepped forward and Dee noticed her look of concern. The sun caused a glare on the woman's glasses that made it difficult for Dee to see her eyes. She was much shorter than her husband and slightly overweight. Her brown hair was medium length and pulled back behind her ears. She wore blue jeans, a tee shirt and tennis shoes. Dee tried to read the wording on the tee shirt and realized she couldn't because she was wearing Mollie's glasses.

Dee took off the glasses, held them in her left hand and put her right hand out to Mrs. Tremane. "I'm Delores, Dee, Dupree." The older lady chose not to shake hands and Dee pulled back. Now she could read the words on the tee shirt. The words were blocked as if they had been cut from different magazines or papers to look like a ransom note and read, *Give me all your chocolate and no one will be hurt.* Dee thought, "If she loves chocolate that much, she can't be all bad."

Frank appeared to be in a trance. Dee looked at Mrs. Tremane and continued, "I'm researching some history on the Tremane family and would like to get some information from Mr. Tremane."

"Those Mollie's glasses?" He became belligerent, "How in the Hell did you come by them?"

"Wait a minute, Frank, let's invite her in before the neighbors get worried about us," Mrs. Tremane suggested. She opened the door and shepherded Dee and Frank into the living room. The room was not formal; it was obviously used often but still was clean and neat.

The television was blaring news about some politician being charged with an ethics violation. Mrs. Tremane quickly walked over to the table by a large overstuffed recliner covered with a large towel, picked up a remote and turned the television off. Dee got the feeling Mr. Tremane had vacated the chair to answer the doorbell since the towel was askew. The afternoon sun was streaming through the front door and the double windows to the left of the door.

The smell of supper permeated the house. Dee's stomach muscles tightened as the aroma of fresh-cooked vegetables filled her nostrils and made her remember the light lunch she had eaten hours ago. She felt like such an interloper. Was the tightness in her stomach hunger or a nervous reaction to confronting Frank Tremane? Or both? The look on his face was dark and uninviting.

Dee defended herself, "I didn't come here to upset you. I purchased these glasses at an estate sale, and . . ."

Frank broke in, "Do you know Mollie? Is she alive?" Dee heard pain in his voice and had to look away as she saw confusion and hurt in his dark eyes.

"I'm sorry, Mr. Tremane. I don't know. I know only that these glasses mean something. I believe they have a story to tell. I'm curious to know who Mollie was or is. Maybe she is alive. But I don't think so. I just don't know. Do you remember what happened when she disappeared? Or, were you too young to remember?"

"I remember a lot. I've spent over forty years trying to forget. If you don't have any good news about Mollie, I don't feel like talking about it. My son and his family are coming for supper. It's best you leave us be." He steered her to the front door.

Mrs. Tremane watched in silence. She barely heard Dee say, "I'll be staying at the Comfort Inn on Highway 123 in Easley tonight. Please call me if you change your mind. I teach school in Elberton." She looked at Mrs. Tremane and added, "Remember, Dee Dupree." She turned and practically ran to her car.

As she sat in the car wondering why he was so antagonistic toward her she realized her grip had tightened on the glasses. She checked to see that she had not damaged them and slipped them into their case, feeling dejected. She looked at the house as she backed out of the driveway and saw Mrs. Tremane watching from the front window. She berated herself for not handling the situation better as she drove back to town. Clouds were moving in from the northwest, darkening the bright sky and adding to her despondency.

She had blown it.

She pulled in at the drive-thru at Burger King and bought a chicken sandwich, salad and tea. She knew she was in for a miserable evening. She wished she had not told them she was staying over. She could have been home in her own bed by bedtime.

After placing her overnight bag on the baggage rack and her food on the round table near the front window of her hotel room, she ate her meal in silence. The clouds continued to move in, but maybe she had enough time for a quick walk. She looked through her overnight bag for walking shorts or something she could use for exercising, but found nothing. She missed her almost-daily yoga routine and longed for the CD in the quiet of the room. She gave up on exercising, changed into her pajamas, found a movie on the television and settled in for the night. She was dozing as the movie finished and the evening news started. She had looked at the phone several times hoping for a call from the Tremanes, while at the same time hoping to never hear from or see them again.

Dee reached over to the nightstand for the remote and cut off the news commentator in mid-sentence. She reached over and turned off the lamp.

She had just settled into a good sleeping position when she remembered she had not put the dead bolt and chain lock on the door. She knew she wouldn't sleep well without locking the door. She turned on the lamp, dragged herself out of bed, stumbled to the door and locked it. She again turned off the lamp and tried to go to sleep.

Dee was unsure if she was almost asleep or if she was asleep and dreaming. Either way the vision seemed real. She felt a part of the scene seeing Mollie walk down the side street to Railroad Street.

She had just left old Mrs. Stewart's house. She opened her small pocketbook, tucked in the dollar and the quarter she had earned for dusting and cleaning for the old lady and walked on. Dee could hear Mollie's thoughts as Mollie remembered Mrs. Stewart digging into her change purse as she admonished, "Now Mollie, you're a pretty little thing; but, always remember, pretty is as pretty does." Mollie smiled, thinking, "She says that to me every week — week after week. She's more afraid of what I might do wrong than Mama is. And Mama's bad enough to stay on my case."

She continued walking and thinking about her mama's way of handling her. In her mind she could hear her mama say, "Now Mollie, you behave." "Behave" covered anything and everything, from not embarrassing her family to not hurting anyone's feelings. Mollie thought, "It certainly means no lying, no cheating, no smooching, no drinking and especially no s-e-x." Before she was six years old Mollie knew that s-e-x could not even be mentioned around Mama and Pa. Even in her thoughts she spelled it out instead of saying it. She smiled thinking about several years ago when she and her friend, Rosemarie, who lived down the street, had written it in the dirt in the back yard and giggled. They made sure they smoothed the dirt over and erased it before her mama came out the back door. It was a washday and her mama had to pass that part of the yard to get to the clothesline.

When she was six she asked her mama where babies came from and her mama replied, "From making love. Babies are made of love." Her friends at school told her babies came from s-e-x. She argued with them and told them, "No way. My mama said they are made of love — not s-e-x." Mollie smiled at how much she had learned since she was six.

She planned just how she was going to use some of the money from Mrs. Stewart. She wanted to go to the movie theater. She had let Rex Jones kiss her the last time she went to the movies. She knew it wasn't s-e-x but it didn't feel like making love either. Rex's kiss left her feeling yucky. It was wet and gross and when she felt his tongue touch hers she felt like throwing up. She wondered if she would feel the same if Ned, her friend's older brother, kissed her. She smiled as she thought about how many years she'd had a crush on him. Just thinking about being kissed by him made her feel warm all over. At sixteen she knew what s-e-x was and she knew she wasn't supposed to think about it, much less do it. Just the thought of Ned kissing her made her think about it — every time.

Her thoughts changed to the promise her Pa had made about continuing to help her learn to drive. She wished he had a car instead of his old beat-up pickup truck. She could hear him say, "Mollie, if you learn to drive this straight shift, you'll be able to drive anything. Let's just take it out again Sunday afternoon. If you do good, I'll take you to the courthouse on Thursday when the state patrolman is there and you can try to get your license." She couldn't believe he was willing to miss work to take her to get her license. She got nervous thinking about it.

Mollie was just a block away from her house when her peripheral vision picked up the red convertible Chevy Corvette as it slowed down. Mollie walked faster. She could hear "Sixteen Candles" playing on the car radio; "Sixteen candles make a lovely . . ." It stopped abruptly. She knew he had leaned over and cut the volume down or off. Even with the tan top up, she instinctively knew who it was. "He is a bully and I wish he would leave me alone," Dee could hear Mollie's thoughts as if they were her own. Mollie hated the name he called her at school. She tried to stay out of his way regardless of the inconvenience. Most of the time she managed to avoid him.

"Well, if it ain't ole Rotten Tamale," he sneered and grinned as if he had just written a great one-liner for a stand-up comedian. His thick blond hair fell down to cover half his forehead. His small dark eyes darted back and forth from Mollie to the car. His full lips carried a perpetual sneer. "Get in the car. I'll drive you home," he ordered. Mollie continued to walk with her head tucked down and with a determination not to talk to him.

Dee could feel Mollie's fear and knew what she saw had really happened. She just didn't know why she was seeing it at five o'clock in the morning. She drifted off to sleep shortly after.

She felt groggy when she woke up the second time. It was raining. If the Tremanes called, she wasn't sure she could deal with either of them, especially Frank. Would she have the nerve to tell him about the vision? She was now convinced these episodes were more than dreams. She felt Mollie's fear all over again.

Dee showered and dressed as she listened for the phone that never rang. She stopped only to get a breakfast biscuit at McDonald's. The rain continued; shopping in Anderson was out of the question. She was back in Elberton before noon.

While Dee was in Easley, she wasn't the only one lost in the past. Across town from Dee's room at the Comfort Inn, Frank felt like he was seven years old and playing in the backyard of the house where he and Mollie grew up. He could see it in his mind as if it had been yesterday. He was looking at the playhouse Mollie had made near the old Chinaberry tree. His face was distorted with anger because he thought Mollie had taken the bag of penny candy Pa had brought home. He was sure she had hidden it so she wouldn't have to share it with him. He didn't like it that she got special treatment because she was twelve years old and she often reminded him that he was *little*.

He had been so angry he'd turned over the cardboard box she used as a table. He smiled as Mollie's can of pretend soup, made of Chinaberries and water, tumbled to the ground. He thought, "That'll teach her to take all the candy. Besides I hate it when she plays like I'm *her* little boy." Sitting in the house in Easley, Frank wanted to quit remembering, but his mind would not cooperate and he thought about how he continued to tear up Mollie's pretend house. He took all the sticks she had used to lay out the rooms and piled them in a big stack. He crossed his arms over his chest, looked at his handy work and felt proud.

He watched as Mollie came out the back door, singing. He saw her big smile turn into a frown. Frankie knew he had hit home. "Gotcha, Moll," he had said to himself.

As quickly as Mollie's smile turned into a frown, her demeanor became smug, "Go to the kitchen, Smarty Pants," she demanded.

Frankie knew Mama and Pa were not at home. He knew there was nothing she could do to him. He walked past her at the door and stuck out his tongue. He looked back as Mollie shook her head and rolled her eyes.

As Frankie sauntered into the small kitchen, his eyes went to the gray Formica table with matching patterned chairs in the middle of the room. At his place at the table he saw the penny candy. Mollie had arranged the small peanut butter logs and Mary Jane logs as if they were train cars. She had rolled up small pieces of paper to attach the cars together. It was obvious she had spent a great deal of time arranging the candy to look like a train. Frankie loved trains.

Mollie had left her portion of candy piled at her place. He felt awful about demolishing her pretend house, but not for long. He didn't hesitate to start playing with his candy train. He couldn't resist eating the train car at the end. He quickly forgot what he had done to Mollie's playhouse. He did remember to give her a sly look and a quick smile.

Remembering Mollie's make-believe-house made Frank think of how he often climbed that old Chinaberry tree. Mollie was the one who showed him how to use a forked stick from the tree and two or three rubber bands to make a slingshot and how to use the tree's hard berries as ammunition. He impressed his friends with his cool slingshot. He kept it a secret that

Mollie had made the slingshot and taught him how to use it. His friends would not have been impressed if they had known a girl created such a neat weapon, so he took credit for making it.

Frank had kept memories like this at bay all these years. He thought he would drown in them now. "Frank Albert Tremane! Don't you ever go through my things again!" He remembered how he was taken aback. Mollie hardly ever got that angry about anything and she always called him Frankie. He had never seen her so furious, not even when he had messed up her playhouse under the old Chinaberry tree. He knew he wasn't supposed to be in her room, much less go through her chest of drawers. She had reminded him often enough to leave her stuff alone. He remembered thinking he was eleven years old and she still treated him like a baby. Soon after the dresser incident Mollie disappeared.

All he could think about were the times he had made her angry or unhappy. He wanted to remember the good times — the times they laughed together or had fun. There were times he felt that Mollie had taken her memories with her when she disappeared, but he knew better. He had pushed them away and not allowed them to surface until that girl from Elberton showed up. Like Dee, Frank went to bed that night consumed with thoughts of Mollie.

Chapter Six

"Rainy Days"

The next day it was raining one of those rains that reminded Nancy Tremane of the song refrain, *"Rainy Night in Georgia . . . it seems like it's rainin' all over the world."*

She found Frank sitting at the kitchen table with his head in his hands wondering for the umpteenth time about Mollie.

"Frank, you've been more quiet than usual. What're you thinking?" Nancy had seen that dejected look many times because he often became withdrawn this time of year. When they first married she felt he would overcome the propensity to pull into himself; however, over the years he talked about Mollie's disappearance less and less. Not that he had ever been a man of many words. She knew more about the circumstances of Mollie's disappearance from the Elberton newspaper than from Frank.

"I've been thinking about Mollie. Did she live near here?" He said as he looked at his wife. "Maybe she ran away with someone and moved here to South Carolina." He shook his head. "I know better. Mollie's dead. Mollie's been dead a long time or she would'a come home. Mama knew it. Mama said it."

Frank had chosen not to work in the granite shed as his father had. He made the trip back and forth for months to the Athens Technical College to be trained as a bricklayer. He could lay brick anywhere. He and Nancy decided to move to South Carolina, and Nancy's favorite uncle and aunt in Pickens had helped them find a place to live.

Uncle Jim also helped Frank get a job with a local brick company. The company sold brick and supplied brick masons for residential and commercial jobs. After getting established in Easley, Frank started his own business. He named his company "Tremane Brick Masonry." Nancy kept the books and paid the bills. Except for a few weeks of bad weather in the winter, business had been good and steady.

Rainy days meant no work for Frank unless he had a fireplace or other inside work to do. Nancy dreaded rainy days at this time of year.

They did not help Frank's melancholia that always set in during the anniversary of Mollie's disappearance. She often made plans to keep him busy if rainy days were forecast. This time she didn't have a contingency plan. Frank continued talking about his childhood.

"Mollie was a good sister. I remember her singing a lot. She taught me to sing all those children's songs like *Row, Row, Row Your Boat.* She sang in the choir at church. At Christmas she and Mama would drive me and Pa crazy with that *Twelve Days of Christmas* song. Mollie and Mama would alternate singing the days through to the twelfth day. Then they would harmonize when going backwards. Mollie loved holding the *'golden'* on *'five golden rings.'* Pa and me would cover our ears pretending we hated it. It became a family tradition for them to sing it and for us to pretend it drove us crazy."

Frank continued, "Mollie would have been sixty years old a few weeks ago. She would be a grandmother by now. Maybe a great-grandmother. She was five years older than me. Did I tell you why there was such a difference in our ages?"

"No, your mom did. That is if you're talking about the baby she lost."

"Mollie told me about the baby. Mama never did. Mollie took care of me while Mama worked. Mama worked hard in the sewing plant across town. She sometimes had a sad look and I once asked Mollie why. Mollie told me Mama lost a baby between the two of us. She said Mama didn't have sad eyes near as much after I was born. As a kid, it made me feel good that my being born took some sadness from Mama." Nancy sat quietly, waiting and wondering if Frank would continue talking. He already had given her more insight to his thoughts than he normally shared.

After a few seconds he added, "After Mollie disappeared, I was afraid we would lose Mama too. She cried at the drop of a hat. She would be making biscuits and would seem fine when the tears would start. I'd run to her and hug her tight. I would hide my face in her apron so she wouldn't see my tears. It got so bad she had to quit work.

"When I was older," the words spilled out of Frank as if a dam had burst, "Mama told me if she had not had me bringing her back from the edge of insanity, she would have gone mad. She had to make herself get up in the mornings. She wasn't even in her forties. She looked like an old woman long before her time. Pa tried to pick up the slack when she couldn't cope. But he had about all he could handle. He worked hard all day, came home with granite dust in his hair and on every inch of his clothes. I would see him walking down Railroad Street and pretend he was a gray ghost coming to visit. I would run up to him to hug his legs and he would say, 'Hey, son. Let me get cleaned up first or you'll be as dusty as your old man.' It didn't matter how tired he was, he spent a part of almost every night with me and Mollie. It hurt him real bad when Mollie disappeared."

Frank quit talking for a while. Nancy didn't say a word as she waited quietly. After a while he related his thoughts in a voice so low it was a mere whisper. He told her how the police had searched their house and his pa's truck. Some one had reported they saw Pa and Mollie in the truck on a back road in the county just a few days before she disappeared and his pa had to explain that he was teaching her to drive. He knew it had hurt his pa to know he was a suspect in Mollie's disappearance.

He told Nancy that he would walk into a room and find his mama sitting against the wall on the floor, crying. "Mama?" Frank would say and she would look around as though she could not figure out how she got on the floor. She would give him a smile and say, "Frankie, honey, I'm all right. Now don't you worry about your mama. I just got lost for a minute. Tell Pa I'll have supper ready soon."

He told Nancy, "There would be times I would hear a hurt come from the pit of her stomach and make it's way out of her body sounding like an animal in pain. She didn't know I was there. She didn't know where she was. She only knew the agony of the moment and the pain of losing a child. I would watch as she bowed her head, wrapped her arms around herself and dropped to the floor in slow motion. I wouldn't know what to do. Should I try to console her or leave her alone in her grief? Sometime I would go to her and just sit with her until she realized I was there. Other times I missed Mollie so much the hurt left me with nothing to give — even to Mama."

"I heard Mama tell people, 'To lose a child is the hardest thing to survive.' She would tell me, 'Frankie, without you I couldn't make it.' She always ended with, 'You're such a good boy.'

"After Mollie disappeared, I felt I had to be good and wondered if my badness caused Mollie to disappear. Maybe Mollie would come back if I was good. I tried to be the best. The best sweeper, the best reader, the best to mind Mama and Pa. If I wasn't the best, I knew Mama would die and leave me. Pa always held everything in. I learned to do that, too. I did that the best, too, even better than Pa."

Nancy could not believe he had talked so long. She had been holding his hand while he talked. She let go of his hand, pulled him to her and hugged him tightly. Her Frank, the one who never complained, never cried and rarely shared his deepest thoughts, cried like a baby. She held him for the longest time.

His words helped her understand why he had been so adamant with the boys when they were in their teenage years. He came on like a prison guard, always wanting to know where they were going, what they planned to do, who their friends were, and when they would be home. His fear of something bad happening was extreme.

Even now, with the boys grown and out of the house, he sometimes interfered in their lives. Nancy could now understand more clearly some of Frank's behavior. "Imagine living with a man for almost thirty years and not knowing so much," she thought. Not that it mattered. Nancy had never thought of leaving him. She knew he cared deeply, more deeply than most men. She knew he was honest and she knew he had never cheated on her.

Nancy remembered a sermon she heard once at church on Mother's Day. The preacher said, "Fathers, the best thing you can do for your children is to love their mother." Nancy knew she had Frank's love. Now she had some understanding she had been missing before. He was quiet like his father, caring like his mother and still grieving for the sister he lost when he was eleven years old.

Nancy made the decision to call Dee Dupree. Dee had Mollie's glasses and appeared to know more than she said. She felt bad about how they treated Dee and hoped she could make up for it.

Chapter Seven

"You Need a Friend"

Dee was back in Elberton, yet the vision she had in Easley was clear and definite, and she found it difficult to get her mind elsewhere. Mollie was terrified of the driver who was big, blond and wicked. He had small brown eyes so dark they looked black. It didn't seem natural to have such light hair and dark eyes. However, natural was not a word she would use to describe the young man.

Dee told Emmy about the vision and how she couldn't get her mind off the driver and the fear he caused. Emmy suggested they have a night out on the town in Athens and started making phone calls.

On Saturday evening, Dee and Emmy drove into Athens to hang out with a friend and have dinner downtown. They were both wearing sandals and were dressed casually with Dee wearing khaki slacks, a black tank top and an open shirt with a pattern of black vines mingled amongst beige and white flowers. Emmy's love of bright colors showed in her choice of red Capri pants and a red and white striped top with three-quarter-length sleeves and a straight neckline.

Dee's former roommate, Janet Dayson, met them at The Winery on Broad Street across from the UGA campus. The perfect description of Janet was "shades of chocolate" that showed in her dark chocolate-colored eyes and the milk-chocolate color of her brown hair. Her tawny complexion looked like creamy milk with a light touch of chocolate syrup blended to make a smooth and flawless background for long black lashes and thick eyebrows. Dee had forgotten just how striking Janet's features were until she saw her waiting for them near the entrance to The Winery.

When Janet saw Dee, she straightened her shoulders, making herself look even taller than her five feet, seven inches. Janet ususally carried herself as if she were the leading lady in a movie. Dressed in a red-wine-colored pants suit and wearing black two-inch, open-toe heels, she flashed Dee and Emmy a killer smile, showing perfectly straight white teeth encased in generous lips. She was gliding toward them with grace unlike most in the Athens night scene.

A theater major, Janet was always in the process of either auditioning for a part or participating in one of the plays at the Town and Gown Theater. A natural, she had a knack for learning her lines and flawless performances. She had a good voice and could assist with musical numbers, but, her forte was acting. She could cry real tears — happy or sad — as the lines required. She could be so enraged or sad or happy or nonchalant to the point the audience, even Dee who had lived with her, believed she was the character. She belonged in the theater.

Her voice carried, causing several people waiting to go through the ID check point in front of The Winery to look as Janet exclaimed, "Dee, you dog, I haven't seen you in ages!"

Janet gave each of them an exaggerated hug and lavished welcoming remarks to the point Dee was ready to ask her to chill out. She had forgotten just how dramatic Janet could get. Dee once referred to Janet's overwhelming personality as being "Janetized," and it stuck. Emmy's thoughts apparently mirrored Dee's. She leaned over to Dee and said, "You know. We've just been . . ."

Dee helped her finish and they said in unison, "Janetized."

Janet laughed and said, "Well, girl friends, you just don't know how much I've missed you two."

They walked to the end of the round metal piping used to cordon off those wishing to enter The Winery. Dee didn't recognize the young man checking identification. Mostly seniors and graduate students hung out at The Winery since no one under twenty-one years was allowed inside. There was a time she knew all the check-in people as well as the bartenders and would not have been asked for identification. The man recognized Janet and let her go through with only a cursory glance. He checked Dee's driver's license and motioned her through. When he looked at Emmy's license, he looked up at her, back down at her license and then at her again. He gave her back the license and motioned her to go in.

As Emmy joined the other two, Dee was saying, "Remember? Emmy is always checked more than us. She has that face that results in double-checking her age. She will be carded when she's forty years old."

"To be so fortunate!" Janet said wistfully.

They walked into the room and looked around for a table. It was still early, but it would be crowded in a few hours. It was a favorite hangout for the college crowd and young professionals. As they entered the large room, the tables in the front near the windows were empty; however, they chose a table near the back on the right. The long wooden bar stretched down three quarters of the room on the left. Several colors of wood created a pattern below the counter top. The bartender caught Janet's eye and raised an empty glass in hello. Janet walked over to speak with him as Dee and Emmy headed to their table.

Janet joined them shortly with a glass of red wine. She asked Dee and Emmy what they would like and returned to the bar for their drinks.

"I asked J.J. to run a tab for us. Hope you don't mind?"

"Fine with me," Dee said.

"Me, too," Emmy added.

Both Dee and Emmy knew that Janet's friendship with the bartender and running a tab would keep the costs down. They could enjoy the night without emptying their bank accounts.

As the evening progressed, more and more young women and a few men arrived. The three girls agreed nothing had changed since their college days. Their favorite hangout still had an overwhelming ratio of probably eight women to each man. Janet knew most of the people. She stayed in Athens after Dee moved away. She had to drop out of college because she couldn't afford tuition. She had gotten a job with a temp agency and hoped to save enough money to move to California.

Janet leaned toward Dee, glanced at a nearby table and asked, "Isn't that Marty with those two girls?"

Dee spotted Marty. "It is. I wonder if one of them is his new girl friend. I heard Angela got an internship at some TV station and moved to New York after finishing at UGA last May."

"Well, Honey, can't you tell? If my gaydar is working right tonight, and it usually is, those girls are not interested in Marty," Janet surmised.

As if on queue, one of the girls placed her arm around the other one with what appeared to be more than just casual interest. Both Janet and Dee looked to see Marty's reaction, but they were all laughing, obviously friends.

"Janet, you seemed interested in Marty at one time. Maybe now's your chance," Dee said.

"Marty and I mostly studied together. He helped me learn my lines for a couple of plays we did on campus. He's a good guy, but not for me. Did you see that? My gaydar *is* working tonight."

Dee laughed as she agreed with Janet that the girls were definitely *together*.

They were finishing their second round of drinks and beginning to make dinner plans when Emmy stopped talking in mid-sentence. Dee and Janet had their backs to the entrance, sitting across the table from Emmy who faced the door. Dee followed Emmy's gaze. "Oh damn," Dee thought. "If that's not Fred Rafferty, it's his twin."

Fred had walked in with two guys Dee didn't recognize. They spoke to several people and headed toward the bar.

"Dee. We have to go." Emmy said with conviction.

"Okay," Dee said. She turned to Janet. "I hope you don't mind, but we need to leave."

Janet looked puzzled, but reached down to retrieve her purse.

Fred caught sight of the girls before they were able to get up from the table. He made his way over and said, "Hey, Em. How are you?"

"Fine." Emmy replied.

"I haven't seen you around Athens for a long time. Are you still teaching in Elberton?"

"Yes."

Fred politely nodded to Dee and Janet. "What are you all up to? A night on the town?"

"Hi Fred. We're just visiting some of our old haunts. Not much has changed has it?" Dee answered.

"I don't know. I see a lot of new faces in here. Younger faces. Have you seen how young the freshmen look these days?" Fred directed the question to Emmy.

"Oh, I hadn't thought about it," Emmy replied.

"The watering hole seems to be the same. Did Emmy tell you this is where we met?" Fred asked Janet.

Janet answered, "Remember? I was here too."

"Sorry. I forgot. We all go back a long way, don't we?"

"We were just leaving," Emmy said.

"Don't leave on my account."

"Don't worry. We wouldn't let *you* run us off," Emmy said unconvincingly.

They all pushed back their chairs and took a couple of steps away from the table. Fred headed Emmy off and quietly asked, "Em, could I call you sometime?" He placed his hand on her arm.

Emmy looked as if his touch burned her arm and quickly replied, "Don't touch me. We really don't have anything to talk about." Dee saw Emmy reach toward a glass of water sitting on a nearby table. "Oh, no!" Dee thought, holding her breath. "Emmy's going to douse him."

Emmy stopped her reach inches from the glass. Dee exhaled.

Fred, undeterred, continued, "We could talk about old times, maybe. Or, just to catch up."

"Dream on, you jerk," Emmy said as she walked through the crowd and joined Dee at the door. "Thank God I got away from him. I wanted to scream, 'Dream on, you damned idiot.'" She shuddered. Dee knew that Emmy had a reputation for being outspoken, but she had become very careful as a teacher about how she presented herself, especially in public and in the classroom.

Emmy's shudder gave way to a smile, and she said, "I should have called him a shit head. That would have worked. After all, as Granny Nida always says, 'Shit is not a curse word — just a nasty word.'" She and Dee waited outside for Janet, who stopped at the bar to pay their tab.

The line outside had grown, and the sidewalk was crowded at the ID checkpoint where people mingled with those who were waiting to be seated at DePalma's Italian Restaurant next door. The trio had not decided where they wanted to have dinner but had agreed to eat somewhere nearby.

Since DePalma's had such a line, they decided to walk up to the next block and check out the crowd at the Taco Stand. They squeezed in just as people at a booth near the front window were leaving. "We're lucky," Dee thought. She asked the others what they wanted so she could order for all three. They would have lost the table had they all vacated it to order their food. Dee and Emmy agreed to pay for Janet's dinner to offset some of the amount they owed her for the drinks at The Winery.

After placing their orders, Dee returned, maneuvering through the crowd with three large soft drinks. They talked about plans for the Fourth of July. Janet invited them to a picnic at Watson Mill Park with plans to see the fireworks in Athens that evening. Dee accepted; Emmy was non-committal, saying, "I think my parents have a party planned and expect me to be there and help with it."

They heard Dee's name called, and she and Janet went to the counter to pick up the food. They all were quiet as they ate. After a while Dee asked Emmy, "Do you think Fred will call?"

"Probably not. I wasn't exactly encouraging and he didn't ask for my phone number."

"Well, that won't stop him if he really wants to talk with you or see you."

The three girls talked about the changes taking place on campus including the location for Health Services. Janet said, "The new building is awesome. I understand they have a lot of new programs for women, including date rape information and the latest in birth control. I understand the drug companies are developing a new patch that will solve all our problems. Have you heard about it?"

"No," Dee said.

"I haven't heard about that one, but years ago my Granny Nida told me about one that is very effective." Emmy seemed to have shaken off the funk Fred had given her.

"Better than the patch?" asked Janet.

"*Oh, yes.*"

"Well, girl, aren't you going to tell us?" Janet asked.

"Granny Nida said take one aspirin." Emmy paused to see the effect her words had on her companions.

"An aspirin?" Janet questioned. "No way."

"Granny Nida said 'as soon as the fever' — and Granny Nida pronounced it as fe-ver, like it's two words — 'as soon as the fe-ver of love starts, take one aspirin, place it between yore knees and leave it there till the fe-ver passes.'"

Janet and Dee looked at each other, shook their heads and laughed. Emmy was back to normal.

After finishing their meals, they left the Taco Stand and walked by The Winery where Janet said her goodbyes and joined several friends she saw inside. Dee and Emmy continued walking to their car parked at the end of Clayton Street across from the Bluebird Café.

"Fred looked good, didn't he?" Emmy asked as they got in the car.

"He did. Maybe Fred has grown up some in the last two years."

"Maybe," Emmy replied, "but I've obviously got some bile left in me from our breakup. Obviously more than I thought."

Dee left Emmy to her thoughts about Fred and concentrated on finding music on the car radio. She stopped surfing and inserted a Mariah Carey CD into the player. She kept toggling through songs, as each one seemed to mourn the loss of a lover. *Any Time You Need a Friend* floated through the air. Dee thought that particular one was good considering their friendship; however, the lyrics, *"Even though I try I can't let go. Something in your eyes . . ."* made her realize it would remind Emmy of Fred. Dee immediately switched to another song, *Fantasy,* but when *"When you walk by every night"* flowed all around them, she switched again and was finally happy with *A Hero Lies in You.* She hoped it would make Emmy feel better. It was amazing how many songs were about lovers and lost loves.

The apartment was dark as they drove into the driveway. They forgot to leave on the porch light. It wasn't the first time and, as they had previously agreed, the driver stayed in the car until the other one unlocked the door and turned on the porch light. Dee waited for the light to come on, turned off the car lights and entered the apartment behind Emmy. Dee was ready to call it a night; apparently, so was Emmy as they went their separate ways.

The night out on the town had served its purpose. Dee spent the entire evening without thinking about Mollie Tremane's disappearance or the frightening visions.

Chapter Eight

"Ramblings of Grief"

Dee went to church on Sunday then spent the rest of the day piddling around the apartment. Dan called to let her know he had purchased the tickets for the trip to Abbeville. He reminded her she owed him a trip to Atlanta for dinner. After discussing his work schedule, they decided on Friday of the upcoming weekend. She had spent very little time with her parents and agreed to have dinner with him and then drive to Marietta to spend the weekend with her mom and dad. The thought of seeing him again raised her spirits.

She had planned to spend the rest of the week sorting her clothes. Winter and summer clothes were all mixed together and she was having a difficult time finding cool summer things to wear. Tuesday afternoon she and Emmy decided to walk in the neighborhood. They stopped several times to talk with Emmy's friends and acquaintances and were gone longer than expected.

As Dee and Emmy entered their apartment, they heard the answering machine turn off. Emmy went to her room and Dee walked over to the machine. She pressed the message button and immediately heard, "I'm calling Dee Dupree. This is Nancy Tremane. I need to talk with you. Please give me a call at 864-555-1250. My sister lives in Elberton and she helped me find your number. If you can see me, I'll drive down on Wednesday afternoon. Maybe we can get together Thursday morning. Please call me. I really do need to see you."

Dee called her back immediately and agreed to see her on Thursday morning. They set a time and Dee gave her directions to the apartment on Tate Street Extension. Nancy knew Elberton well and assured Dee she would have no trouble finding it.

Just before bedtime, Connie called to check on Dee. "How are you, Sweetie?"

"I'm fine now. Aunt Connie, I have so much to tell you. I went to Easley and met the Tremanes. I had a more involved vision and I still have a lot of questions."

"I think some of the answers are in the newspaper articles."

"That makes sense," Dee agreed. "You'll never guess. Well, maybe *you* would. Frank Tremane's wife is coming over on Thursday."

"What for?" Connie asked.

"I'm not sure. It will be interesting."

"Let me know what that's all about. I'll let you get to bed, Dee. Take care of yourself, Honey,"

"I will. And, Aunt Connie, thanks for everything,"

"You bet. Keep in touch. Love you. Bye," Connie said just before hanging up.

No visions had come to haunt Dee since she left Easley. "That's Okay," Dee thought. "I could feel Mollie's fear even though I don't know what happened. It's as though Mollie felt very threatened." Her last thought before going to sleep was about fear and the feeling of an urgency to run. She slept for several hours before the vision picked up where it had left off.

"Rotten Tamale, get in the car or I'll tell my grandpa to fire your ole man."

Mollie knew immediately he would do just that. His grandpa wouldn't hesitate to fire her pa, even though Pa had worked in his granite shed for several years. Everybody in town knew he got what he wanted from his granddaddy. Mollie gave up and walked around to the other side of the car. Before getting in, she tried to make it clear she needed to go home. "It's just a block. I can walk that far . . ."

"Get in, Mollie. My granddaddy owns your ole man and you know it." He removed his sunglasses from the front passenger seat and pushed them behind the visor on his side of the car.

Mollie bit her lip and got into the car. He drove down the road, looking at Mollie more than the road. Mollie was afraid he would have a wreck. He drove by the corner and past her house without slowing down. Her head turned as she continued to look back at the house and yard, hoping Frankie or her mama had seen her. No one was on the porch or in the yard. Her heart sank; she knew she would have to deal with him on her own. She looked down at her lap, twisted her skirt between her fingers and said nothing. He reached over and grabbed the skirt and forced her to give it up. Mollie tried to stay still, but after a while she started fidgeting with her pocketbook and biting her lower lip.

"Take off those hideous glasses," He commanded.

In a small voice Mollie said, "No, I can't see without them."

"If you don't take them off," he threatened, *"I'll take them off."*

Mollie opened her pocketbook and pulled out the glasses case and placed the glasses inside. She was afraid he would break them and he had no idea how much the glasses meant to her. Several years ago her family moved to Elberton for a new start and their finances were tight. A teacher from school told her parents she needed glasses rather desperately. After finding there was no money for glasses, the school contacted the Lions Club. The Lions Club had paid for the examination and her first pair of glasses. Mollie's grades had gotten a whole lot better after the glasses, and her parents scraped up enough money to pay for the pair she had in her hand. She was always extremely careful with them.

Mollie sat quietly holding the glasses and waited for his next command. She hoped to be able to put the glasses back on — soon. She looked at him with surprise when his voice softened, "Mollie, you ain't half bad looking without glasses. Slide over here," He motioned with his right hand as his left elbow was propped on the window ledge and his left hand barely touched the steering wheel. It was obvious he thought he was cool. "Here, I'll take the glasses. We'll take good care of them. Open it," he pointed to the front of the glove compartment. She opened it and he threw them in from his side of the car. It surprised Mollie when the glasses case went in. "See what a good shot I am?" he boasted. "Just like football and basketball. I'm a dead ringer every time. Come on. Slide over."

Mollie slid just a little closer. He leaned over and turned the volume up on the radio, not as loud as before. Mollie tried to concentrate on the song, the words competing with his words. She heard the words to Brenda Lee's Sweet Nothins. He pushed a strand of her dark hair back from her forehead. She flinched and the coldness returned to his voice, "You thinking you too good for me?" Mollie stiffened and said nothing.

"Well, Miss Rotten Tamale, I'll show you just what you're good for!"

By this time he had driven through town via the back roads and was headed down Highway 72. Shortly after passing the Granite City Motel he veered to the left, staying on Highway 72; after the city limit sign he turned onto a dirt road, just before the wooden board fencing started. He drove into the woods for a few yards on the dirt road until he came to an opening. Mollie saw a pond ahead and hoped he wasn't planning to drown her.

Dee woke up feeling the same fear Mollie had felt in the car and the tune to *Sweet Nothins* rolling around in her head. "What on earth is going on here?" she thought. At first she felt disoriented but felt better when she realized she was safe in bed. She turned over and punched the pillow as if the motion would make the dream or vision go away. She sat up in bed for just a few seconds, reminded herself that nightmares are not real and tried to settle in and sleep. It was five-fifteen in the morning when she drifted off to sleep. A few hours later she woke up, tired.

The visions were taking a toll on her. She was lethargic all day. Emmy spent the day with her grandmother, so Dee had the apartment to herself. Emmy called during the day to tell her she would be late coming in. She also said that she was going with her mother to a doctor's appointment in Atlanta the next day and that they planned to spend some time at a new shopping center in Midtown.

Dee hoped to feel more energetic the next day, so she went to bed early on Wednesday evening, before Emmy came home. Even though she didn't have visions during the night, she tossed and turned and didn't get the restful sleep she had wanted. She heard Emmy come in but didn't get up to talk with her. She went back into a light sleep. Early the next morning, Dee heard Big Mabel pull into the drive and, shortly after, she heard the door close behind Emmy. Her mind kept her from going into a deep sleep and she finally got up and showered. She felt the same tiredness of the day before.

Dee wished she had been able to talk to Emmy and tell her about the last vision. Emmy could be a good listener if she was interested in the subject. She had listened to the Easley vision without once interrupting. Dee needed to tell someone about this last one. Each vision was getting more disturbing. She didn't think she should tell Mrs. Tremane. Besides, for all Dee knew, Mrs. Tremane was coming to tell her to leave them alone and forget their family and its history.

She didn't have long to wait. Nancy Tremane was prompt, ringing the doorbell precisely at nine-thirty a.m. Dee was surprised to see her holding a box. She opened the door wide, said, "Good morning," and ushered Mrs. Tremane inside.

"Thank you for letting me come today," Nancy said. "After the way you were greeted and sent away last week I wasn't sure you'd agree to see me."

"That's okay. I shouldn't have come. I have no idea what your family has been through. I should never have brought up Mollie. I am so sorry, Mrs. Tremane," Dee said.

"No, no, Frank needs to deal with this. I believe your bringing it up is a good beginning. Please call me Nancy. When someone calls me Mrs. Tremane, I look around for Frank's mother and she died years ago."

"Thanks. Call me Dee. I have no idea why I used the name Delores at your house the other day. Even though it is my real name, I'm only called Delores when my mom is really provoked with me. Then she calls me by my full name. I suppose I used it because I was so nervous." Dee looked at the box and then at Nancy.

"Oh. The box. I remembered you said you wanted some family history. Here it is. It's not much, but maybe it will help with your research. Frank and I would like to know why you're doing the history."

"Well, I have Mollie's glasses . . ."

Nancy didn't wait for her to go further, "I believe there's more to it than checking the history of a girl's glasses." She paused and gave Dee a quizzical look. "Are you okay?"

Dee knew she looked a little ragged. She'd noticed dark circles under her bloodshot eyes in the mirror earlier in the day. "I'm fine. It's just that I've had some sleepless nights."

"Want to tell me about it?" Nancy asked.

"It's hard to explain. Let's see what's in the box." Dee just could not bring herself to share the visions. Nancy might think she was totally crazy. "Here. I'll take the box to the kitchen table. We can go through it."

"Are you writing a history?" Nancy questioned.

"Not yet," was all Dee offered.

Nancy pulled out a small white Bible and explained, "This was Frank's mother's Bible. It was given to her as a wedding gift. She kept all the birth records in it." As she handed it to Dee, papers fell out.

"Those are the birth certificates," Nancy explained.

Dee placed the Bible on the table and picked up three papers. She looked at Nancy and said, "I thought Molly and Frank were the only children."

"They were the only children who lived. One was a stillbirth. Frank and I talked about that last night. Poor woman. His mother lost one child at birth and lost Mollie at sixteen years. It's a miracle she survived. She was a strong Christian."

Dee looked at the birth certificate of the stillbirth child. "I guess they didn't name the baby," Dee said, thinking out loud. She noticed the date of birth as September 12, 1946. She looked at Mollie's birth certificate dated March 25, 1944. "Mollie wasn't born in Elberton. How old was she when the family moved to Elberton?"

"I think she was about three. It was around 1947, after the second baby. Frank was born in Elberton." Nancy seemed eager to supply the information.

Dee looked at Frank's birth certificate dated February 2, 1949. She felt all these dates should mean something to her. She couldn't quite put her finger on what it was.

As she placed the birth certificates back in the Bible she noticed a card with only a quarter of an inch showing. She flipped to the page where the card was inserted. The top of the card was brown with age; however, the portion below was off-white and obviously had not been exposed to light for some time. The words were hand written and slightly faded. She looked at Nancy and asked, "Did Mrs. Tremane write this?"

Nancy looked carefully at the three-by-five inch card. "I think so. She had a recipe box with those same type cards. The writing reminds me of the recipes she wrote out by hand. She enjoyed writing. Her grammar was not the best in the world, but she used writing as a way of coping. I shouldn't say anything about her grammar when mine certainly isn't perfect. She didn't have much of an education; but she was smart in her own way. I wonder what she could have accomplished if she had been educated. This looks like it's hers. She probably wrote it after Mollie was gone."

Dee was moved by the words. It appeared to be a poem written to her children and never finished. It was titled "The Very Heart of Me" with some words underlined.

> **The Very Heart of Me**
> *Sometimes <u>out</u> of my sight*
> *But <u>on</u> my mind*
> *And <u>in</u> my heart*
> *Yall will always be.*
> *There you are my loves*
> *The very heart of me.*
> *I felt yall grow so near my heart.*
> *Yall*

The last line showed erasure marks after *"Yall."* It was not signed or dated. As Nancy handed Dee three spiral-bound composition notebooks she said, "These are about the tremendous grief Mrs. Tremane was trying to cope with. Frank has told me stories that would break your heart about his mother and father's grief. About his, too."

Dee opened one of the notebooks and thumbed through it. Some of the writing was consistent and easy to read. Other parts looked liked scribbling, as though the pencil or pen was like the writer's thoughts, often running together with no cohesiveness. Some parts were written in cursive with other passages in a childlike printed fashion. It was plain to see the author had not written the words for other's eyes. Dee went back to the first page that was titled "Ramblings of Grief" and carried no author's name. She again flipped through the pages and noticed most entries were dated. An entry dated June 3, 1960, 11:30 p.m., read: *I broke down at work this week and felt I was dying. Mollies been missing now for weeks. I can almost hear her asking me, 'Mama does this blouse look all right with this skirt?' I close my eyes and think of Mollies smile. My heart hurts.*

June 5, 1960, 1:10 a.m.: *I broke down at the grocery store yesterdy and had to leave the cart and groceries behind. I had picked up a box of Mollies favorite cereal and then realized no one else would eat it. I put it back. Will I be able to carry on? What will happen to Frank James and Frankie? I got to get out of this. How can I? Frankie needs me and so does his daddy. Did I tell Mollie I loved her that morning?*

Dee flipped through more pages. She came to one that simply said, *Mollie, I miss you. I miss you. I miss you.* "*I miss you*" was repeated through the end of the page.

July 15, 1960: *I woke up around 5:00 and couldn't go back to sleep. I got up at 5:30 to get all the pitcher books from the shelf. Frank James found me on the floor in the front room holding Mollies pitchers to my chest. He left for work without breakfast. What kind of wife am I? I straitened myself out enough to feed Frankie. A neighbor was goin to take him swimming at Cold Water Creek. Frankie had tried to make me laugh when he told me I didn't have to fix him a sandwich to take. I had already started making a peanut butter and jelly sandwich. I asked him why not and he said, "Cause I can eat the 'sand which' is there." He did make me smile. He's such a great boy, but he left worried about me. What kinda mama am I? I can't let Frankie feel less of a person cause he didn't disappear.* Part of the writing and date were not clear. It looked wrinkled as though it had water damage; several pages were spotted from teardrops.

Another notebook, much the same as the other, described Mrs. Tremane thinking she saw Mollie six months after her disappearance. *I was shor I seen Mollie today. I was walking in front of Rose's Five and Dime. She was just ahead of me carrying her books and talking to a girl I didn't know. My heart raced. I walked fast so I could catch up with her. Tears started running down my face and I couldn't call out to her. I could hardly get my breath. A strange sound came from my throat. It made the girls turn around. When the one I thought was Mollie looked at me I felt distroyed. She was Mollies size. She had Mollies dark hair. She was not Mollie. I had dropped my pocket book and left it on the sidewalk in my rush to get to Mollie. A young man tapped me on the shoulder and handed me my pocket book. I hope I thanked him. I don't know.*

Dee turned the page and read: *If I could just touch Mollies face or if she would find a way to say to me mama I'm all right. I seen the clothes in her closet today and I knowed I need to get rid of them. I can not. I long to see her face, touch her hair and hear her singing me a song.*

The third notebook with dates of one year after Mollie's disappearance was filled with similar entries. The first one started, *I feel like a stone is on my heart and will make my heart heavy fore ever. After a year I know I'm still dealing with Mollies death – yes death cause Mollie died or she woulda come home by now. It seems to me that death has to be delt with on three levels – the spirit the phsycal and the emotional. Spirit is the easy one. The phsycal is the hardest and won't let the emotional part of me get well. Oh to touch her face and hold her to my heart.*

Yesterdy, I forgot about dealing with Mollies death on a mental level. I know I'm gettin older, but things just don't sink in like they use to. My brain don't hold things in the same way and I know its cause of Mollie – not age.

Death has to be handled on four levels: spirit, phsycal, emotional and mental. Dee looked at Nancy and said, "I'm glad she was able to write down what she was feeling. I hope it helped her. I've never read about or felt such grief." She closed the third notebook.

A small recipe-sized card had numbers printed one through five and read: *1) emotionally naked 2) phsycally empty 3) totally vulnerable 4) barely able 5) drained.* Dee knew Mrs. Tremane was describing how she felt at the time.

Dee bundled all the notes and notebooks up and placed them back in the box. She knew she would never forget Mrs. Tremane's "Ramblings of Grief."

Also in the box was an old faded photo album. When Dee opened it, she wasn't surprised to see the sheets had yellowed and some of the pictures had fallen out of the small triangular tabs that had been placed at each corner of each picture to hold them in place. "These are really old. I've never seen these little things before," Dee said as she touched one of the triangles.

Nancy walked around the table to Dee and sat down. "They are old and we haven't taken black and white pictures in years. Did you know they are coming back into style?"

"No. But I'm not surprised. It seems everything comes back around eventually. I hope those little triangular holders don't come back. I much prefer today's photo albums."

"Let me tell you who these are. Even though I don't know some of the cousins, aunts and uncles, I'll do my best," Nancy said as she looked at the photograph in which Dee was interested.

Dee was looking at a photo of a dark-haired girl and boy, about thirteen and eight, respectively, holding Easter baskets and dressed in their Sunday best. "Frank and Mollie?"

"Yes," Nancy said. "Mollie may seem old for a basket, but Frank said he got something for Easter until he left home." She waited for Dee to give the okay to turn the page. They spent a good deal of time going through the album.

"This picture of Mr. Tremane makes me think he's Italian, yet Tremane sounds more English to me."

"I believe the dark skin came in from Mr. Tremane's mother's side of the family. See here?" Nancy pointed to an old faded picture of a young man in a military uniform with his arm wrapped around the shoulders of a young girl. "This is Mr. Tremane's daddy who met his wife in Europe. It's so old it's hard to see their features." Nancy pointed to a picture on the opposite page. "This is Frank's mother and father before they had children." The man in the picture wore a hat and stood almost behind the woman.

"I can see that Mrs. Tremane was fairly tall and thin and from her writings I believe she was a deep thinker. What was her personality like?" Dee asked.

"She was shy, but not as shy as Mr. Tremane. Look how he is holding her more in front of the camera, as though he wants the attention focused on her. You and I may be the only ones to read her writings about grief as well as the poem she started. Frank may have read them just after her death, but he's never mentioned it. She was a great cook. People who knew her felt fortunate to place their feet under her kitchen table. I learned how to cook some from my mother; but, most of my best recipes came from Mrs. Tremane."

Several items in the box were older than the album and appeared to be things Frank's mother had kept from her mother's family. There was an old brooch and a string of pearls that had long ago lost their luster.

"I know I should throw some of this stuff away. There's a lot more in Mrs. Tremane's old cedar chest. It doesn't seem right to throw it out. If Frank's mother held on to them for so long, I feel like we should too," Nancy confessed. "It's almost lunch time and I told my sister I would meet her. I mostly wanted to make up for treating you so badly the other day."

"You have, Nancy. And, I want to be honest with you. I don't know if I will ever write a book about the Tremanes. I probably shouldn't tell you this, but I'm going to. I've been having dreams about Mollie." Dee didn't want to get into the complications of telling Nancy she considered them visions.

"The dreams seemed real," Dee added.

"Maybe they were more than dreams."

"Maybe. They certainly were clear, like Mollie was telling me something."

"Are you clairvoyant?" Nancy asked.

"I don't think so. I have an aunt who is, but she has found it best to not advertise it. Most people do not understand it. Some even think of it as evil," Dee tried to explain. "I've never had anything like this happen before. That's why I don't believe I'm clairvoyant."

"Do you know what happened to Mollie?" Nancy asked directly.

It was apparent to Dee that Nancy was always direct and didn't beat around the bush about anything. Still, she was not ready to divulge the visions. They weren't facts. "Not for sure. I dream about things I don't understand. I came to your house to see if Frank might help me understand."

"I don't think I can get Frank to talk with you. He has a difficult time talking with me and we've been married for more than thirty years. I'll see if he'll talk with you."

"That's okay. He seems shy like his mom and dad. I really appreciate you coming over today. I enjoyed getting to know you and the family better." Dee hoped to end the visit on a positive note.

"By the way, how did you get Mollie's glasses? If you told us, I didn't hear or remember it."

"From an estate sale at the old Dunsman place. Do you know anything about the Dunsmans?" Dee asked.

"My grandfather was in the granite business and knew the Dunsmans. Old Mr. and Mrs. Dunsman's son and his wife were killed in a plane crash. I believe their company was sold years ago. When my grandpa died, his business was taken over by two of his sons. There's only one branch of our family in the business now, my brother and his youngest son. My brother has just about turned the business over to my nephew. But the Dunsmans didn't have anyone in their family interested in the business. I think they all moved away. Well, if you want more information about the Dunsmans, you can get in touch with Miss Wilma Jones. Her mother was their housekeeper."

"Thanks. I might do that. Do you know how to get in touch with Miss Jones?"

"I'm sure she's in the phone book. If not, give me a call." Nancy wrote her number on the back of a receipt and handed it to Dee. "Just in case you didn't keep it."

"Thanks. You really have been helpful,"

"I wish I could have been more help. If I learn something new about Mollie, I'll call you," Nancy offered.

They placed all the remaining Tremane memorabilia in the box. Dee walked out with her and helped put the box in Nancy's car. Nancy drove away.

Dee closed the door and thought, "What do I do now? All this seemed anti-climatic after the visions."

Chapter Nine

"Keep It to Yourself"

The next day was Friday, June 25th, and Dee made good on her promise to have dinner with Dan in Atlanta. She had hoped to get ahead of the rush-hour traffic but didn't quite make it. The downtown connector where I-75 and I-85 came together was backed up all the way to the Peachtree Street exit. The traffic was stop-and-go on both the south- and north-bound lanes. She realized how lucky she was the weather had cooperated and it was clear and sunny; otherwise the traffic would be even more congested. When it rained in Atlanta, the wrecks soon followed and caused the traffic to grind to a complete halt.

She looked at her watch. It was almost six p.m. "No wonder," she thought, "this is the worst time to be driving in Atlanta." She usually didn't use her cell phone in heavy traffic, but the traffic was more stop than go, which made her feel sufficiently comfortable to call Dan and let him know she was running a little late. They had planned an early dinner to ensure she wouldn't be too late driving to Marietta.

He answered quickly, "Hey Dee."

"Caller ID strikes again," she thought, then answered, "I'm running a little later than I expected."

"That's okay. It'll give me time to pick up around here. As usual I left the place a mess this morning. I'm not exactly the best housekeeper. I'll make a path for you, though."

"Don't worry. After the last few weeks my priorities have changed. The traffic is moving again. I just passed the Peachtree Street exit. How many exits now before I get to yours?"

Dan was trying to think. He wasn't exactly sure. He told her, "Not many. Just stay near the right hand lane." He realized the directions were too complicated for her to remember them all. He decided to make it easier, "Wait. Just call me when you see the Williams Street exit and I'll talk you all the way to my door."

"That's good. Otherwise I don't know where I'd end up for dinner." She managed to change lanes as she finished her sentence.

She called him when she was driving under the Williams Street sign. With his directions she found his apartment complex easily and found a parking space near his building. He waved to her from the second-floor breezeway. She ran up the steps, met him on the landing and was happy with the reception she received. He took her in his arms and kissed her deeply. She hadn't seen him for some time, and when he kissed her she realized just how much she had looked forward to his touch. She had been involved in relationships before; however, she had never felt the strong chemistry she felt with Dan. His touch left her breathless and thinking about and hoping for his next touch.

Dan showed her around his apartment. She was especially impressed with the view of Centennial Park. Dee loved Italian food and was delighted to learn Dan had planned the Old Spaghetti Factory as their dinner destination.

They were quiet as he drove the short distance through still-heavy traffic to the huge historic house where the Old Spaghetti Factory served Italian cuisine in several large rooms. Dan requested to be seated in the railway car in the middle of the main dining room. Conversation was light as they enjoyed their house salad and shared their entrees of Chicken Parmesan and Lasagna. Dee was delighted when the waiter brought them a dish of sherbet at the end of the meal even though it had not been ordered.

As they drove back to the apartment, Dan asked her teasingly, "Just why is it you always call me Daniel instead of Dan? You're the only one who does that."

"I'm not really sure. It started off being something fun to do. Later, it felt right. When I call you, you know who I am immediately and it gets your attention. Also, you are special. I hope it will always make you feel special."

"Okay. I'll go for all that," he said with a smile and reached for her hand.

Soon they were at his apartment. "I would try and talk you into staying and maybe get to know more about what makes Dee Dupree tick, but I have a feeling you wouldn't make it to Marietta tonight and I don't want to make a bad impression on your parents before they meet me."

"I almost forgot. Mom invited you to lunch Sunday. The Girls are all coming. We'll eat about one o'clock. That gives everyone a chance to go to church and then to Mom and Dad's for lunch. What do you think?"

"Sounds fine. Who are 'The Girls?'" he asked curiously.

"Oh. I forgot to tell you. The Girls are my mom and her sisters. Actually they call themselves 'The Reynolds Girls.' The family refers to them as 'The Girls.' I'm told I inherited a look from them that can be daunting and they accuse me of perfecting it and making it even more daunting." He seemed puzzled, so she continued, "You obviously haven't been seared with the 'Dee Look' as my cousins call it. Otherwise you would be hiding in a corner by now. Thought I'd warn you. The Girls are a hoot — different as night and day. You won't be bored. And don't be surprised at what's said or done."

"I'll be there."

After giving Dan directions to her parents' house and their phone number, she ended with, "Call if you get lost. I'll return the favor you did tonight and talk you through. I'm not sure I could have found you without your play-by-play assistance."

He gave her a hug and a kiss and sent her on her way. The traffic had finally thinned, and she drove to Marietta in much better time than she made driving into Atlanta. As soon as she arrived, her mom insisted she have something to drink and settle in, as long as she promised to spend some time tomorrow catching them up on what was going on with her.

Dee was so thankful she didn't have to get into the task of trying to explain her visions until tomorrow. Her dad gave her an extra hug and said, "You know we're here for you, don't you, Deedle Bug?" He hadn't called her by her pet name in a while. He sat down in his favorite chair. "You've always been independent and we don't want to step on your toes. We just want you to know you can count on us." His words made Dee wonder if he and her mother had somehow picked up on the fact that everything was not exactly right in her world.

"Daddy, I know. I know, too, how independent I can act. But I still need you and mom. I'm so glad I'm still your Deedle Bug." She leaned down and gave him a kiss on his forehead near his receding hairline. His dark hair started ebbing a few years ago. He had been concerned he would go bald; however, the last couple of years the hair recession had stopped.

She went to her room. It wasn't the room in which she grew up, but it was the next best thing. She and her parents had moved her bedroom furniture and many of her childhood treasures from the other house and set it up almost exactly like it was in the old house. She settled in and slept all night without a dream or a vision.

The following day, they all slept late and had breakfast at nine-thirty. As soon as breakfast was over they went to the Florida room on the side of the house with the morning sunlight. Windows with small blinds adorned all outside walls. Dee's mom pulled the blinds up all around to let in the light.

White wicker furniture was placed against the inside wall with a wicker table in the middle. Live green plants placed around the room along with the bright tropical pattern on the cushions showed different shades of green and gave the feeling of being outside. The golf course was just beyond the property line and added to the illusion of being outdoors. At the end of June golfers were on the course early in order to ensure they would be finished before the midday sun's glare and heat set in. It was going to be a great retirement house.

As soon as they settled in with the second cup of coffee, both her parents said at the same time, "Okay, Dee . . ." They all laughed. Dee knew it was time to fill them in. Her mother gasped when she heard about the visions. She interrupted Dee, "Honey, you should have told us. Our family does have some experience with this."

"I know, Mom. I remembered someone teasing Aunt Connie about her visions many years ago. I talked with Aunt Connie about this. She was most helpful and thinks this may be a one-time thing."

"I hope so, for your sake. However, many people don't understand at all. How does Dan handle it?'

"I don't think he knows unless Emmy has told him." She tried to continue telling them about the fear the visions caused but her mother interrupted again.

"Well, don't tell him," Anna Marie said. "Connie's visions made it hard for our whole family. Dad made a good living but with four girls to feed and clothe, there wasn't much left for extras. He and mom somehow got enough money together to send Connie to a couple of different doctors. I was young and didn't understand until later what a hardship it was for them. Just keep it to yourself and talk with us about it, but don't share it with anyone else. Connie finally got over it and you will too."

Dee could see how upsetting it was for her mother. She knew there was something between Aunt Connie and her sisters but didn't understand why until now. They thought Connie no longer had visions; however, the threat was always present. Dee found herself feeling sorry for Connie. Not only was she misunderstood when she was younger, but even now if she had visions about harm to her own family she couldn't share them. What a dilemma.

"Dad, you've been awfully quiet through all this."

"Honey, I don't know what to say. All your life I've thought I could fix whatever went wrong in your life, or at least help you carry whatever trouble you ran into. But this? I don't understand and don't know how to help you. I'm at a loss."

"I know, Dad. I don't understand it myself. It just happens." She spoke to both of them when she added, "Just don't get upset with me and try not to worry."

They both said they would try and understand regardless of where this led.

She didn't tell them about Frank Tremane and felt it would upset her mother even more if she told them about her trip to South Carolina to visit Mollie's brother. She decided it was time to change the subject, "Mom, who will be here tomorrow besides The Girls?"

"Just us and The Girls and your Uncle Boyd. Well, not Charlie, of course. Pat and Charlie's divorce should be final within the next couple of weeks. Dan will be here. Right?"

"He'll be here."

"Sam, how about going to your favorite store for me?" Anna Marie asked. They all laughed, knowing how much Sam liked to spend hours at the store he claimed as his namesake, Sam's Club. Anna Marie handed him a list that included croissant rolls and Sam's Club's delicious potato salad made with red potatoes and sour cream. Sam took his car keys off the hook near the back door and left as Dee and Anna Marie headed to the kitchen.

"I'm planning to have mostly salads and cold things for lunch tomorrow. It's too hot outside to do heavy hot recipes. We'll make your favorite pie. Hope you don't mind if we use Splenda instead of sugar. I've gained a few pounds lately and am trying to cut back."

"That's fine, Mom. I assume you are going to make 'Peach Silk' pies. Right?"

"Well, I was hoping you would help me. It's an easy recipe but even easier if you help."

"Sure," Dee agreed as she walked to the pantry for the Splenda. She looked over her shoulder and asked, "How many pies are we making?"

"I think it will take three. What do you think?"

"Three should be enough." Dee walked to the food pantry and reached for three graham-cracker-crumb crusts. After placing the piecrusts on the counter, she opened the refrigerator and took out six cartons of peach yogurt and a carton of orange juice.

"I wish we didn't have to make them one at a time, but I tried mixing the ingredients for three several weeks ago when I hosted my Bunco's group and they didn't turn out as well," Anna Marie said. Just before Dee closed the refrigerator door, Anna Marie added, "Hand me those peaches. The ones on the second shelf."

Dee found the peaches and handed them to her mother. "I'm surprised you played cards, Mom. You've always said you didn't want to work that hard."

"Thanks," Anna Marie said as she reached for the peaches. "Honey, it's not a card game — no cards at all. We use dice. It's a game of luck. We play with three dice and in the first set we start out trying to roll three ones, second set three twos and on through six. If a person rolls three of anything they get extra points. But, the player rolling three of the number assigned for that set scores Bunco and the one receiving the most Buncos wins the game. I like that it moves fast and I don't have to think about what another player has played. You should come play with us sometime."

"Bunco's sounds like fun. Let me know when you're hosting again. Maybe I can make it. I'll chop the peaches if you'll mix up the other stuff, Mom."

"Remember they need to be cut in really small pieces." Anna Marie had taken a large four-cup glass bowl from the cabinet, placed one cup of Splenda and one package of unflavored gelatin into the glass bowl and dissolved the dry mixture with half a cup of orange juice. After heating it in the microwave for less than a minute to ensure the gelatin had dissolved, she added the remaining ingredients of yogurt, whipped topping and the peaches Dee had prepared. She whipped it all together with a whisk, poured it into a piecrust and handed it to Dee who placed it in the refrigerator. After making two more pies they made slaw from shredded cabbage, onion, carrots, light salad dressing, salt, pepper and a touch of garlic powder.

"What's happening in your art world, Mom?"

Anna Marie placed her arm around Dee and led her down the hallway. "Let me show you, Love." She took Dee to a bedroom she had designated as her art room to show off her latest project. Anna Marie was just finishing a series of paintings inspired by the last trip she and Sam had taken out west. She was in the process of creating a watercolor painting of a buffalo.

Anna Marie was a self-taught artist and had several paintings in galleries in and around Atlanta. She was best known for her "Kudzu Art" created in watercolors. The kudzu leaves took the shapes of animals or people, similar to seeing shapes in clouds. "Three Monks" was her most famous painting, with the monks' covered heads bent, their faces in dark green shadows. Their long light green robes draped their folded arms at their waists and flowed gently to the ground. A peaceful background of light blue sky and fluffy white clouds gave the monks an ethereal appearance. It was hanging in the lobby area of the State Public Broadcasting Company in Atlanta and was a part of the permanent Georgia art collection owned by the State of Georgia.

Dee's favorite "Kudzu Art" was an elephant with its long narrow trunk hanging between two huge ears in lighter green with darker green shadows completing its shape. Her mom had given the painting to her for her eighteenth birthday. It hung in her bedroom in Elberton.

Anna Marie started painting when Dee was in elementary school. It took years and dozens of paintings before she tried to sell anything. Dee remembered after her mom's father died, The Girls had to place her grandmother in an assisted living home. They had a huge garage sale before they sold Moms' and Pops' house. The Girls had chosen items they wanted to keep and had placed them to the side with "not for sale" signs on each. Two of Anna Marie's paintings she had given her parents were in the batch. Her sisters had claimed them. After the sale, The Girls discovered the painting of day lilies had been stolen. Anna Marie's sisters expected her to be devastated. Instead she smiled. They looked at each other and then at Anna Marie and Becky asked, "Why on earth are you smiling?" Anna Marie said, "I can't believe someone wanted something I painted badly enough to steal it!" She took the theft as a compliment. The others looked at each other and said, "Go figure."

Her artistic abilities influenced their new home. She had created a colorful, informal, loving atmosphere. Dee remembered just how much she appreciated her mom's talent and wished she had inherited some of it. If she had any artistic ability, it hadn't shown up yet.

Late that afternoon Dee and her dad went for a walk. It seemed like old times. It was easy to push visions away in the company of a man who was the epitome of security. She knew she could count on him.

When evening came they pulled out the old family photo albums. Dee wanted to be surrounded by family and good memories. She couldn't help comparing her life with Mollie's. More than ever, she was thankful for having had a good childhood and thankful her parents never had to experience the loss of a child and hoped they never would.

There were pictures of Moms and Pops, her maternal grandparents, as well as Gran and Granpa, her paternal grandparents. Her mom and dad had come from such different families. Her mother had a big family, not only with the sisters, but also with aunts, uncles and cousins. Her parents had passed away a year or so apart when Dee was a teenager.

Dee loved the pictures from her mom and dad's wedding in 1971. The pictures taken with their parents showed younger grandparents than Dee

remembered. The picture of the bride and groom listed their names —
Anna Marie Reynolds & Samuel Richard Dupree. They waited nine years
for Dee.

Her dad was adopted and, like Dee, an only child. Gran and Granpa
Dupree were older when they adopted her dad and passed away when Dee
was a toddler. They had been able to give Sam a good life; however, they
had not been wealthy. Sam finished high school in Atlanta and graduated
from a community college with a business degree. He was still struggling,
trying to get his own business started when he met Anna Marie.

By the time Dee was born, her dad had taken a partner into the
business and the future looked bright. He inherited his parents' house and
a few investments that had done well. After his parents' deaths, he
continued to make good investments, making it possible to send Dee to
college without putting a strain on their finances. The Duprees had lost
touch with their only cousin who lived somewhere up north.

Dee's mom had been consistent about picture taking. There were
pictures of Dee's first everything from birth through college. Sam said,
"Look at this one," pointing to a picture of Dee on the soccer field. "You
were the best player on the field. And, I'm not saying that because I'm
your proud papa."

"That's true. You were the best player," Anna Marie added. "You
hated to lose. Remember the time you fell and broke your finger? You
didn't even tell your coach and you refused to cry in front of the coach or
the team. I had forgotten just how stubborn you were. You certainly had a
mind of your own." She gave Dee a warm hug.

Her dad continued to point to the pictures of her playing sports
through high school. "I remember this one like it was yesterday," he said
as he looked at a picture of Dee holding a basketball in the air at the foul
line. "They almost threw me out of the gym."

"No wonder. Later in that game when the referee made a wrong call
against Dee you kept saying over and over and louder and louder, 'We've
got a rope. We've got a tree. All we need is a referee.' I was so
embarrassed even though I agreed with you about the call." Anna Marie
added, "You and Dee both have always been too competitive." The
pictures clearly indicated that not only did Dee inherit her competitive
streak from her father, she also got many of his features including the
black hair, green eyes and tall, thin stature.

Chapter Ten

"You Heard Too Much"

The next morning was busy, and the weather continued to cooperate with no rain in sight. Dee's mom gave her dad a "honey-do" list that kept him on the run — including an errand to the grocery store to pick up ice and fried chicken; a request to get the cushions from the closet and place them on the patio chairs, and to open the umbrella over the patio table.

Anna Marie decided at the last minute to add another vegetable to the menu. The recipe was one her mother had given her — a way to make canned green beans taste as if they were fresh out of the garden. She sautéed a large sweet sliced onion in olive oil, added four cans of drained green beans, seasoned them with salt, pepper and a small amount of garlic powder and cooked them until the remaining liquid disappeared. Dee and her mom made iced tea, set the tables inside and visited.

Dan arrived before The Girls and their families, which made his introduction to her parents easier. Dee left Dan and her dad to talk while she went to the kitchen to help her mom. She heard Dan's distinctive laugh as her mom whispered, "Dee, Dan does have red hair . . . and is he ever good looking! I like him."

"I am so happy you like him." She didn't acknowledge the remark about the red hair. She didn't want to get into a conversation about her childhood declaration.

"Does he play golf?" Anna Marie asked, hoping Sam and Dan would find some common interest.

"He does. But it's not the same kind of golf Dad plays. He plays Disc Golf."

"I've never heard of it," Anna Marie said as Dan and Sam walked into the kitchen."

"Dan, tell Mom about Disc Golf. I only know what you told me. And, that's not much."

"It's similar to the golf you play, Mr. Dupree," Dan said.

"Call me Sam. Anna Marie and I don't do the formal stuff. Sam's fine. We walked in on the tail end of their conversation. Did Dee say you play Disc Golf?"

"Yes, Sir, when I have time, which is not too often. There are a few courses in and around Atlanta. I don't know of one in Marietta. I usually play at the Redan course. Sometimes my buddies and I go to Cumming to play."

"What's the difference in your Disc Golf and regular golf?" Sam was interested in golf, regardless of the differences.

"Mostly the equipment. We play with a Frisbee and the course is set up differently. The course has concrete tee areas about 150 to 250 feet from the basket and the baskets are often placed on a slope or a drop off."

"That does sound different. I'd like to see the set up sometime," Sam said.

"They have tournaments fairly often. I'll find out when Redan is having their next one and we'll check it out."

"I want to go too," Dee said to ensure she didn't get left out. She was happy Dan and her father had something in common, other than herself, even if it was two different type golf games.

"Don't leave me out," Anna Marie said.

"I'll find out more about the schedule and let you all know."

The doorbell rang and before anyone could get to the door, Becky and Boyd came in the kitchen door. The others came in at almost the same time, making introductions to Dan a bit confusing. Dee introduced her Aunt Becky and Uncle Boyd first. In the past ten years, Uncle Boyd had lost his hair and gained a lot of weight. He had teased Dee unmercifully as she was growing up. She learned to take it well and occasionally gave it back. Aunt Connie's introduction was second and Aunt Pat last. It all happened in such a short time Dee felt sure Dan would never remember who was who.

As they were leaving the Florida room, Dan and Dee overheard a conversation between Uncle Boyd and Aunt Connie. Uncle Boyd said, "Connie, it's time you put the past behind and find you a good husband to help take care of you in your old age."

Connie reacted hostilely. In a very loud voice she said, "Boyd, lay off. I'm not interested in a man, married or otherwise. I am not interested in sex, married or otherwise. I am interested in creating — songs and gardens — not procreating. Besides, I'm way too old for any of that. Thank you very much." Connie walked away. Boyd shook his head as if he still couldn't believe a woman would want to live without a man.

Dee looked at Dan and shrugged her shoulders. She said, "I need to help Mom with lunch. Want to wash up?" She gave him directions to the bathroom.

Shortly, Dan joined everyone else in the kitchen as Dee and her mom were placing food on the island in the middle of the kitchen, buffet style. She heard Aunt Pat telling her dad about the upcoming divorce, stating, "They say when life gives you lemons, make lemonade. That's what I'm trying to do."

"Well," Dee's dad put his arm around Pat's shoulders, "when you're talking about Charlie you have to remember — you can't take shit and make peanut butter."

The room became quiet and the conversations all stopped. They looked at Sam and Pat. Connie started laughing, "You're so right, Sam." She looked at Pat and added, "You are lucky that narcissistic prick is leaving you. Every time that bastard had an affair he exposed you to every sexual encounter that person had. I'm just glad your AIDS test came back negative."

"Me too," Anna Marie and Becky said in unison.

"You were smart to get tested so you won't have to worry about what Charlie exposed you to. Count your blessings, girl," Connie said.

"I know I should. I have no idea how many affairs he's had. I just want to be fair to the Audra and Andy. I chose their father years ago. They didn't. Hopefully, they are old enough now to handle the divorce without too much trauma," Pat said.

Dee looked at Dan across the room and gave him an "I-told-you-so" smile. He made his way to her side near the island and they filled their plates with chicken, green beans, slaw, potato salad and sliced tomatoes.

Dee saw very little of Dan after lunch. He was much in demand by The Girls, who kept him laughing. By the end of the afternoon they knew more about Dee's boyfriend than she did.

As Becky and Boyd were leaving, Becky said to Dan, "Well, I'm glad Dee finally found her red-headed man. As a little girl she said she was going to grow up, get married and have red-headed children. Now maybe she can concentrate on those red-headed children."

Dee was horrified and gave Becky the "Dee Look." She wanted to crawl under the table.

Dan smiled. "Aunt Becky," he said, using the name by which she had been introduced earlier, "I'll have to talk with her about that — sooner than later."

Dee's dad laughed and tried to help, adding, "I think there's plenty of time for that, son. It can wait another ten years."

They all laughed.

After her aunts and uncle left, Dee pulled Dan aside and offered an apology. "I am so sorry. Things tend to get a little out of hand when The Girls get together. Just ignore it, please."

"I don't think so," Dan disagreed. "I kinda like the idea of a couple of red heads added to our family tree. Who knows, maybe there's a little black-headed 'Deedle Bug' there somewhere, too. I heard your dad call you that today."

"You heard too much today!" she said emphatically and playfully punched his arm.

"You warned me. You said I would not be bored. I was not. Wait till your family meets Granny Nida." They both laughed.

"I wonder which joke she will tell them," Dee said.

"I'd rather not think about it. I'm not sure your family is ready for Granny Nida."

"How about having that dessert we missed earlier?" Dee asked. "I was too full to enjoy it right after lunch, but I'm ready now." She told Dan about the refrigerated pies she and her mother made the day before.

"Sounds good. I've never had 'Peach Silk' before." He followed Dee from the Florida room to the kitchen.

Dan left to drive back to Atlanta while Dee stayed long enough to help her mom with the cleanup and have dinner before getting on the road. They had leftovers and ate on the deck overlooking the golf course. It was a beautiful evening highlighted by a gold-tinted sunset.

The red geraniums had bright orange-red flowers, and the green foliage had taken on a shade of bright green they had not had only moments before. The wooden deck glowed as though the wood had an inner light. The sky was tinged with shades of gold with a hint of pink; Dee and her parents had golden tans. The golden clouds had silver linings. It looked as if God had changed nature's light bulb from a regular light to amber, and it affected everything for a matter of moments, then it was gone.

Anna Marie filled a bag with leftovers which Dee was happy to take with her. She drove home in the dark and used her cell phone to talk with her friends to make the time pass more quickly.

A car she didn't recognize was in the drive. When she walked into the apartment she noticed Emmy had her "do not disturb" sign on her bedroom door. It suited Dee fine because she was tired and ready for bed. She snuggled into the bed with thoughts of Dan and her family. It had been such fun, and he had not been put off by The Girls' antics or the

"Dee Look." She thought of Mollie and how sad it was she had missed out on so much.

The following morning she walked into the kitchen and saw the refrigerator door open with a man's butt sticking out from behind it, showing only white undershorts with "UGA" logos and two hairy legs.

"Who is that?" she thought. She cleared her throat rather loudly. A head with tight dark curls popped up above the lower refrigerator door. Fred was short for a guy, with his head not quite reaching the top of the refrigerator. His hairy chest showed above the opened lower door. "Hi, Dee," he said without a trace of self-consciousness about his attire. "Y'all don't have much in here in the way of breakfast foods. Come to think of it, there's not much in here for lunch or dinner either. You two on a diet?"

"Hi, Fred. I didn't recognize your car when I came in last night. No, we're not on a diet. How are you?"

"Better."

"I assume you and Emmy have made up?"

"Somewhat, but not completely. She acted so cool when we broke up; it never occurred to me that she was so hurt. You wouldn't believe the names she called me on the phone the first time I called her Friday night. Then she hung up on me. It may take her a while to trust me like before. I really made a mistake when I walked away. I called her back and begged to see her. She finally gave in. We still have a few hurdles to overcome and she was right, I was a real shit head."

Dee looked him straight in the eyes and said, "If you hurt her again like that, I will do more than call you names." Then she laughed and added, "If you're looking for orange juice, look in the freezer. There's some there you can use." Dee wasn't sure what she meant by the threat she made, but whatever it was, she meant it. She would find a way to make his life miserable if he hurt Emmy again.

"Thanks," Fred said and added quietly, "I think."

"You might find a frozen waffle in there, too. Just pop it in the toaster."

Dee decided to change from her pajamas and run some errands, giving Emmy and Fred more time together. The grocery store was first on her list of stops.

Chapter Eleven

"Girl Talk"

Dee spent the Fourth of July weekend with Janet and other friends in Athens. She joined them for the picnic at Watson Mill Park located between Elberton and Athens at the county line between Madison and Oglethorpe counties. They spent the hot day sunning on the rocks, playing in the water and eating picnic food. It was only slightly cooler in the evening as they sat in fold-up chairs in the parking lot at the YMCA on Hawthorne Avenue and watched the awesome fireworks at Bishop Park. During the park's grand finale they could hear and see fireworks from the Athens Country Club just above the treetops. Dee remembered thinking, "Two for the price of one." Only it was better than that because they saw the fireworks free of charge.

Several of their friends joined Janet and Dee at Janet's apartment for dinner, ordered from Jason's Deli. The extremely hungry group quickly devoured the selection of sandwiches and sides.

After dinner, Janet insisted they unwind with her favorite pastime, karaoke. In the past year since Dee had moved to Elberton Janet had collected many of the classic pop and country songs to use with the equipment she had bought second-hand from a local disc jockey.

Dee enjoyed the camaraderie; however, she realized Janet was a far better singer and she went along for the fun of listening rather than participating. She missed Emmy being there. She and Emmy would sometimes attempt a song with Emmy's talent carrying the load or they would just cut up, have fun and be silly. But Emmy was spending the Fourth with her family and Fred. She and Fred had become a couple again and were constantly together. Emmy had told her that this time her parents had no doubt about Fred and Emmy's relationship, and she didn't have to hide the way she felt about him from anyone. Dee had never seen her so happy.

She would have also liked to have had Dan there. Dan's firm was considering taking on a huge project in Brownsville, Texas, and had sent him there for preliminary research. He did call Dee several times, and, given all the things he had listed on his agenda, she felt honored he called so often.

The following week, Dee and Emmy got some time together. They had an entire day ahead of them to have some serious girl-talk. It had rained the night before and the weather had cooled slightly from the low nineties to the high eighties.

Emmy was reading a book of poems and pictures when Dee walked into the living room, "I've been planning to talk with you about Dan. You know he's a regular guy, don't you?"

"Sure. That's one of the many things I like about him," Dee agreed.

"Well, you don't know what guys are really like. You've never had a brother. Guys are on their best behavior when they are trying to impress us and you haven't been around Dan much. Sooner or later Dan will do or say a guy thing and it will gross you out — or worse."

"Wait a minute. I've lived with my dad for years and he's a guy. I've dated guys who didn't care what they said *or* did. I have to admit, I didn't go out with them many times. And, Dad can be obtuse sometime."

"No, Dee. I'm not talking about being blunt or insensitive. We all can manage being those things at one time or another. I'm talking about things guys would do that girls would never do. Like crude . . ."

Dee interrupted, "I just can't imagine Daniel being crude or offensive. He is so thoughtful."

"That's exactly what I'm talking about. You're placing him on a pedestal and he's bound to disappoint you. He's still trying to impress you and he just hasn't slipped up. I'm not saying this to make you *not* like him. I only want you to be realistic about him and not let the slip up, when it comes, ruin your relationship. Remember Doug? You stopped going out with him because he said the dreaded "F" word. He only said it once and, *bang!* he was gone. And, remember that guy you dated who stopped to pee on a side road on the way home one night from Atlanta between Conyers and Walnut Grove? Obviously he couldn't wait, but you were so grossed out you wouldn't even take his phone calls. You need to lighten up and move into this century.

"And, oh yes. Poor 'what's his name?' The one who beat you at tennis one afternoon and then had the audacity to beat you playing cards that night. He was sooooooo cute and adored you. You let your need to win outweigh your better judgment when you marked him off your list. You're the most stubborn person I know."

"Like I said, I can't imagine Daniel doing or saying anything to hurt our relationship," Dee said adamantly. "Besides, all my life Dad told me

that people who use bad language usually do so because they don't have a good vocabulary. Actually, it wasn't only the F word. He gave me the creeps one night. He was a great kisser. He and I had some good times together. One night — now don't you ever tell anybody this, Emmy — "
She looked at Emmy, who raised her hand as if pledging. "One night we were making out on the sofa at his place. Things were getting pretty steamy when he leaned away from me and said in a deep husky voice, 'You would make a beautiful corpse.' He freaked me out so much I almost ran out of his apartment."

"Oh, you know he was teasing."

"No, I didn't. If he had laughed when he said it I might have thought it was funny. But, no he was *dead* serious. Pardon the play on words. But it wasn't funny and I got the feeling he thought he was giving me some kind of compliment. I didn't stay around so he could see me as beautiful some day."

Dee didn't tell Emmy she had been called a prude before. One guy told her she was a "good" girl and followed it with, "There's just no demand for good girls."

"I hope it would have been different if I'd felt anything for any of those guys. The chemistry just wasn't there." Dee thought she had already shared too much about how she felt about Dan. The chemistry *was* there. Just the thought of Dan made her heart beat faster.

"Once I walked out the back steps at Mom's house and heard Dan and Ward, a friend of his, talking about the things that gave them a hard on. They didn't know I had walked up on them till I started laughing. They were furious and tried to make me feel bad. They accused *me* of eavesdropping." Emmy said. "Really, I wasn't. The point is, sooner or later Dan will do or say a guy thing. Just be prepared. Want to see what made me bring this up?"

"Sure," Dee said.

"Actually the author was writing it for her son. See the illustration beside it?" She held the book up for Dee to see a woman, after falling backwards off a pedestal and landing on the boy, all one could see of the young man were feet and hands. A big "S-P-L-A-T" was placed where his torso would have been. Dee read the poem:

Don't Put Me On A Pedestal

Don't put me on a pedestal.
I might fall off you see.

The person to get hurt the most
may not be me.
If I fall off a pedestal
I could break a bone or two.
But, the person I fall upon
might be you.
You may get a few little
bruises all around.
Or, you might end up a greasy spot
left on the ground.
So, don't put me on a pedestal
high up in the air.
You could get wounded
more than your fair share.
I do not want to hurt you
on the ground or in the sky.
So, don't put me on a pedestal
until I learn to fly.

"I love the illustration. Thanks, Emmy. I don't think there's a problem. I will try and remember your advice. Do you think I do?" Dee asked.

"Do what?"

"Do you think I give Dan a hard on?"

Emmy laughed so hard she could hardly answer, "Dee Dupree! I can't believe *you* asked such a question. That cracks me up. But, to answer your question — I expect you do. But, I'd rather not go there." She continued to laugh.

Dee turned red as a beet. She couldn't believe she had given Emmy ammunition she knew Emmy would use to tease her forever. She changed the subject. "We need groceries. How about we make a list, turn it into an outing and include lunch somewhere?"

"Great! Sounds good."

They stopped by the Jacksons' on their way to the grocery store. Emmy had left her checkbook there the night before. Dee had been contemplating contacting Wilma Jones and wondered if Mrs. Jackson knew her. She might offer a link to find out more about the Dunsmans.

"Mrs. Jackson, do you know Wilma Jones?" Dee asked.

"Oh yes. Miss Wilma lives just down the street on Oak Street. She worked for our local pediatrician until she retired two years ago. She retired when he did. She knows more about the people in Elberton than anyone. Has a memory that's unreal. She must have started with Dr. Smith just out of high school. Most of us would say we were taking our children to Smith & Jones. She was as essential to that office as he was." She reached for the telephone book and searched for Miss Wilma's number.

"Thanks. I may call her about some of the things I picked up at the Dunsman estate sale. I understand her mother knew the Dunsmans well." Dee saw no reason to be specific about why she was contacting Miss Wilma. Besides, she wasn't sure herself.

"Just tell her Dan and Emmy Jackson's mother gave you her phone number. I'm sure she'll remember Dan and Emmy." She handed Dee a small piece of paper with a phone number.

Emmy found her checkbook, and she and Dee started toward the back door when they heard, "Hey, Emmy Lou." Granny Nida was holding the back door open. The words came out between small gasps of breath as she stepped into the den. She had worn herself out getting out of the car and walking to the back door.

"Hi, Granny Nida. You okay?" Emmy inquired.

"Shore am, Honey. Just gittin' old and out of breath." Granny Nida and Dee exchanged smiles.

Emmy took her grandmother's arm and walked with her to the kitchen. Dee followed behind them.

"Hi, Mom," Mrs. Jackson said as she set a glass of water on the table. She had pulled out a chair for her mother.

Granny Nida sat. "You girls aren't leaving, are you?"

Emmy replied, "We were, but we'll visit with you for a minute."

"Good. Cause I want to tell you both to be careful. I read in today's paper where they're finally sendin' that rapist to jail."

"What rapist?" Emmy asked.

"The one that was all over Athens when you were in school. I use to worry myself to death over yore bein' in the same town with him."

"Are you talking about the one that broke into the homes behind the hospital?"

"Shore am." Granny Nida pursed her lips together for a few seconds and added, "There was another one out there breakin' in houses and rapin' back in the mid-eighties when we lived on the farm near Bowman. Remember Ida Mae? She was our neighbor."

"No, Granny Nida," Emmy said.

"Mom, are you talking about Ida Mae Street?" Mrs. Jackson asked.

"Yep. That's the one. Her husband died in the early eighties and left

her on that farm by herself. I told her she better start lockin' her doors
'cause that rapist could leave Athens to go someplace like South Carolina
and stop right in Bowman on his way." Granny Nida waited for a reaction.

"Well, he never did. Did he?" Emmy asked.

"No. But, Ida Mae said if he did come to her house she would say
'Mister, you have to leave and you have twenty-four hours to git out'a
here.'" Granny Nida smiled as she innocently looked up at Emmy and
Dee.

Emmy returned the smile. "Granny Nida, that sounds like something
you would say."

"Well, Emmy Lou, Ida Mae did say if he wasn't *too* much of a toad,
she would tell him he had just twenty-four hours to git out. You know Ida
Mae was the one who told me 'bout the remedy for my dry skin."

Without thinking, Dee asked, "What was that?"

"She saw my legs just a-peeling one day and said, 'Onida, you'ar
taking too many baths. You just need a few PTA baths to quit drying out
yore skin like that.' It was the best advice she ever gave me."

"PTA?" Dee asked.

"Pussy, tits and armpits. That's what I wash when I'm in a hurry or if
my skin's too dry."

"Mom, stop. That's enough. Girls, you'd better leave while you can.
Mom's on a roll."

Emmy smiled and kissed her grandmother on the check. She and Dee
said their goodbyes and left Granny Nida telling Mrs. Jackson about one
of her friends who lived at Elsburg Towers. Her friend had fallen in love
with a man who moved into the complex just a few months before and
they were making plans for a wedding. Just before closing the back door
Dee and Emmy heard Granny Nida say, "And I'm probably gonna be
asked to be a bridesmaid, Em-Ily." She always made her daughter's name
sound like two names.

They had a quick lunch at the Dairy Queen Brazier where Dee had
her favorite chili cheese slaw dog; Emmy chose a cheeseburger.

"You always order a hot dog with chili, cheese and slaw, Dee. It's
kind of like a ritual with you," Emmy said.

"Well, you could say I'm made of them. My dad loves to tell the story
about how Mom would talk him into going to the Dairy Queen when she
was pregnant with me. She craved chili cheese slaw dogs. He said some of
the Dairy Queens and fast food places around Atlanta had never made a
hot dog with that combination. Remember, we're talking about a long time
ago. He said he would be embarrassed because she wanted him to tell

them it had to be made that way: chili, cheese with the slaw on top. She didn't want the slaw *under* the cheese. They would look at him like they thought he was weird. He would say, 'She's pregnant . . . you know that pickle and ice cream thing.' He said some places refused to make it the way she wanted it. Anyway, I love the combination." She laughed as she used her napkin to wipe the last signs of the slaw from her lips and added, "It's Mom's fault."

Emmy laughed with her. "Everything has a history, doesn't it? Do you know what Dan's made of?"

"No. But I'm sure you're going to tell me."

"He's full of bologna."

"Why would you say that?"

"Because, when he was growing up he refused to eat anything except bologna sandwiches. He truly is full of bologna. You can tell him I said so."

"And, what are you made of, Emmy?"

"Oh, you know that sugar and spice and everything nice stuff," Emmy said, laughing.

They enjoyed a leisurely walk through the Bi-Lo grocery store, just a block from the Dairy Queen, picking up all the items on their list.

As soon as they were back in the apartment and the groceries were put away, Dee called Miss Wilma Jones. Miss Wilma answered right away, and Dee talked with her about Dan and Emmy. Dee asked if she could stop by and see her. Miss Wilma invited her to visit the next afternoon.

Dee decided to spend some time working on the curriculum for the coming year. As she looked through books from the estate sale, the books she had been given as guidelines from the State Education Office and other books she had purchased about Elberton and Georgia, she was drawn to a book from the 1960's that had the seal of the City of Elberton on the cover.

The words "CITY OF ELBERTON" were included in the outside circle at the top of the seal with "GRANITE CENTER" at the bottom. The next small circle had "GOD • COUNTRY • INDUSTRY • COMMUNITY • SCHOOL" wrapped within the outside circle and around the top with "EVER EXPANDING ELBERTON" at the bottom, reminding Dee of her feeling of how Elberton changed after granite became its most promising industry in the early 1900's. The center contained four stars to the left with the shape of Elbert County above a skyline of buildings that included a church steeple and industrial and government buildings. A small outline of the State of Georgia was located to the right of the outline of the county.

Dee hoped she could pass on her love of history to her students and planned to take them on a field trip to the Elberton Municipal Center to view the original seal located in the City Hall. A trip to the courthouse and other government buildings would be included. She confirmed an earlier decision to assign each student an existing historical government building or a personal home or business building to research who had built it, including information as to past and current uses.

The idea took root when she attended a funeral at Hicks Funeral Home on Heard Street. Emmy's cousin had died from ovarian cancer last January. Dee accompanied Emmy to the viewing the night before the funeral. As soon as she saw the house it sparked a need to know more about it.

She asked Emmy, "How long has this building been a funeral home?"

"I don't know." Emmy answered. "It's a family-run business. Mr. Hicks ran it for years. That's why it carries his name. It's been a funeral home all my life. I don't know who built it. I'm not the history buff you are, and history doesn't stick to me like it does you. Dad probably knows. He's kinda like you . . . loves old stuff."

Chapter Twelve

"Call Me Miss Wilma"

The next day, Dee arrived at the small, white, frame house a couple of minutes before four p.m. Miss Wilma's front wooden door was opened, and Dee could see through the glass storm door. Miss Wilma came to the door before Dee could ring the doorbell. She unlocked the storm door and held it back for Dee to come in.

Miss Wilma was ready for company. She was a darling little woman who obviously took a great deal of time with her personal care. Her hair was dyed jet black and pulled into a *chignon* at the nape of her neck. She wore bright pink lipstick on lips that had thinned with age. Her makeup was light with just the right touch of rouge on her smooth cheeks. Wrinkles showed around her eyes and mouth as her dark blue eyes lit up when she smiled at Dee and invited her in. She was dressed impeccably in a stylish lavender blouse and white Capri pants. Her flat open-toe shoes matched the lavender in her blouse. As soon as Miss Wilma spoke, Dee knew she was southern from the tip of her dyed black hair to the tip of her pink painted toenails.

"Dee Dupree, do come in," Miss Wilma said with a drawl. "I'm delighted to see you."

"Thank you, Miss Jones," Dee stepped into the cool living room.

"Oh, Honey, call me Miss Wilma. Everybody else in this town does, including all my children I helped take ca-ah of all these yea-ahs." Miss Wilma made Dee think of the characters in *Gone With the Wind*. Dee loved it. She knew her time had not been wasted. Miss Wilma was one of those characters that made a small town interesting. She was quite proper and the epitome of a "Southern Lady."

She motioned to Dee to sit in a chair opposite the one she was using. "Come join me, Sweetie. I'm fixing to have my afternoon tea." The silver service sat on a low coffee table between them. *A formal tea.* Dee didn't know anyone else who entertained formally anymore. Her mother talked about the times her grandmother and aunts used their silver service pieces and their fine china. It was rare to see it used today. Dee knew why Miss

Wilma kept her house cool. Hot tea was much more enjoyable in a cool room.

As Miss Wilma poured the tea, she asked Dee about her background. She told Miss Wilma she was teaching history at the middle school.

"You mentioned the Dunsman family when you called. Are you a relation?" Miss Wilma questioned. "I don't rememb-ah any Duprees in that family."

"No, Ma'am. I'm not related. I purchased a few things at the estate sale and became curious about the family. None of the family was there the day of the sale. I wondered why so much of their memorabilia was sold. It seemed like there was no family left to want the heirlooms."

"You'ah right about that, Shug. There's only one left I know of and he's somewhe-ah out in California, I think," Miss Wilma continued in her slow southern drawl and Dee noticed how she changed many of the words ending in "er" to sound like "ah."

"My moth-ah worked for the Dunsmans. She was Mrs. Dunsman's companion, which means she did whatev-ah she was asked to do. She was asked to do almost everything imaginable. She became the housekeep-ah, maid and at the end she was the ca'ahgiv-ah for the old couple. She wore herself out taking ca-ah of the Dunsmans and they-ah grandchildren."

"Tell me about their grandchildren." Dee tried to remember if they were listed in Mrs. Dunsman's obituary.

"They had two and they were both old-ah than me. They-ah granddaughter, Bea, was the oldest. But, Moth-ah would tell me things you wouldn't believe. Until I was eleven or twelve years old, I would accompany Moth-ah to the Dunsmans' house. I use to read or do my homework while Moth-ah worked."

"Why did you stop going with her?"

Miss Wilma leaned over toward Dee and said quietly, "It was because of the boy. Moth-ah didn't tell me until much lat-ah, aft-ah I was a grown woman, that she was afraid he would hurt me." Miss Wilma leaned back in her chair. "The girl stayed in touch with Moth-ah until Moth-ah died. I still have her lett-ahs somewhere. It was after one of Bea's lett-ahs came that Moth-ah told me. She said, 'That family has more skeletons in they-ah closets than the Elmhurst Cemetery.' When I asked her what she meant she wouldn't elaborate." She shifted, pulled idly on her slacks and waited for Dee to comment.

"I suppose the grandson ended up with the estate."

"Oh, no. Bea inherited the house and the land. The grandparents sold the granite business and used what Dun didn't spend to live on in they-ah old age. Bea deserved the house and land. They had gobs of antiques. She inherited those too. I don't know why Bea didn't sell all that stuff off before she died, unless it was just too painful for her to deal with it."

"Why just Bea when she had a brother?"

"A broth-ah?" Miss Wilma's expression was indignant. "She had a monst-ah is what she had. Poor Bea. Her grandfath-ah doted on Dun. Dun could do no wrong. When I said my moth-ah stopped taking me to the house, it was for a very good reason. Now that they-ah all gone, I guess it doesn't matt-ah if I tell you. You aren't going to write this up or use it anywhe-ah, are you?" Miss Wilma leaned forward, apparently eager to tell her story.

"No Ma'am," Dee assured her. She realized Miss Wilma had already let one of the larger skeletons out of the Dunsman's closet.

Miss Wilma went on, "The reason I couldn't go back to that house was Dun. He had raped his sist-ah. I know that's true 'cause Bea told my moth-ah. Near the end of her life, my moth-ah didn't hold back on any secrets — hers or the Dunsman's. When Bea became pregnant, the grandparents sent her away to North Carolina for an abortion. That was about the only state whe-ah you could get an abortion back then.

"Old Mr. Dunsman blamed Bea. Imagine that! He said, 'Boys will be boys' and blamed Bea for enticing her broth-ah. He was a mean old man and I nev-ah knew when he was watching me 'cause he wo-ah dark glasses all the time. It's a shame they-ah parents were killed. My moth-ah said many times that Dun would not have gotten away with hurtin' Bea if they had lived. I suppose, at the end, they felt like they owed her somethin', so they left the house and land to her. Like I said, Dun had already gone through most of the money they got when they sold they-ah granite company."

Dee realized she, too, had leaned forward, meeting Miss Wilma's eyes. "How about the grandmother? Didn't she care about Bea?"

"Old Mrs. Dunsman was not a strong person. If she spoke up for the girl, my moth-ah nev-ah knew about it. She held that against the old woman until the day she died."

"What happened to Bea?"

"She went to a girl's finishing school aft-ah the abortion and seldom came home. She married a dentist and lived in Atlanta. They nev-ah had children. Her obituary was in *The Elberton Sun* about a ye-ah ago. I understand her husband was in charge of the estate. I read somewhe-ah that the proceeds from the sale were going to charity. I think it was something like Project Safe. Are you famili-ah with the one in Athens?"

"Yes," Dee replied. "It's a great program. I knew someone's sister who took advantage of it. I was amazed how much assistance they give to women who have been abused. They took my friend's sister and her two children in the middle of the night and helped her get out of an abusive marriage. It's too bad Bea didn't have such support back in the '50s and '60s. Do you know what happened to Dun?"

"Moth-ah said he tried to get into the University of Georgia but couldn't. He enrolled in a junior college and dropped out aft-ah the first ye-ah. Moth-ah use to say he was the perfect example of 'all brawn and no brain.' He got into the real estate business in Atlanta by marrying the daughter of a real estate broke-ah who owned one of the largest firms in Atlanta. That's the only way he could-ah made it — on someone else's coattail. That wife died in a ca-ah accident on I-85. Moth-ah always thought Dun caused it in some way. He took all he could from his wife's death and moved to the west coast. He had a substantial amount of life insurance on her. He's been through a few mo-ah wives since then and the splits usually involved domestic violence. I think Bea kept up with him just to be shu-ah she managed to stay out of his way."

Miss Wilma stopped and had that look of someone getting caught. "Good gracious, I really shouldn't 'ave told you all that. It's a sad story and I can be such a blabbermouth. Moth-ah often called me 'Blabber Box.' She would say, 'BB, watch that tongue!' I knew what the 'BB' meant."

"That was hard for you, wasn't it?"

"Being called BB? Not too much. Moth-ah always laughed when she said it. I suppose that took some of the sting out. She nev-ah called me that in public. I was about twelve or thirteen when she quit. I hardly ever talked back to her; but one day I couldn't resist. She said, 'BB, watch that tongue,' and she turned to walk into the hallway. Moth-ah was stout and had a rath-ah large backside. I said, 'Ok, BB One.' She turned around quickly and asked, 'What does that mean?' I laughed and said, 'I'm BB Two. You know, for Blabber Box. That means you-ah BB One. You know for . . .' and I pointed to my backside and mouthed 'Big Butt.' I thought she was goin' to have some kinda fit. She turned red, shook her head and to my surprise she laughed and said, 'It is big, isn't it?' She nev-ah called me 'BB' again. Lordy mercy, I hadn't thought about that in ye-ahs."

Dee laughed and felt she had misjudged Miss Wilma. She wasn't quite as straight-laced and proper as Dee thought. "That is a funny story. Your mother obviously had a great sense of humor. Thank you for explaining how the Dunsman estate ended up like it did." Dee looked at her watch. She had been there for more than an hour. "By the way, do you know if the grandson had a red convertible?"

"I don't rememb-ah a red ca-ah. I believe he had a black one. Actually, he had several ca-ahs. He wrecked his first one a few weeks aft-ah he got it for his sixteenth birthday. The new hadn't even worn off it. He might 'ave gotten a red one aft-ah that. I just don't rememb-ah. Before you leave, young lady, tell me about Dee Dupree. You were quite vague early-ah."

Dee explained her new teaching job at the middle school. She told Miss Wilma about growing up in Atlanta and attending the University of Georgia.

"Do your folks still live in Atlanta?"

"No, they moved to Marietta to a small house at the edge of a golf course. Dad hopes to retire in the next year or two, and the new place is perfect for Dad to play golf and Mom to do her art work."

"I forgot to tell you that Bea asked Moth-ah to make a list of the things she might like to have from her grandparents' house. Moth-ah never did, so Bea brought her this silv-ah tea service. She said enjoying tea with Moth-ah and her grandmoth-ah was one of only a few good memories she had of her childhood." She gave Dee a hug at the front door, "Do come back to visit me."

"Thank you so much for your information today and the tea was wonderful. I look forward to another visit." Dee waved as she walked to her car.

Dee drove home and settled in for the evening. She made a sandwich and placed it on the end table beside the comfortable cushioned side chair. She sat down and used the remote to find and start a movie. She munched on her sandwich and finished it before the first commercial. Her eyelids became heavy. She started dozing off during the commercials and slipped farther down into the chair. After a while the noise of the movie was in the background as the last scene of the vision played in her head like the movie playing on the television.

Mollie's fear was escalating. They were at the pond. He got out of the car, grabbed Mollie's left arm and forced her out of the car with him. She had a difficult time getting past the steering wheel and pulled back. As she pulled back, she hit the volume knob on the radio and the music got louder as the song changed to the Everly Brothers version of Cathy's Clown. *He yanked her the rest of the way out. Mollie started begging, "Please. Please," is all she got out as she cleared the door on the driver's side with her pocket book clutched in her hand.*

"I'll please you all right," Mollie felt his spit hit her cheek as he

threw the words in her face. He pulled Mollie around to the front of the car and picked her up like a rag doll and pushed her onto the hood of the car. As the metal took her full weight, she whimpered and tried to get up. He pushed her harder against the bright red metal. Mollie moaned.

"That's it, bitch. I know you been wanting this longer than I been wanting to give it to you."

Covered in perspiration, Dee sat straight up in the chair. "This is too real," she thought. The details. So clear. Her head lolled to one side as she slipped back down into the big chair. The television noise continued to play in the background.

Mollie was dazed and pinned under his one hundred eighty-five pounds as he pushed her skirt up and ripped her underpants. He had one hand on her throat as he continued to molest her with his other hand. The pain was so intense as he entered her and the pressure on her throat increased to the point she felt herself passing out. Even though Mollie had gone limp, he continued raping her.

Dee was crying. She was there and could not return to the safety of the room. She could feel his breath on her face. Or was it Mollie's face?

As he climaxed, he loosened his grip on Mollie's throat. Her panties fell to the ground near her pocketbook when he took his weight off her and her limp body slid down the front of the car and lay motionless on the grass. He looked at her with disdain and gave her a kick. When she didn't respond, he kicked her harder. He bent down to take a closer look and swore, "God, you little wimp. Wake up, bitch!" He took his hands and held her face toward his, "Damn you! Wake up!" He saw she was breathing and let her head fall to the ground.

Mollie felt him near her as she slowly regained consciousness and was glad when he moved away. Shortly afterward she thought she heard a car door close. She moved slightly and immediately felt something hit the side of her head. She felt the roughness of the grass and saw a bloody shovel on the ground as she was dragged to a car, lifted and thrown into the trunk along with her shoe that had fallen off earlier. Blood was running into one eye. With the other eye she caught a glimpse of his sunglasses. Something had changed and she couldn't figure out what was happening. Pain was shooting through her head. She heard the sound of her pocket book being opened and closed and then felt it hit her arm. She reached for it and held it tight. She tried to reach out to him and remove his sunglasses, hoping to look directly at him and beg him to take her home. He was even more frightening since he stopped talking. He closed the trunk lid and shortly after she felt the car move away from the pond back toward the road.

Even though she moved in and out of consciousness, Mollie was certain the driver never made it back to the main road. She felt the car bumping as it turned off the beaten path onto rougher ground. Mollie tried to stay conscious as the driver stopped, got out and opened the trunk. She saw the vague outline of her attacker as he walked to an old wrecked car that was almost hidden by pines and hardwoods. She strained to lift herself up. When he got to the old wrecked '57 Chevrolet, he tried to open the trunk without success. Mollie felt her body go limp just before he walked back to the trunk of his car. She felt like she was outside her body watching the scenes unfold. Her body shifted as he pushed her legs and arms aside, looking for a crowbar. As soon as his hand found the tool, he pulled it out and continued with the job of forcing the trunk lid open on the '57 Chevrolet. After applying pressure in several places, the lid creaked open slightly. He took his right hand and forced the lid all the way up, exposing the junk inside.

He went back to his car, lifted Mollie and placed her in the trunk of the abandoned Chevrolet. He went back to his car and retrieved her belongings. He gathered the small pocket book and the shoe and threw them on top of her body. He checked his car a second time to make sure all her stuff was out. Feeling certain there was nothing left of Mollie's in his trunk, he went to the other car and slammed the trunk lid down.

In a half-wakened state, Dee was briefly herself, although she was crying. "What kind of animal did this?" Dee knew it happened. Why was she seeing it? She drifted off again.

Mollie moved. Her arms and legs hurt. Her head hurt. She wondered if she was blind. "No, it's just dark," she told herself. She was weak and disoriented. She changed positions in order to be on her back and lifted her arms to push. She pushed hard. At least she thought she pushed hard. She felt so weak she was unsure as to how much strength she had applied. Her weakness wouldn't let her lift the trunk lid. She tried to lift her leg to give herself more leverage; however, she didn't have room enough to bend her knees.

"I am going to die." She panicked and felt around for something — what? She didn't know. She found her pocket book and managed to open it enough to feel the panties he had picked up and stashed in her pocket book. She closed it and held it close against her chest. She started to cry but didn't have the strength to cry hard or long. She turned on her side as much as possible trying to get into the fetal position. She brought her hands together in front of her chest and started to pray. "Please, God.

Mama. Mama, I'm sorry. Please don't cry." Her head ached as she drifted into oblivion.

Dee woke up. Her face was drenched in tears. She was in a fetal position. Her heart was racing. She got up and looked around, trying to remember where she placed the folder with the newspaper articles. After finding it on the coffee table in the living room, she flipped through all the copies and with shaking hands pulled one out. She thought about how when someone gets a new car for graduation or for going to college, the old car gets cleaned out before it is turned over to a dealer or is sold. Things left in the glove compartment would be removed along with whatever else was in the car. The box on the Dunsman's back porch held the items that had been in the glove compartment of the red convertible. After the last vision and talking with Miss Wilma, she knew who raped and murdered Mollie. She just didn't know what to do with the information. And there was no body. How could she prove what she saw in her visions really happened?

Chapter Thirteen

"Karaoke Fun"

Saturday, July 10, was Janet's birthday. Dan joined Dee, Emmy, Fred and Janet in Athens for part of the weekend. Emmy spent most of her time with Fred but they joined Dee, Dan and several Athens friends to help celebrate the occasion. They decided to take Janet out for dinner at a restaurant of her choosing.

She opted for an evening at the Beef Baron Restaurant with karaoke to follow. Dan volunteered to be a designated driver.

They drove north on U.S. Highway 441 through Banks Crossing and continued north almost to Cornelia. They arrived at the restaurant just before ten o'clock. The dinner crowd had gone and the remaining rooms were empty except for the wait staff cleaning tables, rearranging chairs and preparing the rooms for the next day.

They walked through the lobby into the darkened lounge area. The spotlight at the front of the room was on a young man singing his heart out as the lyrics to a Hank Williams, Jr. song appeared on the monitor. Dee couldn't decide if he was drunk or if he was doing a great job imitating *Bocephus.*

The singer was a light-skinned African American with a short beard that seemed to be the only thing he had in common with Hank Junior. Unlike the superstar, the young man was tall and thin with an air of sophistication he couldn't completely hide and *Bocephus* would not have possessed. A loud crowd sang along as the performer held the microphone close to his lips. They howled as he sang, *"All my rowdy friends are coming over tonight."* The fun was well under way when the Athens group arrived and found seats in the back of the room.

The customers in the lounge were able to order from the menu and, as the name indicated, beef was the specialty. Soon after finding seats and tables, most of the young people ordered hamburgers with home-made French fries; Dee and Emmy ordered their favorites, small filets. Emmy had her steak split in order to get her meat cooked the way she liked it, medium to well done. When she asked if they could butterfly the filet mignon, Janet looked at her and asked, "What does that mean?"

"It means they will cut it in such a way that I get a piece that is twice as big, but half as thin and it looks like a butterfly with its wings open. You know. Both sides the same and still attached."

Janet still didn't understand exactly what it meant and was looking forward to seeing what a butterflied steak would be. She ordered the beef kabob with peppers and onions. By the time they finished eating, not so much as crumb remained, leaving no doubt about the restaurant's culinary expertise.

It wasn't long before the early karaoke fans were interacting with the Athens people. Soon after eating, Janet signed up to sing Shania Twain's *I Feel Like a Woman.* All the women in the room joined in each time Janet sang, "Uh, uh, oh, I feel like a woman." She was the hit of the evening; everyone in the crowd clapped or whistled. When Janet finished, Emmy took the microphone and asked everyone to sing *Happy Birthday"* to Janet. The crowd's momentum increased as they sang loudly and boisterously.

"Bocephus" asked Janet to sing a duet with him. They chose *Written In The Stars* by Elton John and accompanied by LeAnn Rimes. Janet and her new singing partner made a striking couple and, even though he didn't sound exactly like Elton John, he came close enough. Janet had a knack for sounding like almost any female singer. The crowd responded positively as they finished, screaming "More, more, more!"

Janet brought Bocephus over and introduced him, "Hi ya'll. I want you to meet Judd. Don't you think we were made for each other?"

Dee laughed, knowing Judd didn't know the tiger he had by the tail. Janet had a way of taking over and Judd had been "Janetized." He just didn't know it yet.

Dan left Dee sitting with the group, walked over to the young man who was signing people up for the upcoming songs. Dan flipped through the voluminous notebook, chose a song and was on stage before Dee realized he planned to sing. She leaned over to Emmy and said, "I didn't know Dan could sing."

"I didn't either," Emmy said, looking puzzled.

As Dan took the microphone, Janet and her new singing partner started looking through the notebook of songs. Janet looked up to see Dan on stage.

The music started; Dan watched the monitor bring up *The Mississippi Squirrel Revival* on the screen. He didn't miss a beat as he sang Ray Stevens' song. Dan's movements and facial expressions were hilarious. He had the entire room rolling with laughter.

When he finished and was making his way back to the group, Dee looked at Emmy and said, "I've never seen that side of him. He is *funny!*"

"He is, isn't he?" Emmy agreed.

When Dan returned to the table he looked at Dee, "Well, it's your time. Almost everyone here has done at least one song. How about it?"

"You might think that's what you want, but believe me, it is not. I loved your song. I never knew you were such an entertainer."

Emmy seconded Dee's comment. "Dan, she's right about singing. She has many talents, but singing is not one of them. Plus, she doesn't normally have a sense of humor. I can't believe you had her laughing like crazy." She looked at Dee and apologized, "Sorry, I meant, you have a weird sense of humor."

Dee couldn't be angry. She knew Emmy was right. She didn't see the humor in a lot of things that seemed to be apparent to others. Plus, when she laughed, it was normally more inside than outside. Once in a while something or someone was hilarious enough to elicit a real belly laugh, such as Dan's karaoke performance.

Emmy added, "Dee is great at sports. And card games. She's terribly competitive. Hates to lose. You'd better watch out if you're not her partner. She shows no mercy."

Janet and Judd sang the last song of the evening with the most popular duet in country music history. Kenny Rogers and Dolly Parton could have been in the room singing *Islands in the Stream.* Janet and Judd looked and sounded as though they belonged together.

They closed the bar down at one a.m., said their goodbyes to their new friends, piled into their cars and drove back to Athens. Most the passengers fell asleep before the trip was finished. Dee tried desperately to stay awake and talk with Dan all the way back; however, she found herself nodding before the trip was over. Fortunately, she had no visions of Mollie.

Dan and Dee, along with several others, stayed overnight in Janet's small one-bedroom apartment. People slept wherever they could find a place to stretch out. It was past two-thirty before Dan and Dee crashed on the living-room floor with only an old sleeping bag beneath them and a couple of sofa pillows for their heads. Privacy was as hard to find as a soft bed.

Dee wanted to confide in Dan and tell him all about the visions and problems she had encountered regarding Mollie. Those thoughts disappeared as his arm came around her waist followed by his light sleep-induced breathing. She thought about how good it felt to be close to him. She smiled and drifted immediately into her own deep sleep. Again, Mollie did not crash into her dreams.

Sunday was hectic. All the crowd slept late and left in small groups. Janet didn't wake up until after one o'clock, just in time to say goodbye to Dee and Dan as they left to find a place still serving breakfast. They waited forty-five minutes to be seated at the IHOP restaurant on Baxter Street.

It was mid-afternoon when Dan and Dee went in opposite directions. After a long goodbye kiss Dan told Dee he would call her when he was back in Atlanta. Dee drove to Elberton knowing she would not tell Dan about Mollie on the phone. She wanted to do that in person and at the right time.

Chapter Fourteen

"I Aim to Please"

True to his word, Dan called that evening, shortly after eleven o'clock, "Hi Dee, how's my favorite history teacher?"

"Oh no! Do you think of me as a history teacher? I can think of many things I would like you to think of when you think of me. They are not words like history or teacher."

"Oooops. Didn't mean to hurt your feelings. I actually called to ask if you are ready for bed and ask you what you're wearing. Do those sound like history teacher questions?"

"No." She laughed and asked, "They sound like the beginning of phone sex. Are you trying to have phone sex with me?"

"I hadn't planned on it. Didn't know you were into the kinky stuff. What do you have in mind?"

"Daniel!" Dee laughed at how easily he had turned her teasing around. "I'm wearing my pajamas — light blue cotton pants and an old white tee shirt."

"When you're alone, do you sleep on your back or on your side?"

Dee couldn't figure out where this conversation was leading. "I normally sleep on my side. Why do you ask?"

"Do you sleep with your hands together under your cheek?"

"No, I sleep with one hand under the pillow and one on top of the pillow. You *are* trying to have phone sex with me." She giggled and added, "Pervert."

"No. I'm trying to get a picture of you in my mind. Just before going to sleep I want to picture you sleeping and if I dream, it will be dreams of you."

"That is *so* sweet."

"If kinky sex comes with the dream, I won't complain," Dan teased through one of his infectious laughs.

They talked about the trip to Abbeville and what to pack. Just before ending the conversation Dan said, "Dream of me tonight. Okay?"

"I hope so. Goodnight, Daniel."

"Goodnight, sweet dreams."

Dee curled up on her right side with her right hand under her pillow and her left hand resting on the top of the pillow in front of her face. She felt Dan's presence around her and fell asleep thinking of him and how much she enjoyed being with him. The future looked bright and in her dreams she saw herself floating in the air on a huge white cloud feeling safe until she opened her eyes expecting Dan to be by her side. Instead he was slowly floating away from her on another cloud. She had no control over her cloud and could not force it to move in Dan's direction. When she woke up the next morning she couldn't remember the entire dream. She knew she had been floating on a cloud but couldn't recall any other details. Dreams and visions differed that way.

The subsequent Saturday trip was a welcome reprieve. Dee had spent too much time on the "Mollie Mystery." She had not figured out how she would tell Dan without making it sound like she was an idiot or a psycho. She thought of him constantly, yet Mollie and the visions were always near. She smiled as she thought about how she had enjoyed seeing the many facets of Dan's personality up to this point in their relationship.

Dan had driven from Atlanta and was at their apartment well before noon. Dee and Emmy helped him load their things into his SUV for the trip. They were on their way out of Elberton when an old service truck about two car lengths in front of them attempted to cross on a yellow light. In order to do so, the driver gunned the truck and it backfired. A ball of black smoke shot out of the tail pipe toward Dan's vehicle.

Dan laughed. "Wow. That was some kind of truck fart!"

"What?" Dee asked and gave him one of her looks.

"You know. The big pop. The black smoke. The odor. Think about it. It was a giant truck fart." He looked at her a second time. The Dee Look had not been wasted on him.

"Daniel!" Dee exclaimed. "That is so gross."

"You can't tell me that's not the perfect description of what just happened," he justified his remark.

"It may be the perfect description, but it's still gross." As she finished her sentence she glanced back at Emmy. Emmy gave her a smug smile and made a motion with her hands to indicate a pedestal and a fall. Dee knew she shouldn't blow this all out of proportion even though it *was* gross.

She added, "Okay. It's a guy thing. Let's leave it at that." She almost told him her earlier "pedestal" conversation with Emmy. She thought better of it and wanted to change the subject.

Dan gave her a sheepish grin. "You're right. It's a guy thing. Don't hold it against me."

"Don't worry. I'm sure I can take a small dose of gross if you can survive a Dee Look."

"Yeah. I saw The Look."

"Sorry. I understand it can be intimidating. I don't even know I've done it until I see the reaction it causes. I just saw your reaction."

"It's intimidating. It certainly leaves no doubt about how you feel."

Ten minutes later Dan turned off the main road into the parking lot at Clifford's Restaurant. He parked the car alongside several other vehicles and the three of them got out of the cool car and into the hot sun. The restaurant was not very busy and the menu offered a wide variety. They were back in the car in less than an hour. They continued their trip and made comfortable small talk as they crossed into South Carolina.

Dan appeared to know where he was going as he drove into Abbeville. He entered the square and took an immediate right. The building on the right at the end of the block was the historic Belmont Inn.

The front porch started at the street and continued down the side away from the street. The front entrance was at the far end of the porch with planters of Impatiens blooming in soft pink and white on the steps. Several empty large rocking chairs waited for the weather to cool when the patrons would return to relax on the front porch.

Parking was in the back. The trio quickly exited Dan's SUV and met at the back to unload luggage. Dee and Emmy each had a small piece of luggage with wheels plus a hang-up bag. Dan traveled much lighter with just a suit bag with pockets. It seemed strange to be doing something without Fred since he and Emmy had been inseparable since their reunion. Emmy had explained he had to visit his mother and stepfather for the weekend, and Emmy had committed to the Abbeville trip before she and Fred reunited.

They entered the inn through the back, a floor below the front entrance. The office was just inside the door. Dan had made the arrangements and stepped to the registration desk. After a brief exchange with the person on duty, Dan joined the girls. He held up an envelope and teased, "Only a loving brother would let this be a threesome." He opened the envelope and showed them the itinerary for the day plus the next day.

The envelope held tickets for the three of them to attend a tour of a historical house; wine and cheese party; dinner in the main dining room; a play titled "The Foreigner" at the Opera House; dessert after the play in the main dining room of the bed and breakfast, and a continental breakfast Sunday morning.

Dee was floored at the busy schedule. "This did not come cheap," she spoke solely to Dan. "I insist on paying my part." She was perusing the brochure about the bed and breakfast and noticed it was built in 1903.

"I invited you. Remember?" Dan replied.

"Emmy, help me here. You know it's not right for him to pay for all of this," Dee appealed to her roommate.

"I'm not complaining," Emmy offered. "Besides, you keep on and I'll have to pay. It suits me fine for him to pay."

"You're no help at all," Dee countered. "Besides, he's your brother."

"Lucky me," Emmy said sarcastically.

Dan teased, "You're correct. She's my sister. This will mean she's indebted to me. I insist on paying for yours also. And, you know what that means. Right?"

"Sure," Dee replied. "You just might be surprised. Being indebted to you just may not bother me." She hoped she sounded nonchalant. That's how she planned to be this weekend. She loved the schedule. The play. The history. It all sounded too good to be true. She needed a break from her obsession with Mollie Tremane and decided to make herself stop right then and there thinking of Mollie. She had promised herself she would enjoy this weekend no matter what happened. She had even made it through several days and nights without hearing the music and words from *Sixteen Candles*, the sound of the red convertible engine slowing down or feeling the fear that always accompanied the visions.

"It's already one o'clock, you two. If we are going to make the tour of the house and get back here by four o'clock, we had best move on." Emmy added, "And I am not going to miss the wine and cheese party. That is high on my list of priorities."

Dee and Dan looked at each other and smiled.

"Spoken just like the little sister I know and love," Dan laughed. He reached into the envelope and gave them each a key. They were not key cards that were so common in hotels, but were the old fashioned, heavy metal keys with the room number on each. "Let's find our rooms."

Each of them carried luggage up one flight of stairs. At the top of the stairs a large public room with cozy furniture seemed to be placed just right for a gathering place. The inn's front entrance was on the opposite side of the room from where they entered. Windows to the right of the front door allowed a view of the town's square. A long hallway ran off to the right at the backside of the building. The three guests headed in that direction checking the numbers on the doors with the keys. Dan came to his room first. "Two-oh-six. This is mine. See you in about thirty minutes. Okay?"

"Sure," Emmy replied. Dee just smiled and headed down the hallway. She and Emmy were sharing room 210.

The girls wheeled their luggage in and found a small lovely room with twin beds. "Do you have a preference, Emmy?"

"I'll take this one, if that's all right," Emmy said as she placed her purse and hang up bag on the bed nearest the window.

"That's fine. I'll be happy with either. Isn't this great? I love this place."

"I do too," Emmy agreed. "But, I wouldn't let Dan know. I'd be even more indebted." She laughed.

They each took turns freshening up in the bathroom and putting out their toothbrushes, lotions, and other toiletries. They would change later for the dinner and theater.

Dan came to the door on the first knock. Dee thought he had never looked more handsome. He let Emmy walk down the hallway ahead of them, allowing Dee to walk beside him. They talked about insignificant things as they made their way out of the building.

"It's easy to forget how hot it is out here," Dan commented as he clicked his remote to unlock the truck. Dan opened the door for Emmy and she got into the back seat as she had done on the trip over. Dan opened Dee's door, waited for her to settle in and then gently closed the door. He walked to the driver's side without making another comment.

The historic Burt-Stark mansion built in the 1830's was a few blocks away from the public square. They probably could have walked except for the heat. Several local senior citizens were available at strategic areas of the house with tons of information about how and when the house was built, the owners and the furniture. David Lesley, an Abbeville District judge, planter and lawyer, built it in the Greek Revival style for his wife. The tour guides painted a picture of Lesley's love and dedication for his wife in the building of the house that was later sold to Armistead Burt.

Since the Ordinance of Secession was held in Abbeville before the start of the Civil War and Jefferson Davis chose to hold the final Confederate War Council meeting at the home of his friend, Armistead Burt, Abbeville earned the distinction as being the place to witness the beginning and the end of the Confederacy. The well-kept house displayed original furnishings preserved by donations and sales of tour tickets within the theater packages like the ones Dan purchased.

As they drove away, Dee felt obliged to tell Dan, "Thanks, Daniel. That was great. You really know how to please a history buff, don't you?"

"I aim to please, Miss Dee," he said with an exaggerated smile, lifting his eyebrows up and down like *a la* Groucho Marx.

At the wine and cheese party held on the lower floor in the bar and lounge area of the Inn, they sat at a table near the bar and could see across the street. Several other guests were already enjoying glasses of wine and talking amongst themselves.

Pointing to the building across the street, Dan said, "That's where the play will be tonight. Isn't this handy? The building is called the Opera House. Anyhow, tonight — it's the theater."

All the guests were friendly and interesting. One couple with Australian accents asked questions about the history of the area. "Where are you from?" was the question asked most often. An older couple came from Connecticut to celebrate their fortieth wedding anniversary. A couple from Atlanta had their teenage daughter with them, and two ladies from the nearby town of Calhoun Falls said they were regulars and came often to enjoy the plays. There were a few locals in the bar who were not a part of the package group. The gathering set a laid-back pace for the weekend.

Dee and Emmy had an earlier understanding that Dee would return to the room first in order to shower and dress for the evening. When Dee left, Dan took advantage of the opportunity to get Emmy's take on Dee's feelings for him, "Well, little sister, what do you think about Dee and me?"

"Dan, I've never known you to be insecure about anything. Don't worry. Dee may not admit it, but she is crazy about you. The last time I went home with her to Atlanta, her mother asked me about you. You know, the sorta stuff a mom would want to know. Are you a good person, what kind of job do you have and where do you live? You owe me. I gave her all the right answers. Evidently Dee had mentioned you more than once to her parents. That was before you met them."

Dan looked relieved, "Thanks. I do owe you."

"Dee doesn't know, but her mom told me something else of interest."

"What?"

"If I tell you, will it unobligate me for this trip?"

"There is no such word as *unobligate*," he said in a superior older-brother tone.

"It doesn't matter, it says what I want to say."

"Anyway, it all depends on how important it is to me," Dan refused to unobligate her so easily.

"Oh, it's good. Before she met you and before Dee talked to her mom about you, Dee's mom asked me if you had red hair. Only after I told her your hair color did she tell me about when Dee was a little girl she always said she was 'going to grow up, get married and have red-headed children.' Who do you know could help her get her red headed children?"

"That's good. Did she say how many red-headed children? That might make a difference," Dan teased Emmy. He didn't tell her that Dee's Aunt Becky had already let that cat out of the bag.

"Nope. Sorry. You know you do have to work some things out for yourself. I can't do it all."

"Okay. You're off the hook. Debt free," Dan laughed because he knew she would be calling on him soon for something.

After they finished their wine, they left to go upstairs and parted at Dan's room. "Let's meet at the restaurant a few minutes before six-thirty," Dan offered.

"Suits me. See you there," Emmy agreed.

In room 210 the bathroom was vacant. Emmy had it all to herself. Dee seemed to be in another world as she was getting dressed. Her thoughts wandered from Dan's kissable mouth to his laughing eyes. There was no room in Dee's mind or heart for anyone else tonight. Not even Mollie.

Chapter Fifteen

"A Sanctuary"

The dinner consisted of several courses. The menu was fantastic and offered things they had never eaten, such as sweet potato biscuits, roasted garlic-Vidalia onion soup and cold melon soup. All three were low key, intent on enjoying their food with little conversation. Time for the play slipped up on them, and they had to rush to get across the street to the Abbeville Opera House before the lights went down. During intermission they got a quick tour of the theater and learned it was built in 1908 with an impressive list of past performers including Jimmy Durante and Groucho Marx.

Emmy and Dee had seen *The Foreigner* in Athens at the Town and Gown Theater. With a totally different cast, it was like seeing it for the first time. They all laughed a lot. Dee sat in the middle and for the first time in her life did not feel like an only child. Her best friend had become like a sister and Dan was quickly becoming the love of her life. Several times Dee looked at Dan only to find him looking at her.

After the play, they walked across the street to the front entrance of the bed and breakfast. "I'm going to turn in," Emmy informed the others. "Take your time, Dee. I will be asleep as soon as my head hits the pillow."

Dan couldn't believe it. Emmy, without any coaching, had accomplished what he had been contemplating all evening — a chance to be alone with Dee. He leaned over and gave Emmy a hug. She smiled at him conspiratorially.

Dan took Dee by the arm and said, "I want to show you something you've never seen before." He led her to the rocking chairs, moved two of them away from the rooms on the end ("Someone might be wanting to sleep," Dan explained) and placed them closer to the front door and away from too much light.

"You seem to have a need to show me things I've never seen before. I like that, but rocking chairs?" she questioned. "You want to show me rocking chairs? Daniel, I . . ."

He didn't let her finish, moving her to one of the chairs and insisting she sit. "You certainly have seen rocking chairs before. However," he said as he sat in the chair very close to hers, "you have never seen us in rocking chairs before."

Dee laughed. Sitting to his left, she started rocking, her hands resting on the arms of the chair. He placed his big hand over hers and they rocked with the same cadence. The only noise came from the rockers and tree frogs. Dan was first to speak. "I hope I was right tonight."

"About what?" she asked.

"I think I picked up on something earlier. I thought you were sending me a message a couple of times during the play tonight. It was more than just a casual glance from your beautiful eyes. Right?"

"Right," was all she offered.

He was quiet. She had said a lot in that one word.

"Daniel, I'm not quite sure where this will lead. I am enjoying your company a lot. Actually, more than a lot. There is something I need to tell you about myself before either of us gets more involved."

Dan's face contorted. "Let's see, you love someone else? You have another commitment? Well, let's hear the bad news."

"It might be bad news in your eyes," she replied with a degree of concern. "But it's not another man."

"Then, Dee, it can't be that bad."

"I'll just tell you. I don't know of any other way than to just come right out with it." Dee watched his expression closely as she continued, "Since I moved to Elberton I have had what I thought were dreams. Lately they seem real and I believe they *are* real. They are more like visions than dreams. I don't know why it's happening to me."

His expression didn't change. She continued, "Somehow I have become connected with a person who lived in the 1960's. She disappeared when she was sixteen years old. I believe I have seen how she died, and it wasn't pretty."

She waited for some reaction from Dan. All he said was, "Go on."

"One reason I think I have visions is Aunt Connie was considered by some to be clairvoyant. I've talked with her about it and she confirmed she has visions; however, most of the time she ignores them unless she feels someone is truly threatened."

"So, you're clairvoyant?" His tone said he was trying to get a grip on exactly what that meant to them.

"I don't know," she said honestly. "I've never had this happen before and it may never happen again. The last few days and nights have been vision and dream free. Maybe I will never have such weirdness again. I just don't know." Again, she watched and waited for a response.

"Is that the worst thing you can tell me about yourself?" he asked.

"Right now it is. It has kind of consumed me lately. The visions are so real."

"Have you talked to anyone? Maybe a counselor of some sort?"

"No. Normally I'm really pragmatic about things in general. I have talked with Aunt Connie and she has helped. If this makes a difference I understand."

"Dee, I don't think I'm that shallow. I'm not saying I want to make a permanent commitment right this minute — and dealing with visions is foreign to me. But I do know that I have been interested in you for some time. Come here."

Dan beckoned for her to come sit with him. They were the only ones on the porch and she gave in to sit on his lap with her legs hanging over the arm of his rocker. She pulled her long skirt over her knees. He kissed her lightly and said, "Now, isn't that better?"

"Ummmmmm. It is," she agreed, very willing to try it again. The next kiss was deeper and she felt it all the way down to her toes. She started laughing.

"Woman, you laugh at me?" he teased. "That's not exactly the effect I was counting on. I was hoping bells would ring or fireworks. But . . . laughter?"

"Actually, it was better than bells ringing or fireworks. That kiss made my toes curl." She held her sandaled feet up for him to see her toes curled downward.

"I wish I could take credit for that, but the chair arm probably cut off the circulation to your feet. It was a natural response to poor circulation. But I look forward to disproving that theory — sometime soon." He helped her turn around and get to her feet.

"I believe it's time for twinkle toes to go to bed. I know it's time for me to call it a night," Dan said as he placed his arm around her. She returned the gesture and they walked into the bed and breakfast.

They walked past his room to hers. He gave her a quick goodnight kiss. They both knew it had to end quickly or they would backtrack to room 206 for the remainder of the night.

"Goodnight," she said quietly as she inserted her key.

"Wait," she hesitated. "What time do you want to meet for breakfast?"

He walked the few steps back, "Breakfast is over at ten-thirty. Let's meet about ten o'clock. I expect to sleep late. Someone kept me out late tonight." He tapped his watch and leaned over for one more kiss. As he pulled away, she looked into his eyes. They both knew it was too late to back away and without a word, she withdrew her key from the door and walked back to his room with him.

Within seconds they were undressed and in bed. Slowly and quietly they made love as the light from the outside parking area cast a pale glow on their bodies. The light turned into a brighter glow as perspiration covered their bodies and they lay exhausted in the antique bed. Dee uncurled her toes and went to sleep beside Dan, who had already slipped into a quiet contented slumber.

Later, Dee dressed, slipped out of Dan's room and made her way back down the hallway to her room. "This feels good," she thought. She was quiet as she entered the room and made every effort to not wake Emmy. She brushed her teeth, changed into pajamas and smiled as she crawled into bed.

Dee slept without dreams or visions. Recalling being in Dan's arms, she was smiling when she turned over and opened her eyes. She looked over and saw Emmy sitting on the other bed, her legs crossed, looking in her direction. She looked as though she had been waiting for Dee to wake up.

"Good morning," Dee smiled. "What's up?"

"You tell me what's up. I'm not sure when you got in, but it was late. Anything I need to know?"

"Not really, unless you need to know you have the most terrific brother a girl could have."

"Really? That's nice. Let's go eat. Is he meeting us for breakfast?"

"Yes. He said ten o'clock. We have to check out shortly after breakfast. Maybe we should go ahead and pack up."

"I've finished in the bathroom. It's yours," Emmy offered.

"Thanks. I shouldn't be long."

They were waiting at the entrance to the dining room when Dan appeared for breakfast. He was quiet and Dee wondered if he had changed his mind after having time to think about her visions. She hoped the sexual part of their relationship meant as much to him as it did to her.

Her fears were alleviated when he took her hand and squeezed it. "Whew. All is well," she thought. He had given her all the right answers the night before; the day after, he seemed the same. She felt confident about their future.

They quickly put away the continental breakfast and retrieved their luggage. By the time Emmy and Dee got downstairs, Dan had checked out and was waiting to walk out with them.

Again, Dan opened the doors for the girls with Dee in the front passenger seat. They talked about the great food and the wonderful play as they headed home.

They were near Elberton when Dee started feeling uptight. It was a feeling of anticipation with some fear involved. It wasn't a vision, but a feeling as strong as the visions, and Dee knew something important was about to unfold. She just didn't know what.

A few miles before Highway 72 turned into the main road to Elberton, they reached the broken fence that ran along the perimeter of the Dunsman estate. They passed the entrance to the drive and Dee felt something like a punch in the stomach. She said in a strange voice, "Slow down. Turn here."

Dan looked at her. All the color had drained from her face. "Are you all right?" He was already slowing the car.

She pointed to the right. "Please turn here." He turned and went through the large cattle-type gate that was open and in need of repair. The grass and weeds showed signs of another vehicle having gone in and out recently. Dee wondered if the new owners had been inspecting their recently purchased property since this was part of the land that had been sold the day of the estate sale.

She motioned for Dan to continue. He traveled about a quarter of a mile, following the tire tracks to where the trees opened up to a pond. For Dee it seemed like *déjà vu*. Mollie had been here. "Turn around here," the strange voice called from Dee's mouth.

Dan turned around and slowly headed back toward the highway. "Stop!" Dee demanded before arriving at the main road. "Try pulling into that opening to the left."

Dan did so and stopped. Dee immediately opened her door.

"Dee, what's wrong," Dan said in a concerned tone.

"I have to look over here."

"Wait. I'll come with you. Emmy, you stay here with the car." Emmy didn't answer. She did as she was told. Her face was blank.

"Dee. Dee. What is it?" Dan continued to ask as he followed her to a large stand of trees. Weeds and vines were everywhere. She walked as if she didn't see or feel them.

She turned to Dan, "See the light coming from in there?" She pointed to an area under the trees where everything was dark except something reflecting the sunlight. Dee quickly disappeared into the dark thicket.

Dan looked back to the car. Emmy had gotten out and was walking slowly toward him. "Stay there!" he shouted.

Dan pulled back branches nearest the spot into which Dee disappeared. It was eerie. It felt like a sanctuary. Everything was quiet and still. No animals scurrying here and there. The clearing had been completely hidden by the low-growing shrubs, yet had a canopy of green above. It was well hidden.

Pine trees and hardwoods covered the area completely except for spheres of sunshine here and there lighting only the areas touched by the sun. Light and dark. Light and dark. He looked around desperately for Dee and saw her standing near the glass that had caused the reflection. The reflection came from pieces of a mirror. Some of the pieces had found their way to the edge of the trees and bushes.

It was so quiet. He pushed away the remaining vines, leaves and limbs until he was in the open space where she stood looking at an old rusted car. Pieces of mirror lay on the ground. They had fallen from the side view mirror. Why they weren't covered with pine straw, dirt and debris was a puzzle. It appeared to be an old 1957 black — more rust-colored than black, actually — Chevrolet with a silver fin. Dee was standing at the back, looking down at the trunk. Dan walked into the clearing and stood beside her.

"She's here."

"Who's here?"

"Mollie. Mollie Tremane."

"How do you know?"

"She led me here. She wanted me to come here all along. I think she was waiting for a time I wouldn't be alone. She waited until I was with someone she could trust." Dee seemed to be in a trance even though her words were clear.

"Who is Mollie?"

"She's the girl who disappeared when she was sixteen years old. She was placed in the trunk of this car."

"Come on, Dee." He took her arm and tried to pull her away from the rusted car. "You can't know that; this is crazy. Come on. Let's go."

"No, Daniel, I won't leave her until she's free."

"What are we to do?"

"We have to open the trunk." Dee started checking the ground all around her feet. "There's a crowbar here somewhere," she said with conviction. Dan could not bring himself to believe she could know that for a fact.

The pine needles and leaves were like carpet. Nothing grew under the trees, and the canopy of shade was extremely thick. Any crowbar would be buried under a ton of pine straw. Dan started kicking around the straw and was shocked when his foot hit something about two feet to the left of the car. He used his hands to dig through the pine straw and found a crowbar caked with rust. Dee looked at the crowbar with no surprise on her face.

"Even though it's rusty it might do the job," he thought, "unless the trunk is so rusty it won't open at all." He tried placing the crowbar in the middle of the trunk under the keyhole and it didn't budge. He tried the right side with the same result. He tried the left; the lid gave a fraction of an inch. He pushed harder until there was a gap sufficient to continue pushing the crowbar in all the way down the length of the trunk. He managed to get some clearance except for the right corner. He banged the area beside the trunk to get enough leverage to force the right side of the trunk lid open. Except for the noise of the crowbar the entire area was quiet. Finally, Dan was able to get his fingers inside the trunk lid just enough to force it up. There was a swooshing sound as if the wind had escaped from inside as the trunk lid was raised.

As if by design, a sphere of light shifted to the contents of the trunk. A skeleton lay in a fetal position with the bones of the hands poised as if in prayer. A small purse with only the plastic lining intact rested between the bones of the hands and the rib cage. The size of the skeleton, the purse, pieces of clothing and shoes led Dan to believe the bones were that of a young girl. One shoe was lodged in place on the bones of her right foot, which lay on the floor of the trunk. The other shoe was farther back in the trunk. Dan knew the purse and shoes were plastic and not biodegradable. *Plastics last forever.* Other items were shredded and damaged beyond recognition.

He quickly looked at Dee, who was standing perfectly still as if in a trance.

Dee felt she was on the outside looking in at events unfolding in slow motion. She watched Dan open the trunk and look inside. She saw Mollie before she leaned over and looked into the trunk. Dee had expected to see exactly that, but nevertheless shook her head and felt dizzy. Dan caught her before she could fall. He yelled to Emmy, "Use my cell phone and call Sheriff Dalton."

Dee recovered quickly and stood up straight. She looked at Dan as if she had seen a ghost instead of a skeleton. She said, "Mollie. It's Mollie."

"We can't touch anything. Emmy's calling Sheriff Dalton. He should be here soon. Can you walk to the car?"

She felt as if she was standing guard. "Mollie's free, but I can't just leave what's left of her — here."

Dan shook his head, then turned as, from the other side of the green wall, Emmy called, "Dan, Sheriff Dalton wants to know what's out here."

"Tell him we've found someone who's been missing for a long time," he responded.

Dan held Dee and didn't ask her to leave. The sheriff should arrive soon. Dee was lost in a fog like she was on sacred ground — a sanctuary. She and Dan were the only living, breathing beings in this sanctuary. She felt nature's elements had conspired to preserve this space for Mollie until Dee had answered Mollie's call.

The outside world intruded soon enough. Emmy came with the sheriff, who asked how they had discovered the remains. Dan started to answer and Dee cut in, "I asked him to stop here. I knew."

The sheriff asked, "How did you know?"

"I saw it in a vision."

He shook his head, asked other questions and received answers that provoked further head-shaking.

The sheriff escorted them out. Dee asked what would happen next. The sheriff told her everything in the trunk would be sent to a lab to be analyzed. Under the circumstances he felt he needed to call the GBI to help with the case. As they were leaving "the sanctuary" another sheriff's car pulled up.

The sheriff took their personal information and said he would be in touch soon. He had other questions and he would update them about the facts as soon as possible. Dee willingly left with Dan and Emmy. She knew she had done her part.

Mollie was free.

Chapter Sixteen

"Strange to Meet You"

Beads of perspiration covered Dan's forehead. "Dee, I'm sure glad you told me about the visions before we started home." He glanced at her as they continued their trip into Elberton. He directed a question to Emmy, "Don't you think we should go to Mom and Dad's? I gave Sheriff Dalton their number. He will call or come by there within the next couple of hours, I'm sure."

"I agree. Plus, we need to tell them what's happened. If I hadn't talked with Dee while she was having these visions, I would never, ever believe this could happen. Is that okay with you, Dee, to go to Mom's?" Emmy asked.

"It's okay." Dee was still not one hundred percent back from wherever it was she had gone when she knew how to find Mollie.

Dan drove the back roads to South Oliver, avoiding town. He pulled into his parents' drive. An audible sigh told the girls he was relieved.

Mrs. Jackson saw their unexpected arrival. She called Mr. Jackson, "Daddy, come to the kitchen. Something's happened."

Mr. Jackson immediately put down the Sunday paper and hurried to the kitchen. He addressed his son first. "What's wrong, Dan?"

"We're all right. Just shaken. The sheriff will be by or will call soon. We found the remains of a girl who's been missing for more than forty years."

"Where?" Mr. Jackson asked.

"At the old Dunsman place just outside of town. She was in the trunk of an old car."

"What were you doing at the Dunsman place?" Mrs. Jackson asked.

"We were on our way back from Abbeville when Dee asked me stop there. She had been seeing things about the girl for some time," Dan tried explaining. "I know I'm not making much sense, but . . ."

Mrs. Jackson picked up his sentence, "You're right, it's been in the works for sometime. Dee, I hope you don't mind that Emmy kept me apprised of the strange situation you've been in. Not that I understand it. I know you've been under a huge strain this summer trying to figure it out. Shall I call your mom and dad?"

"Thank you. Not right now. I think I'll wait till the sheriff comes by. I'll call them when we know more," Dee responded.

"I'd like to be filled in on some of this before John comes. I seem to be the only one out of the loop," Mr. Jackson said, shaking his head.

"Let's sit down first," suggested Mrs. Jackson. "Dee, Honey, may I get you a drink or anything? You look rather pale."

"Thanks. Do you have iced tea?"

"I do. How about the rest of you? Want something?"

Mr. Jackson preferred coffee and made his way to the coffee maker to start a pot. The others joined Dee with glasses of tea.

Dan gave his dad a short update and covered all the highlights he could remember about how Dee had been hearing and seeing things since she moved to Elberton. He touched on the visions without going into detail. Mr. Jackson kept looking at Dee. His incredulous look almost shouted, "I don't believe all this."

"Mr. Jackson, I know all this sounds unbelievable. I wouldn't believe it myself if it had been someone else having the visions. They scared me half to death. They seemed so real." Dee's voice was a bit weak. "I even visited her brother in South Carolina." She turned to Dan, and her voice seemed restored as she blurted, "My gosh, I forgot about them! Do you think I should call them?"

"Let's wait until Sheriff Dalton comes. If he doesn't come soon, I'll call him. He may have already called them or he may not know about a brother," Dan said. Dee gained even more appreciation for her man, who seemed in control even though she was sure his thoughts were jumping around.

They all heard a car. Soon Sheriff John Dalton was knocking on the back door. "Let me get it," Mr. Jackson ordered.

He talked quietly with Sheriff Dalton for a minute or two and then accompanied him into the kitchen. All eyes were turned toward the sheriff. "Well, this is the strangest damn thing I've ever run into." He looked at Dan, "Son, let's go over why you stopped at the Dunsman place."

Dan repeated his story of Dee's visions of Mollie. Every so often Sheriff Dalton would shake his head and glance at Dee. He was of average height with brown hair and brown eyes. Nothing distinguished him from the everyday "man on the street" except his uniform and a large purplish-red birthmark that started below his ear and ran downward, around his neck and into his hairline. When Dan had told him all his details, he

formally introduced Dee to the sheriff. "I didn't properly introduce you to
the sheriff when we were at the car. This is Sheriff John Dalton. He and
Dad were in school together."

Sheriff Dalton acknowledged the introduction. "Nice to meet you,
Dee. Or, maybe I should say, 'Strange to meet you.' This is baffling. We'll
get to the bottom of this."

"What have you done with Mollie?" Dee's voice rang with concern.

"I believe it may be Mollie Tremane," the sheriff answered.

"Did you find her name in the purse?" Dee asked.

"No, I didn't. I didn't touch a thing. I don't know how you know. I
know because there was a bracelet on her arm. It was one of those with the
name on the underside. It was solid where the name was and connected to
a chain. I believe it used to be called a friendship bracelet. I couldn't read
what was on the top. With my flashlight and a magnifying glass I could
make out the 'M' and the 'Tremane.' It was all pitted and discolored. It
appears to be a homicide considering the person was not a small child.
Small children get trapped in cars and refrigerators, but not older children.
Well, I guess I don't have to tell *you.* I've roped the area off and covered it
well to ensure no one gets in there until the GBI come either later tonight
or early tomorrow. I'm not sure how they categorized this one. They may
feel they need to do something quickly. You're the one calling it a forty-
some year-old case. They don't know that and won't until forensic tests
have been run. They do know it's a skeleton. That may influence whether
or not they hurry over from Atlanta."

"Have you talked with Mollie's brother?" Dee questioned.

"No. I thought I would come talk with you first. I believe I'd be
wasting my time if you already have the answers." It sounded more like a
wisecrack than a wise remark.

"John, take a seat," Mr. Jackson offered. He gave him his seat at the
table, handed him a cup of coffee and pulled a stool close by for himself as
he picked up his coffee from the counter.

"Let's talk about what you saw," Sheriff Dalton's tone was matter-of-
fact. "Then you can tell me about the brother."

Dee told him about buying the glasses with Mollie's name on the
inside of the case. She told him about the student's paper describing
Mollie's disappearance. When she finished he said, "Well, that explains
the visions. Your subconscious took those two events and gave you some
pretty bad dreams. I bet you have an imagination that just won't quit."

Dee gave the sheriff one of her Dee Looks, but it was wasted on him.
She wasn't the only one upset with his condescending attitude. She

answered quickly to ensure the others didn't have to defend her. "No. It's not like that. I was already having short vague visions before. Actually, it started shortly after I moved to Elberton."

"I just need to ask a few questions. Who opened the trunk?"

"Sir, I did," Dan was quick to respond.

"Miss Dee, did you . . ."

"Now, John. You can't possibly think these kids had anything to do with this. They're only in their twenties. This happened more than forty years ago." Mr. Jackson's tone was perturbed.

"I'm sure they didn't do anything forty years ago. I'm just trying to establish if the body had always been in the trunk or if it was placed there more recently. Miss Dee, did you help open the trunk or lean into the trunk and place your hands anywhere?" Sheriff Dalton continued his questioning.

"I don't think so," she answered, unsure of herself. She had been in a funky daze at the crime scene. "Did I, Dan?"

"I'm not sure. I believe you had your arms wrapped around yourself. That's how you were when I caught you and kept you from falling. You just looked into the trunk. I remember thinking you didn't even try to hold onto the car or me. You were kind of in a trance. Come to think about it, I don't remember any of us touching a thing inside the car. Sir, I can tell you that trunk was not easily opened. I had to work hard with a crowbar. You'll see the scratches where the rust is missing on the edges of the trunk from my using the crowbar. The crowbar was rusty, too. That trunk had not been opened in a long time."

"Where did you get a crowbar?"

"It was on the ground," Dan responded.

"Convenient, don't you think?" Sheriff Dalton seemed to be pushing for more than answers.

Frustration showed in Dan's wrinkled brow. "It was there. I'm sure it was left when the body was left."

"Sheriff, I have a question. Is it possible there's any usable DNA in the trunk — maybe in her purse?" Dee asked hopefully.

"I doubt it. The lab won't know for a while. I plan to have the entire scene checked thoroughly. I don't mean to be so hard on you young folks. I have to cover every angle. I'd like to be sure this happened the way you've presented it, then I won't have to apologize later for not doing a good job," the sheriff said. "Now, tell me about the brother."

"His name is Frank Tremane. He lives in Easley, South Carolina. He doesn't have family here, but his wife does. She was here not long ago. I don't know her maiden name," Dee said, supplying as much information as she could. "Are you going to call them or should I?"

"I'll do it. I'll let them know it may possibly be Mollie. If it is Mollie I won't be able to tell them when they can have the remains. I won't know till I've talked with the lab guys. Sometimes it takes them weeks to turn everything loose. I may have to wait for some of the tests to come back before we can say for sure it is Mollie Tremane. It could be a friend of Mollie's wearing a bracelet with her name . . . you know, that friendship thing. If the GBI wants to talk to you, will you be here?"

"No, I don't think so. Emmy, will you go with me to the apartment tonight?"

"Sure, but I'd rather both of us stay here. We can sleep in my old room. Please, Dee."

Mrs. Jackson said, "I wish you would, too. It would make me feel better."

"Okay," Dee conceded. She felt outvoted, but maybe it wasn't a time to assert her independence.

"Your overnight bag is still in the car. I'll bring it in. You won't have to leave and I'll feel better if you stay here," Dan added. "I hate it, but I need to leave soon. I have to be at work tomorrow." Dan turned to the sheriff, "Is it okay if I leave?"

"Sure, son. I'm sure your dad can get you back here quick enough if I need you." His tone had mellowed from his earlier third-degree interrogation. "I'll get back with y'all tomorrow." Mr. Jackson walked out with him. The sheriff drove off shortly after.

Dee called her mom and dad and tried to explain the situation without going into excessive detail. She skipped over a huge part of what had happened since she saw them last. They tried to insist on driving over to be with her but Dee wouldn't allow it. Mrs. Jackson talked with Anna Marie and assured her Dee would be fine with them.

Dan stayed until late, spending most of his time with Dee. "I'll stay over if you need me to," he offered. "I might be able to take care of a few things from here."

"Thanks for the offer. I'm fine. I can't thank you enough for believing in me and supporting me with the sheriff and at the car. I could not have made it through finding Mollie if you had not been with me. And, I know it must be terribly weird for you regarding the visions. I'm having problems with it myself." She paused as a new thought entered her head, one, which on one hand, she really didn't want to tell Dan. But she had to say it. "What if I have these kinds of visions the rest of my life?"

Dan looked at her blankly. "You may never have them again." He stopped for a moment, obviously in deep thought, then said, "I have to admit I'm feeling a little overwhelmed by all this."

He visited with his parents while Dee showered and got ready for bed. He tucked her in with a goodbye kiss that felt more protective than sensual. She realized it was exactly what she needed, though. Her last thought before going to sleep was how wonderful he was and how sensitive he had been through the terrible ordeal of the day.

But his statement about feeling overwhelmed bothered her.

Chapter Seventeen

"I Call Them Visions"

The next day Emmy and Dee hung out at the Jacksons' all morning waiting for Sheriff Dalton to call. That call came about noon. Several items in the purse, along with the bracelet, led all the investigators to conclude that the remains were those of Mollie Tremane. He had already notified Mollie's brother in South Carolina. He told her Mr. Tremane asked if Dee was involved in finding the remains. The sheriff told them she was but did not elaborate.

Dee went back to the apartment and called her mom to let her know she was home and feeling fine. She promised to visit them on the weekend. Then she called Aunt Connie and left a short message on her answering machine, requesting a return call. She placed the yoga DVD into the machine and concentrated on yoga positions and meditation for forty minutes. She realized that yoga mediation had become a form of prayer for her, centering her and relieving stress. She lay in the prone position, relaxing her entire body. Once relaxed, she stayed there for a long time.

Around three p.m. Nancy Tremane called. "Dee, are you okay?"

"Dee said, "I'm fine - just a little shaken. I've wondered where all this was taking me and now I know. How about you and Mr. Tremane?"

"Frank and I are okay, maybe a little stunned. We realize it will be a long two or three weeks wait before Mollie's remains are turned over to us, but that gives us time to plan the arrangements."

"That will be hard," Dee predicted.

"Not as hard as all those years of wondering. Frank may never say this so I'll say it for the two of us. Thank you. I know Mollie would still be missing if it weren't for you. It was like she was waiting for someone."

"I felt that way too, especially at the site where we found her," Dee agreed.

"Sheriff Dalton didn't tell us about the car, only she was in a trunk. Frank wanted me to ask you if it was a red convertible?"

"No. It wasn't a convertible at all. It was an old black Chevrolet that was more rust than anything else."

"He was only eleven years old then, but, he's remembering more and more. He mentioned Mollie being on the porch propped against the railing at the top step, reading while he played in the yard with his trucks and cars. A red convertible would come by and the driver would call Mollie an ugly name, laugh and drive on. He said Mollie would always go inside the house and make him go in with her."

Dee debated about sharing the red convertible information from the visions and decided against it. She repeated, "No. She wasn't found in a convertible."

She received a beep on the phone indicating a call waiting. She didn't say anything about it to Nancy. She didn't want to rush her.

Nancy continued, "Well, I'll let you go. Would you like to know about the arrangements when they are finalized?"

"Yes, please."

Nancy said a quick goodbye and hung up.

As soon as she replaced the receiver, the phone rang. She thought, "Good. I didn't lose the call that was waiting,"

She was delighted to hear Dan on the other end. He asked about her day. She told him about the call from Nancy Tremane. She explained about the red convertible and asked him if he thought she had done the right thing by not volunteering the information from the visions. He assured her she had made the correct decision and agreed it would only have caused more consternation for the Tremanes. Dee thought he sounded a little distant.

Two days later Dee went to see the sheriff. She felt she needed to tell him who murdered Mollie even though he probably wouldn't believe her. She found a parking space in front of his office. She had not called ahead and was relieved to find him in. The large wooden door to his office was open and she knocked softly on the thick dark trim. He looked up, surprised to see her.

"You're up bright and early. If I was a teacher with the summer off I'd sleep till noon."

"I need to tell you something about Mollie's murder. Something I didn't tell you at the Jacksons' house."

"It's not another dream, is it?"

"Not exactly. I call them visions. They are clearer than dreams. Also, I have copies of some old newspaper articles I think you will find interesting."

"Okay. Let's have it. I'm still sending information to the GBI."

She opened her folder with the articles about the Tremanes and the Dunsmans. She leafed through them and pulled the one of Dun Dunsman in his footfall uniform and pointed to him. "This is the murderer. His name is Michael — Dun — Dunsman."

The sheriff looked at the picture then at her and said, "And you know this because . . .?" He waited for her to finish the sentence.

"Because I saw it. He picked her up in a red convertible, took her to his grandfather's farm, raped her and put her in the trunk of the '57 Chevrolet."

"How old are you?"

"Almost twenty-four years old."

"You weren't even born when all this happened. Exactly what am I suppose to do with this?"

"I don't know. I just wanted you to know it. Maybe you can match his DNA with something left in the car with Mollie."

"I don't know if there is any DNA. I don't know where this Dunsman guy lives, and even if I did know the GBI would laugh me out of Georgia if I told them Dunsman did it and I know because you talk to Mollie who died more than forty years ago. Even if I believed your story in every detail, none of it would stand as evidence."

"Miss Wilma Jones thinks he lives in California."

"Miss Wilma is probably right, but she's not the one investigating this case. Little lady, you have an imagination like nothing I've ever seen or heard. What's Miss Wilma got to do with this anyway?"

"She knew the Dunsmans. Her mother worked for them and she believed he raped his own sister. And it's not my imagination. Plus, Mollie wasn't dead when he left her in the trunk."

"And how do you know that?"

Dee hated it when she became angry; however, his attitude got to her. She took a deep breath, gave him the Dee Look and said, "I know because I saw it and you should know because if someone dumps a body into a trunk he is not going to place her hands as if she's praying like Mollie's were." Her voice got louder as she continued, "Plus he wouldn't take her knees and pull her into a fetal position with her fingers intertwined in the chain of the purse. Mollie placed herself in that position!" She released the air from her lungs.

He stood up and looked at her. He appeared to be at a loss for words. She picked up her folder, sent him another scathing look and stomped out of his office.

The sheriff watched her walk away and thought he had never met a more stubborn person. He knew she wasn't going to back off from her assertions about the skeleton at the old Dunsman place. He felt he might as well pursue her theory since he didn't have any other leads to follow.

Dan was having his own problems. After leaving Dee with his family and driving back to Atlanta his mind went back again and again to the skeleton in the trunk of the old car. He shivered as he went over the details Dee had given the sheriff and questioned how she could possibly know so much.

The romance he thought had deepened during the trip to Abbeville was overshadowed by a death more than forty years before. He felt guilty when he remembered how Dee had thanked him for supporting her through the discovery of the skeleton and dealing with Sheriff Dalton. On one level he wanted to continue to give her all the support she needed while on another level he wanted to pretend the discovery never happened. He knew he had been vague with her on the phone the afternoon before.

While Dee was talking with the sheriff, Dan found out he had to fly immediately to Texas to do some trouble-shooting on the Brownsville project. He pushed his guilt farther away, happy to be able to put his time and effort into his job. Dan was relieved as he flew over Atlanta and distanced himself from Dee and Mollie's skeleton.

It was almost three weeks later and school had started before Nancy Tremane called Dee to let her know about the arrangements. "Hi Dee. This is Nancy Tremane. Hope you're okay today."

"I'm fine. I'm still adjusting to the new school year."

"I have some information for you. The sheriff called and said Mollie's remains will be back in Elberton in less than two weeks. Frank and I have already been to Elberton and talked with my nephew who is part owner of Monumental Monuments. We saved some time by choosing a stone that was already cut. We had to supply only the pertinent information. The graveside service will be two weeks from Saturday, August 28th, at eleven a.m. My sister is having the family over afterwards for lunch. We hope you can join us for both the service and lunch."

"I plan to be there."

"The newspaper article about finding the remains mentioned a couple of people who were with you when you found Mollie. Would you please invite them to join us?"

"Sure. Thanks," Dee accepted. "See you soon."

"Thank you, Dee. Bye."

Dee wondered if the service would be announced in the newspaper. She called Dan and left a message on his home phone about the service and Nancy's invitation. Dan had not returned a couple of calls she had left on his cell phone. Even though she felt something really worthwhile was slipping away she didn't know how to stop it. She was more determined than ever to pretend she didn't care about Dan. She wondered if their breakup would affect her relationship with Emmy. She was so hurt and for the first time since she met Emmy she couldn't share her feelings with her. She vowed to never let Emmy know how devastated she was.

When Dan returned to his apartment in Atlanta, his message-waiting light was blinking. After listening to Dee's message about Mollie's service he deleted the message and made a quick decision not to call Dee until he had time to talk with her about his feelings. He had been in a quandary the entire time he was on the last trip. He wondered how he could explain his feelings when he didn't understand them himself. He knew it was a coward's way out, and instead of calling Dee he called his mother to let her know he had just returned from Texas and would not attend Mollie's funeral service. He asked his mother to let Dee know he would not be there.

Before the Abbeville trip he told Dee about a Disc Golf Tournament coming up at the Redan course, and he'd wanted Dee and her parents to join him. He was sure they would enjoy watching a tournament but he knew he wouldn't pursue it now. He didn't know how to plan his future and had lost interest in the golf game. He couldn't remember a time when he felt so lost and miserable.

Chapter Eighteen

"Singing With the Angels"

On the day of Mollie's graveside service, Dee and Emmy rode to the cemetery together. Mrs. Jackson had passed the message on to Dee and Emmy that Dan had just returned from a trip and would not attend the service.

Dee saw Nancy with several young people as she pulled her car over and parked at the end of a row of cars near an open grave. She and Emmy got out of the car and walked toward the crowd. Nancy was dressed in a black summer sundress, carrying a matching jacket with her hair in the same neat, casual style she had worn the last couple of times they had met. She was wearing sensible dress flats and stepped away from the crowd to greet Dee and Emmy. She gave Dee a hug and Dee introduced Emmy to Nancy.

"I want y'all to meet our sons," she said as she ushered the young women toward her children. She introduced Albert, the youngest, first. Second, she introduced Stephen, the oldest. When she called to Jake, the middle son, Dee blinked and thought, "I know him." All three boys wore dress pants, white shirts with dark ties. All had removed their suit coats to accommodate the warm weather. Nancy was busy trying to explain to her children how Dee was involved with Mollie's discovery. Dee continued looking at Jake, puzzling over the fact he seemed so familiar.

Dee was still looking at Jake when Frank walked up. He was dressed in a light brown suit, and his ponytail was gone. He looked like a different person without it. As shy as he was, he gave her a hug. Then it hit her that Jake looked a lot like his dad. He had the same dark hair but was not as tanned. Jake obviously didn't work outside as much as his dad. They were about the same height. No wonder she felt she knew him. The other two boys favored their mother.

She had been so busy with introductions she had not looked at the headstone. She was looking at the back-side with *TREMANE* at the very top, musical notes just below and *Singing With The Angels* below the musical notes. She walked to the other side and stood at the end of what would be Mollie's grave. This side of the monument showed Mollie's full name, Mollie Ann Tremane, and the dates of her birth and death. Underneath the dates, the words *"She came back to us"* followed by the date her body was discovered. A wooden box with a crocheted runner and yellow roses on top was aboveground where the casket normally would be. It looked so unusual.

Nancy walked up behind her and explained. "We are using the oversized cedar chest that was always kept at the end of Mrs. Tremane's bed. It will fit into the vault instead of a casket. Mrs. Tremane crocheted the runner. Frank and I decided his mama would want Mollie to have them. Mollie is wrapped in the yellow baby blanket Mrs. Tremane used to bring her babies home from the hospital. Now I know why I couldn't bring myself to get rid of Frank's mother's things." She paused. "When the service is over I want to show you something else."

The pastor from Broadcast Baptist Church had arrived, and the family was gathering. Nancy commented, "I also want you to meet my side of the family, Dee. I'll introduce you after the service."

Dee walked over to join Emmy, who had been talking with the Tremane brothers. The boys joined their parents on the first row near the box. Dee and Emmy stood behind the family. Dee missed Dan and hated the fact that he was avoiding her. He had told her he had several trips in the fall; but she knew it was more than travel keeping him away.

Several people were standing on the opposite side of the grave. Dee recognized Marie Willsen standing with her mother and an older woman. Dee hoped to talk with Marie before she left the cemetery.

The pastor explained, "The Tremane family has introduced me to Mollie. I never met her, but I understand she could sing like an angel."

Dee had not known about Mollie's singing. Now the engraving made sense. As soon as the pastor said the final prayer Dee asked Emmy to walk with her to speak with Marie.

They walked over to the Willsens and Dee shook hands with Mrs. Willsen. "Hi, Mrs. Willsen. It's good to see you again. I'm sorry it's at such a sad occasion."

"Hi, Ms. Dupree. This is my mom, Rosemarie Hines. Mom, this is Marie's history teacher from last year."

Dee shook hands with Mrs. Hines, introduced Emmy, then looked at Marie and smiled, "Hope you've had a fun summer, Marie."

"Yes, Ma'am. I have."

"Marie, isn't Mollie the person you did your report on last fall?"

"Yes Ma'am. Granma knew Mollie."

Mrs. Hines said, "Mollie and I were friends. She lived on the corner of Railroad and Dillon Streets. We lived three doors away and had been friends since elementary school."

"I'm so sorry. It must have been devastating for you when she disappeared."

"I've never forgotten her. Marie found the newspaper articles I kept in a book about Mollie and her family."

"I wondered how she got a copy of a newspaper article from so long ago. That's one mystery solved today," Dee said.

"Speaking of solved mysteries, I understand from Nancy you helped solve the mystery of Mollie's disappearance. You are new to Elberton, aren't you?" Mrs. Willsen asked.

"Yes, I am. And, I can't explain how I got involved with Mollie's disappearance. It just happened."

"Oh, you don't have to explain, Dear. I'm just glad it's over and Mollie has been found. As much as I needed closure, her family needed it even more," Mrs. Hines said.

After saying goodbye to Marie and her family, Dee and Emmy turned to find Nancy walking up to them. She said to Dee, "I want my family to meet you and Emmy." She led them to where her sisters, her brother, and their children were standing and introduced them. Emmy knew some of them from elementary and high school and started talking with them.

Nancy said, "I'm going to borrow Dee for a while." She guided Dee to an older section of the cemetery two blocks away. They walked up the incline. Nancy passed three plots in the second block, then walked past one plot to the left of the pavement. She stopped at the next plot. Dee looked at the marker and was surprised to see "Tremane" in large letters at the top. It was Mollie's parents' burial spot. She turned Dee around. "See?" Dee saw exactly what she was talking about. Mollie's place was directly below their plot just two sections down in the new area.

"Somehow, it seemed appropriate. It made us feel that Mollie's folks would be here to watch over her now that she's been found," Nancy explained. "All this may seem silly. But it makes us feel better."

"I like the thought too."

After Nancy and Dee returned to the group at Mollie's grave Nancy asked, "Have you had more visions or dreams?"

"No. I'm not exactly sure why Mollie got through to me unless I do have some of my aunt's clairvoyance. I haven't had any visions at all since finding Mollie. Mollie's free. I didn't have visions before and expect to not have them again," Dee explained.

Dee started to walk away, when Nancy turned and said, "By the way, Dee, Sheriff Dalton said he got the reports back and they found enough DNA for testing. It seems that Mollie's purse was lined in plastic and kept the DNA intact."

Dee smiled and said, "Thanks for letting me know."

Dee and Emmy joined Nancy's family for lunch after the service. They lived on Elm Street, a few blocks from the cemetery. Many members of the family took the opportunity to express thanks to Dee for her participation. Several tried to talk with her about the visions and how and when they came. She was so evasive they were polite enough to change the subject.

There was a front-page write-up in *The Elberton Sun* about Mollie's graveside service with Mollie's picture and a list of Mollie's family and friends attending the funeral. It described the headstone and explained the words, *Singing with the angels,* as well as the date when her remains were found. Dee cried when she read the article. The paper reflected the outpouring of love for Mollie, who was lost for so many years.

Dan was on her mind constantly, and she immersed herself in her work, pushing away memories and depression when the longing to see him or talk to him became overwhelming. Her natural curiosity about Elberton and Elbert County along with her teaching responsibilities sent her searching for information. The facts she gleaned from the books she purchased at the estate sale, research at the UGA library and information from the Internet filled up a file folder. One article from the Internet stated that miles and miles of a subterranean bed of granite had been found in Elberton and was not very helpful to the farmers in the 1800's. It was used as crude grave markers, gravel, foundations for houses and chimney stones. The first quarry was opened before Dutchy's infamous last stand. She wanted to learn more and felt it was time to visit the museum, to see Dutchy and learn more about the granite business. She would incorporate the information into her class curriculum.

It was a week after Mollie's funeral when she walked into the museum and was surprised to see Dutchy flat on his back on a cart near the entrance to the second floor. An older gentleman, the host that day, told her Dutchy was temporarily placed there. He assured her plans were under way to give Dutchy a place of distinction within the museum. The man showed her how to take a tour of the building in such a way that it would explain the granite process from extracting the rock from the quarry to cutting it into smaller pieces in the granite sheds and sandblasting the letters and designs to create the final product.

She never quite understood the phrase "diamond saw." She did understand it took a special saw to cut the granite. She saw how the equipment used for lettering and designing in the early 1900's was crude compared to today's computer generated designs.

She learned more about Dutchy. Many of the locals viewed him as monstrous instead of just a poor replica of a confederate soldier. It took years for him to receive the credit due him for being the *first statue* carved in Elberton from Elbert County granite. Mollie's murder was hidden and out of sight, just like Dutchy; and, like him, her murder had been buried within the layers of the town's history. Dee was happy that Mollie was no longer out of sight and forgotten. Mollie *and* Dutchy had been resurrected.

She spent time with the museum host who knew the business well. He told her he had worked in the shed just blocks from the museum. She knew he was talking about Railroad Street and wondered if the shed was the same one where Mollie and Frank's father had worked in 1960.

He was proud to show her the mythical "Sea Lion" on display. It had the face of a lion and the tail of a fish and supposedly brought luck to the granite businesses. After she walked around the first floor, took the steps upstairs and viewed the exhibits and huge murals, she joined the older man downstairs. He walked with her to a rack of brochures and publications and generously gave her a printout about Dutchy, a copy of the *Elberton Graniteer* (the official publication of the Elberton Granite Association), a printout of the granite quarrying and manufacturing process and other Elberton Granite Association publications.

When Dee left, she knew she had not wasted her time and planned to take her students to the museum when the older man would be there. His knowledge of the business was extensive and his experience working in the local shed gave him credibility when he talked about the granite business.

She thanked him for the tour, walked out into the smothering heat and got into her car. As she drove away, she realized she had forgotten to ask him about the Georgia Guidestones. She heard a rumor that someone still living in Elberton knew who commissioned and paid for the stones and the land on which they stand. She also heard the man was sworn to keep the information a secret.

Chapter Nineteen

"The Anti-depressant"

Fall brought some normalcy to Dee's life. She had an entire year of Georgia history lessons planned out. Although changes would be inevitable, she knew she could accommodate the needs as they presented themselves. The beginning of the year was assigned to local history. She certainly had information on the local granite business, how it got started and its effect on the community. She planned to spend the end of the year on state history dedicating a large portion of time to Georgia governors and their impact on the state.

The high school football season was in full swing and she enjoyed attending the games in the Granite Bowl that could seat 20,000. It was located behind the government office buildings on the main street into Elberton from Athens. The seats were made from Elberton granite. In 1960 the buildings served as the high school where Mollie walked the hallways carrying her books, talking with friends and being a typical teenager. Mollie, no doubt, had sat in the Granite Bowl and watched football games. She would have attended her high school graduation ceremony in the Granite Bowl if she had lived.

After one of the football games, Dee drove back to the apartment. Emmy and Fred had stopped to pick up pizza for the three of them; they'd be back shortly.

With a few moments alone Dee thought of Dan and a conversation they had when she asked, "Do you think you will ever live in Elberton again?"

"I don't know. Why?"

"Because I cannot imagine living anywhere else. I wondered if you had gotten tired of Atlanta."

"Ummmm," Dan pretended to have a hard time making up his mind. "Atlanta has its pluses. The new office is a definite in Athens, just off the loop. It takes me about forty-five minutes to get to work now. I could drive from Elberton to the Athens loop in that same amount of time. I've thought about it."

"Somehow this place has become such a part of me. Besides, you and

Emmy grew up here. You two turned out pretty good."

"Pretty good?" Dan questioned. "I'd say damn good. Well, I don' know about Emmy," he added teasingly.

"That conversation is history," Dee thought. She had hoped the two of them would live in Elberton together. He had teased her about having red-headed children and raising them here.

Dan had called only once more to let her know he was having a hard time dealing with a skeleton and visions he didn't understand. Somehow he felt threatened. She tried to understand what he was going through and wondered if they could be friends. He had not asked to see her as a friend or otherwise. The hurt of his pulling away was growing.

The day he called had been a bad day. She woke up depressed and on the verge of tears. She was glad Emmy wasn't there to see her feeling sorry for herself. When she answered the phone that morning and heard his voice she automatically thought, "Everything is going to be all right now." By the end of the conversation she knew he had not called to make everything work out.

When she hung up the phone, the tears ran down her cheeks and dripped on her tank top. She sat on the sofa and cried for Mollie and all the things Mollie did not get to experience. She cried for the Tremanes and wondered how they had coped for so long with the unknown. She cried for herself and for a second blamed Mollie for the loss of Dan. She immediately regretted doing so. She finally got angry with Dan and wished she had never met him. If he was such a wimp about this and didn't care enough about her to get past it, she didn't want him in her life.

She remembered how Emmy wanted to call Fred a damned idiot and a shit head when she was so angry with him. The anger and hurt Dan caused was making her do things she wouldn't normally do. She picked up a square pillow cushion and threw it across the room. It hit the television, knocked over a lamp and crumpled the lampshade. She felt better even though she knew she would have to repair the shade. She looked at the pillow and laughed. It literally had become a throw pillow.

She got up to straighten the lamp but instead of walking toward the television she pretended Dan was in the room. She danced around him, jabbed him in the stomach and kneed him in the groin. She was in the process of giving him a kick in the butt and telling him of her disappointment when she heard the front door open.

Emmy came in, saw the lamp and pillow, Dee dancing around like a maniac with red swollen eyes and said with alarm, "Dee, what's wrong?"

"Nothing. Just feeling sorry for myself."

"With all you've been through, I can understand why. You sure look like Hell. If crying is healthy, you're really healthy today. I assume it's the vision stuff. Right?"

"Yes. I haven't had a really good cry through the whole experience. I guess I was due it," Dee sniffed a couple of times to prevent another onset of tears.

Dee straightened the lamp and then sat on the sofa holding the pillow she had thrown. Emmy stepped over to the phone and checked for messages. "Any calls for me?"

"No, unless there's a message from yesterday. I haven't checked this morning."

Emmy was pressing the display button for past calls. "Fred called, but didn't leave a message. I'll call him back. Oh, look, here's a call from Dan. Did you talk with him?"

"Yes. I was here so I took that call."

"Well, are you going to tell me my brother finally came to his senses?"

"If you mean does he want to pick up where we left off before finding Mollie, then no."

"Is that why your eyes have bags big enough to use for shopping. You look like you've been crying all day?"

"No. His call didn't help, but . . ."

"That shit head! I'm going to call him right now. How dare he upset you like this."

"No, Emmy, stop!" Dee commanded. Emmy had already picked up the phone.

"Please don't call Dan. It'll just make things worse. If he can't get past it, I'll just have to live with it."

"Okay." Emmy put the phone down and sat down beside Dee. They both looked depressed.

"It's ice-cream time," Emmy said. "You know all those commercials where women eat ice cream to fix everything? Well, there's something to that. As you know, I ate a ton of ice cream when Fred and I broke up. It helped for a while, but then I became depressed over all the weight I gained from the ice cream. There are about two servings of Rocky Road left." Emmy got up, went to the freezer, dished out all the ice cream and served Dee the larger portion of the anti-depressant.

"I wonder how much ice-cream would not be sold if men weren't such jerks?"

Dee couldn't help but laugh.

Chapter Twenty

"Surprise Birthday Present"

With football season came Dee's dad's birthday, Sunday, September 12. She and her mom were planning a special day with Dee driving over that morning and taking him to his favorite restaurant for lunch. All the gifts were to be golf-related. Golf had become his passion as his retirement date drew closer.

Dee left the gift purchasing to the last minute and had hoped to get something connected with the Augusta Masters. She had not worked it out yet.

As she kept thinking of September 12, her mind brought up the images of the time she and her parents had planned the trip to Italy. It was their first and only trip out of the country and they each needed a passport. Dee helped her mom do all the paperwork. She remembered sorting through the information on each birth certificate. Her dad was born in a hospital near Atlanta. His mother had died in childbirth and he was adopted at two days old. His paper work included his birth information as well as the adoption information involving a name change.

The information kept spinning around in her head. September 12, 1946, Swain's Hospital, Howard County. "Why does this keep coming back to my mind?" she wondered.

She was sitting at the table in the kitchen when she remembered. It was at the same table where she and Nancy went through the Tremane memorabilia and birth certificates. The Tremane stillbirth. September 12, 1946, Swain Hospital, Howard County. That was it; they were almost identical.

The day of Mollie's funeral service, she was sure she recognized Jake Tremane. He favored his father, but he favored her father more. When she and her parents were looking through the family albums, there was a picture of her dad when he was younger and before his hair started receding. He looked exactly like Jake Tremane or Jake Tremane looked exactly like her dad. Dee could hardly contain her excitement.

Aunt Connie had mentioned there had to be some strong connections, in plural, for Dee to see Mollie's visions so well. It took two things: blood kin from her dad's side and the clairvoyant gene from her mother's side. That made sense to Dee; otherwise Mollie would have contacted someone without waiting forty years plus.

She called Aunt Connie immediately. Connie answered quickly and Dee started talking so fast Connie had to slow her down, "Aunt Connie, I figured it out. There are two . . ."

"Dee, Honey, slow down. What is it you're working on to figure out?"

"Oh, I'm sorry. I was getting ahead of myself. Remember when you felt I had to have strong connections with Mollie to see and hear the visions?"

"I do."

"Well, I figured it out." She explained the birth certificates and continued, "I don't know how to prove it, but I know my dad is Mollie's younger brother."

"I think you are right. You will probably never get proof of it from the paper work. Your dad and Frank could have some DNA analysis done. Are you going to tell him?"

"I think I'll let that be his surprise birthday present. I believe it will make him happy. He loved his parents, but they are gone. I'm certain he would love having his own biological family and knowing from where he came. Just think — he has a brother with a family! And Frank is my uncle and Mollie was my aunt."

They discussed several ramifications that could come from this new development. Connie didn't tell Dee she saw a lot of resemblance between Dee and the picture of Mollie when Dee was at her house last summer.

Dee decided she would present the facts to her father and let him do what he wanted with them. She was so excited. But more than for Dad, it was a breakthrough for Dee. She didn't need to worry about constantly having visions. They came only when a close member of the family needed her. Hopefully, there would never be a situation like Mollie's ever again. Except for Aunt Connie and the sheriff, she had never told anyone about the vision showing how Mollie was not dead when she was placed in the trunk. Sharing that vision would cause unnecessary grief. She wished many times *she* didn't know about it.

She wondered if this would make a difference with Dan. Would he be interested if he thought she would never have visions again? She decided not to call him. He had to accept her as she was — or not all. And, there were no guarantees the visions were permanently gone. Her pride kicked in. She thought, "I won't beg and I won't let him know how I long to see him." She made herself stop thinking about him and started thinking about her dad's big surprise.

Dee was certain she had not told her parents very much about Mollie's brother and felt awkward about telling her father about the Tremanes. She decided to go early and spent Saturday night with them and they skipped the normal Sunday church service to drive into Buckhead for a birthday lunch at Maggiano's Italian Restaurant.

They ordered "family style" that included several appetizers and entrees. Dee chose chicken Parmesan, her dad chose a shrimp and mozzarella dish and her mother chose the day's special seafood entrée. After their drinks arrived, Dee presented her dad with a golf shirt in his favorite color — green. She had not been able to find any Masters memorabilia. Anna Marie gave her husband a white dress shirt with a tie covered in golf tees of all colors. Dee had planned to tell him about Frank Tremane after he received his gifts; however, she could not bring herself to do so in a restaurant.

The Mozzarella Caprese (several thick slices of tomato topped with thin slices of red onion, thick slices of soft Buffalo Mozzarella, fresh basil leaves with virgin olive oil and balsamic vinegar sprinkled on top) came first as a salad. When the entrees came it was more than they could eat at one sitting; the servings were humongous. They ate as much as they could and took home two large bags of leftovers including most of the Tiramisu dessert with ladyfinger cookies alternated with a vanilla pudding filling sprinkled with coffee-flavored crystals.

Once they got home, Dee asked them to sit with her in the Florida room. She took an old photo album with her and sat down looking at them without knowing where to start.

Her mom spoke up, "Dee, what's this about?"

"It's about Mollie."

"I thought we had decided that was over." Anna Marie added, "The funeral is over. You have to let go of Mollie and go on with your life. It's already messed up your relationship with Dan." She added in a harsh voice, "Isn't that enough?"

"Mom, it's the past *and* the future I want to talk about with you and Dad. I believe Dad needs to know something, then he can act on it if he wants."

"What on earth are you trying to say?" her mother asked.

"Mom, do you remember when we did the paperwork for the passports to go to Italy?"

"Yes."

"And, we used everybody's birth-certificate information. Well, I saw a birth certificate almost identical to Dad's." She looked at her father who had been quiet since he sat down.

"I expect there are lots of birth certificates that look like mine. They are state-issued. The same forms are used all over the state," her father said.

"No, Dad. I mean the information is almost identical. The one I saw may have had a different pre-printed edge; however, it had the same date, same hospital, same doctor, and I believe the weight and birth time may have been the same or very close. The mother and father's names were different and the one I saw was listed as a stillbirth."

"I don't see how that has anything to do with me."

"I wouldn't either if I hadn't met Mollie's brother, Frank Tremane, and his boys." She opened the photo album and turned several pages before holding up a page for him to see. "See this picture of you? How old were you?"

"About thirty."

"At Mollie's funeral, I met Frank's son, Jake. This picture looks just like Jake."

"I don't understand." Sam seemed unable to follow Dee's line of thought. Her mother sat looking at Dee as though she was hearing a foreign language.

"Dad, I believe the paperwork at the hospital where you were born got mixed up either by accident or on purpose. The Tremanes had a stillborn child on the same day and at the same hospital in which you were born. Haven't you wondered about your birth parents?"

"Yes, but Mom told me the lawyer did all the paperwork and she and Dad understood my biological mother was very young and died in childbirth. Mom and Dad were great parents. I had no reason to go looking for others."

"I know, Dad. I loved them, too. You were lucky to have such good parents. But they are gone now and I believe you have another family in South Carolina."

"Do they know about me?"

"No. I haven't told anyone except Aunt Connie and maybe Emmy about the two birth certificates. Aunt Connie agrees with me. She and I have been trying to figure out why Mollie's visions came to me. We decided it was because I received clairvoyant genes from Mom's side and am blood kin from your side."

"Wait a minute. Don't go blaming me for those awful visions," Anna Marie said. "I do not and never have had visions. You didn't get that from me," she added angrily.

"Okay, I got it from Aunt Connie. Mom, you're missing the point. Dad may have family. Don't you think that's a good thing?"

"We don't know those people. What if they're criminals and spend their time in and out of jail? We don't want to jump into something from which we can't walk away."

Dee was surprised at her mother's anger and negative attitude and never expected the reaction she was getting. She thought she was giving her dad the best birthday present he had ever received.

"I know you met Mollie's family at her funeral," Sam said, "But you don't know much about them."

"I didn't tell you because I didn't want to upset you, but I went to see them the first of the summer when the visions first started. They live in a nice house and seem to have a good life. They aren't rich or anything like it and they have three sons and two grandchildren. He's a brick mason and favors you except his eyes are brown instead of green and brown like yours. He's very quiet."

"How about the son that looks like me? What color are his eyes?"

"Green with some brown. Just like yours and mine."

She stayed with them a while longer. Before leaving she asked them to think about it and let her know if they wanted to pursue getting DNA for testing, if they wanted to meet the Tremanes or if they wanted to do nothing.

She drove home feeling disappointed. She had been so sure her father would jump at the chance to have a brother. Her surprise birthday gift had ended up surprising her more than anyone else.

The September 23 edition of *The Elberton Sun* carried an article about how Michael Dunsman, III, of San Francisco, California, had been charged with killing Mollie Tremane in 1960. The reporter went on to tell how DNA from the articles found in the trunk of the old 1957 Chevrolet had matched that of Michael (Dun) Dunsman, III, connecting him with Mollie's murder.

The report from the sheriff's office confirmed the Georgia Bureau of Investigation had run the DNA results through the FBI's records. Michael Dunsman had been accused of rape in San Francisco twelve years earlier and had been acquitted by a jury. During that trial his defense attorneys were able to create a scenario of consensual sex that left "reasonable doubt." However, the DNA results remained in the FBI's database.

The article continued with facts about finding the remains of Mollie Tremane and how underwear in a small plastic purse had provided enough DNA from semen to be used against the murderer/rapist. Dee thought it was ironic that Dun's placing the underwear in the plastic purse had ensured his DNA would stay intact and would be the evidence needed to connect him with the murder. To Dee's dismay, the story also gave her credit for finding the remains: "Without the assistance of Ms. Dee Dupree of Elberton, Mollie Tremane's disappearance would still be a mystery." There was mention of the visions, but they were played down.

Two days later, *The Elberton Sun* carried the obituary for Michael Dunsman, III, who died in San Francisco, California. It listed him as the son of Mr. and Mrs. Michael Dunsman, II, as well as maternal and paternal grandparents who had predeceased him along with his sister, Beatrice Dunsman Spence. His brother-in-law, John Spence of Atlanta, survived him. No other family was listed.

The article said that Dunsman was out on a $200,000 bail negotiated by his attorney with a local bondsman when he committed suicide by placing himself in his car on a train track. His attorney's statement said Dunsman was depressed over the pending court case in Georgia and had left a suicide note before taking his own life.

A few days before the first article appeared, the sheriff called and asked Dee to stop by his office. When she did, he was especially gracious. "Well Miss Dee, I suppose I need to apologize to you and admit there was more to your dreams . . ."

Dee corrected him, "Visions. They were visions."

"Okay. There was more to your visions than I gave you credit for." He then told Dee about how the DNA matched and how lucky they were to have Dunsman's DNA on file; otherwise, Dunsman would never have agreed to willingly give it, even if they connected him with Mollie's murder in some other way. He said, "I just wanted you to know the facts before the newspaper reports on the findings."

She thanked him and asked if he had gotten in touch with the Tremanes. He said he gave them the information earlier that day.

When Dee got home she had a message from Nancy verifying the information the sheriff had shared. Nancy thanked Dee again for making it all possible.

Within a few days after the newspaper carried the second article about Dun Dunsman, Dee found a package on the kitchen table. It had been delivered via UPS while she was out; Emmy had left it for her. The return address listed the Tremanes in Easley. Dee had not expected anything from them and was puzzled. She opened the package and unwrapped the tissue paper from a silver frame.

A post-it note was on the glass with a message from Nancy stating she thought Dee would like to see the poem Mollie wrote for a school project just a few months before she disappeared. Nancy explained that the words were exactly as Mollie had written them; however, she had her daughter-in-law type it and print it from her computer to make it ready for framing. She took the post-it note off and found a poem titled, "Free." It was printed on light-blue paper with white clouds and perfectly fit the topic of the poem. She read:

Free

I wonder how it feels
To soar to the sky
To leave this earth and
Push away the clouds
With just a fleeting thought
To never have to worry or
Think of human needs
I wonder how it feels
To float in peaceful pleasure
To know all there is to know
To be all I can be
And that be enough
I wonder how it feels
To know no pain or sorrow
And have only tears of joy
To sing with the angels
To be free

Mollie A. Tremane
February 12, 1960

Dee turned the frame over. Taped to the back was a piece of cardstock with the following message: *To Dee Dupree who helped Mollie soar to the sky and all the other things she wondered about, including singing with the angels.*

She placed the framed poem on the table beside the sofa. Her thoughts drifted to Dan and how much she missed him and how much she longed to hear his laugh and see that laugh in his eyes.

It was late that same day when she arrived at the Guidestones. It had rained the day before, cooling the lingering summer heat. She wasn't sure what made her decide to drive out there alone, knowing she had hoped Dan would be with her on her second visit. Maybe it was longing to find a part of Dan and to feel his presence that made her go there.

She found herself looking at the stone arrangement. She walked around it, her fingertips lightly touching each of the four stone slabs as she passed. She stopped to read the English translation of the message. She wondered who kept the grass cut as she backed a few steps away from the stone panels. She sat on the grass in a cross-legged yoga pose with her hands on her knees. As she closed her eyes, she felt the onset of meditation creeping into her mind and body.

She was in a meditative state when a warm breeze drifted around her. She opened her eyes, fully expecting to see the wind blowing the leaves on the branches of the small trees and shrubs within the fenced area and at the edge of the pasture. Even with the feeling of a light wind around her she saw no movement. She looked at the stone panels and felt the warmth that had engulfed her had captured them as well, turning the cold, gray stones into warm, welcoming participants within her meditation. The warmth stayed. She felt its healing penetrate every part of her being. She sat for a long time, feeling peaceful. She placed her hands in front of her heart with her palms together, bowed her head and quietly spoke the word that sent gratitude and respect for her life and the life around her to all those she loved: the word she associated with the peace and health of yoga, "Namaste" (nah-mah-stay). She left the Guidestones and headed home.

The phone was ringing as she walked to the front door. She managed to get her key out, open the door and get to the phone, getting in an out-of-breath "hello" before the call was disconnected. The caller identified himself as John Spence, the husband of Bea Dunsman Spence. Dee was cordial but wondered why he would be calling her. He asked if he could talk with her about Bea's wishes regarding her brother, Dun Dunsman. He said he would drive to Elberton, or if she were planning a trip to Atlanta, he would take her out for lunch or dinner. They agreed to meet in the middle in Gwinnett County for lunch at the Olive Garden on Saturday.

Dee called Miss Wilma and told her about Dr. Spence's call. "Do you think it's safe to meet him, Miss Wilma?"

"Oh, Honey, he wouldn't hurt a fly. Bea had a good life with him even aft-ah she told him about her horrible childhood. You have nothing to fe-ah from John Spence."

"Thanks. I told him I would meet him even though the meeting depended entirely on my conversation with you."

"Well, Sweetie Pie, you let me know what he wants. I'm sure-ah it has to do with Bea even though I can't imagine what it is. Promise to call me aft-ah you talk with him. Okay?"

"I will. Thanks again. I'll call you. Bye now."

"Bye, Sweetie."

Dr. Spence's request seemed strange to Dee. She couldn't think of anything she could add to his family's situation. As soon as Dee entered the restaurant she saw a small, thin, white-haired man with friendly blue eyes standing off to the side. She took a chance as she approached him and asked, "Dr. Spence?"

"You must be Dee. Please call me John; otherwise, I'll think I should put you in a dental chair and check your teeth."

They both laughed, happy to be over the initial discomfort of meeting as strangers. The waitress ushered them to a table.

He started the conversation. "I know you must be wondering what this is all about."

"Yes. And, I can't think of any way I can help you."

"Let me tell you up front how sorry I am you had to go through so much."

They stopped their conversation as the waitress came to the table. After taking drink orders she promised to come right back for their food order. Dr. Spence asked her to bring the salad with the drinks.

He continued, "I know what was in the paper. Maybe you can fill me in on other details; however, I'm here to get your input on some personal issues I have. I realize you are under no obligation to me, but you might be able to help me out with a couple of dilemmas."

"I don't know if I can help."

The waitress arrived with tea, salad and breadsticks. They ordered from the lunch menu. As soon as the waitress left, Dr. Spence made his first request. "Dee, I know you are responsible for getting a violent man out of the picture. First, I would like to know more about how you knew about a murder that happened forty-some years ago."

While Dee was telling him about the visions, their entrées came. They ate in silence for a few minutes, and then she finished the story of how she had two connections with Mollie.

She decided to tell him about her disappointment with her parents' responses to the blood-kin issue. After telling him about the birth certificates and how one of the Tremanes' sons looked like her father, she concluded, "Mom and Dad still haven't asked me to pursue DNA testing or asked to meet the Tremanes. If I thought I had a brother or sister I would be ecstatic. I totally do not understand their reactions. I was sure they, especially Dad, would be so excited."

He had listened quietly with his only response being the occasional shaking of his head from side to side. When she stopped talking, he said, "What a monumental undertaking."

"Well, I didn't know I was taking it on until it was too late. Besides, it needed to be done. How did you know about me?"

"From the newspapers. I'm sure the visions were hard for you. Especially since you haven't had them in the past."

"They were. And I've never been so frightened."

Again he apologized. "I am so sorry. I wish someone had taken care of him years ago. Someone should have. As I said, I am here on behalf of my wife who would be here with me if she could. I know she would want me to do this. I've ended up as administrator of her estate. She specified that any monies from the Dunsman house and land be used in some way to help women who have been abused. Her brother abused her too."

Dr. Spence was surprised when Dee said, "I know. At least I heard that from someone whose mother worked for the Dunsmans."

"Miss Wilma Jones?"

"Yes. She told me in confidence. Please don't hold it against her."

"Not to worry. Her mother was the only one to defend Bea. Bea would never agree to have children because of him. She was terrified of bringing a child into this world with his genes. We talked about adopting and never did. That gets me back to the estate money. I wonder if you would mind if it's given in your name. I haven't worked out the details."

"Before you go further, I would like to say no. It was Mollie who suffered the most. It was Mollie, too, who just wouldn't quit until he was unable to hurt another person. Any credit or any money given to any cause should be given in her name."

"Okay. I'll honor your request. It's hard to believe that I've ended up the administrator of his estate also. He made out a will before Bea died. At the time, he owed more than he owned and thought she would have to deal with his debts after his death, knowing she would hate it. She was his only living relative and that's how he listed it in his will. After Bea's death, I became his only living relative. His lawyer led me to believe his status changed a lot since he made out the will. He told me Dun was in the process of changing his will, but didn't get it completed and signed before his death. I plan to use any money from his estate for victims who suffered at the hands of monsters like Dun. If you have any ideas now or later about how best to use the money, I would love to hear them."

"I love it. I think it would be *apropos* to use his money to help such victims. I believe Mollie would like that too."

"There's one more thing. They are sending me his cremains. I will hate having them. Bea made the statement that if he died before she did, she would have him cremated and would flush his ashes down the commode."

Dee laughed. "That seems appropriate. Do you live in the house you lived in before her death?"

"Yes."

"Was her bathroom separate from yours?"

He looked puzzled and answered, "Yes."

"Why don't you flush them down *her* toilet?"

"I can hear Bea laugh as his ashes flush into the sewer where they belong. Let's have a dessert to celebrate," he offered.

She accepted. Later, as they parted in the parking lot, they had another good laugh about Dun Dunsman ending up where he belonged. He was walking away when he turned and said, "Dee, you know *you* could have DNA tests run. You really don't need your parents DNA to find out about that blood kin."

"You're right. I was so disappointed that my parents weren't interested, I hadn't thought about my own *direct* connection."

The next day Dee called Miss Wilma, "Miss Wilma you won't believe what Dr. Spence and I decided yesterday."

"I can't wait. Tell me everything, Shug."

"First, he wanted to send a memorial gift to a women's shelter in my name, but I convinced him he should give it in Mollie's name."

"But, Sweetie, you did so much. You should've let him do just that."

"No, Miss Wilma, Mollie is the one who suffered at the hands of that monster. But, you're going to love the other decision we made," Dee said and then hesitated.

"I can't wait. Tell me now."

"Dr. Spence is going to end up with Dun Dunsman's cremains. He ended up the executor of Dun Dunsman's estate and he can do whatever he wants with his money and his ashes."

"What does he have in mind?"

"He is going to flush those ashes down the toilet in Bea's bathroom."

Dee waited for Miss Wilma's response.

Miss Wilma stood in her kitchen with a strange look on her face until she realized the impact of Dee's words. "Honey, that's the funniest thing I've ev-ah heard. I bet Bea and my moth-ah are laughing like crazy."

Dee smiled; unknowingly, she accurately pictured the look on Miss Wilma's face. Miss Wilma continued, "I think you-ah right. Dun Dunsman is getting his just rewards. His spirit will spend eternity whe-ah it belongs, you know — down below, and his ashes will be whe-ah they belong — in the sew-ah." After Miss Wilma said goodbye and before Dee's phone disconnected, Dee heard Miss Wilma laughing.

Chapter Twenty-One

"Unfinished Business"

Dee went to sleep that night thinking about Dr. Spence and Miss Wilma. Her mind was jumping from one person and one event to another. She sat straight up in bed when she thought she heard someone call her name. She got out of bed and walked to Emmy's room to see if she had called. Emmy's door was open. She peeked in to see Emmy fast asleep. She hadn't had a vision since they found Mollie. It seemed like Mollie had called her name but it got all mixed up with the conversations with Dr. Spence and Miss Wilma and blood tests.

She went back to bed and tried to go to sleep. Again, her mind kept so many thoughts swirling around in her head she couldn't relax. After another hour of tossing and turning she got out of bed and went to the kitchen, found a notepad and pencil and wrote down some of the words that kept coming to her mind. She wrote the names of the people involved in her life since she moved to Elberton. She looked at her list and thought it described the mind chatter that had been buzzing in her head for hours. She then did something that had never come naturally to her. She wrote about how she felt about the mind chatter. After that she went back to bed and fell asleep.

The following morning she found the poem on the kitchen table. She knew it was her writing; however, the circumstances seemed vague. As she read it for the third time, she wondered if Mollie had influenced its writing. She looked at the words again and read them out loud:

mind chatter - stop
you drive me crazy
you won't let me sleep

mind chatter –
you keep me from hearing
 things I need to hear

Amazed at the writing, she sat there thinking how she had never kept a diary; she was not prone to writing poetry and wondered again if Mollie had inspired the crazy poem. She remembered looking at the Tremane memorabilia and Mollie's mother's attempt at writing poetry along with all the "Ramblings of Grief." She thought, "If Dad is Mollie's brother, then Mrs. Tremane is my grandmother. Maybe I inherited a poetry gene like Mollie did and didn't even know it until now." She wondered what it was she "*needed to hear.*" The poem was a puzzle. When she showed it to Emmy, Emmy said it looked like two Haiku poems at first glance. Then she explained that Haiku was about nature, i.e., seasons or flowers, and went on to explain the style as a traditional Japanese poetry — always short and simple. Dee decided she didn't really want to write poetry. It was too complicated.

Monday, October 4, Dan left messages on Dee's answering machine at home and on her cell phone. She checked her messages during lunch period at school and was excited to hear his voice. He said, "Dee, I need to talk with you. I am miserable and I miss you. Please call me." A similar message was waiting at home. Her first instinct was to call him back immediately. She remembered the hurt and the pain she felt when he distanced himself from her after finding Mollie's skeleton. It had been about eight weeks since they found Mollie in "The Sanctuary." It felt like eight months. She waited to return his calls and the more she waited, the easier it was to ignore them. Her stubbornness took over and she erased the messages.

In mid-October Aunt Connie called and told Dee she wanted her to be careful. She called it "feelings" she was getting, but Dee felt sure she was receiving visions. She told Dee she thought someone in a car was watching and waiting for her. She felt it somehow had to do with Mollie even though all the loose ends had been taken care of when Dun Dunsman killed himself. She said it was probably nothing, but asked her to be careful.

A week later Dee thought about Aunt Connie's warning when she walked out of the Bi-Lo grocery store on Saturday afternoon and stopped to let a car go by before heading to her car. The driver slowed and lowered his window and asked, "Can you tell me where the Granite City Motel is?"

"Take a left as you leave this parking lot. The motel is less than a half-mile down on your left. By the way, it's now the Budget 8 Motel."

"Thanks. Have a good day." The driver made his way through the parking lot and exited. Dee watched him take a left toward the motel. There was something familiar about his thick white hair covering half his forehead and his small dark eyes. She surmised the blue compact Chevrolet Cavalier was a rental car because of a small sticker on the bumper, and because he had asked where the motel was.

She made her way to her car and placed the grocery bag inside. As she drove home, her mind kept going back to the old man. He had specifically asked for the Granite City Motel, which meant he had been to Elberton before. It hadn't been the Granite City Motel since the Olympics came to Georgia in 1996 although most of the locals continued to call it by its old name.

Dee remembered the first time her parents spent a weekend in town after she moved in with Emmy. It was hunting season and the motels were full of hunters in their pickup trucks with gun racks. When her dad called to make reservations he was told he could have one only because they had just received a cancellation. He was surprised and asked what was happening in Elberton. The hotel personnel told him it was hunting season and the hunters used all the rooms in Elberton, especially on the weekends.

He told Dee he got a good laugh at the sign on the bathroom counter: "PLEASE DO NOT CLEAN YOUR GUNS WITH OUR TOWELS. CLEANING RAGS ARE AVAILABLE AT THE FRONT DESK."

Dee laughed with him and said, "Wait until you visit me in the spring when it's fishing season. The parking lot will be full of pickup trucks with their fishing boats. Now that's a challenge. They use twice as much parking space as the hunters. The sign changes to 'PLEASE DO NOT CLEAN YOUR FISH IN THE BATHTUB.'"

Her thoughts came back from the past, leaving her with a feeling she did not like, a feeling she was being watched. She looked in her rear-view mirror, then into the oncoming traffic; she saw nothing to justify the feeling. She drove to her apartment. Emmy was spending the weekend with Fred in Athens. She planned to join Emmy, Fred, Janet and a few other friends for dinner and possibly a movie or to hang out at The Winery later in the evening.

She took the groceries in and put them away before showering. She left the apartment around seven o'clock and stopped for gas on her way out of town. She had the feeling of being watched again. She locked the doors, picked up her cell phone and called Emmy. The call went to Emmy's voice mail. She left a message telling Emmy she was on her way and asked her to please call back. She called Janet's apartment and talked with her. She felt better talking with someone; however, she didn't tell Janet she felt someone was following and watching her. She verified the time she thought she would arrive at Janet's place. She had no logical reason to believe she was being followed. She felt she was safe with her cell phone nearby.

The clouds that had gathered in late afternoon made the darkness of night come sooner than expected, requiring Dee to use the headlights as she took the road to the right toward Athens and drove under the bridge. Her nervous fingers drummed on the steering wheel; her mind raced back and forth trying to find logical reasoning for the agitation she felt. She had driven several miles and was in the right lane when a blue car started to pass. Instead of passing, it came over into her lane. She blew the horn and concentrated on holding her car in the road. The driver forced her into the parking area of a strip mall. She checked to be sure the doors were locked and grabbed her cell phone. She almost ran into a tree as her car stopped at a ditch just past several businesses. She couldn't go anywhere.

The man with the white hair who had asked for directions was outside the car with a tire tool. She turned her head to ward off the broken glass as he smashed the window. Her hands were shaking as she pressed 911 and the send button on her phone. She didn't wait for an answer she said, "Help. The Athens Highway. Send Sheriff Dalton. It's in front of the . . . " Dee looked to her right and saw a "Hardware and 'lumbing Supplies" sign beside a tire store and several other small stores. All the businesses were closed. Without taking the time to explain the P was missing from "Plumbing," she said, "Hardware and something. Help me." She didn't see the granite company's sign near the road with an arrow pointing toward the dirt road behind the stores.

The stranger reached in, unlocked and opened her door. He had left the door on the passenger side of his car opened. He grabbed her by the arm and hair, dragged her to his car and placed her in the front seat. She thought they were far enough off the road the other cars didn't see what he was doing. He had placed his car between her car and the road. Dee held on to her cell phone as if her life depended on it. He closed the door and locked it with a remote. Dee was surprised how fast he got around to the driver's side and into the car. She thought he moved fast for an old man. He was laughing.

"Ain't it great they make cars with locks that prevent children from getting out? Ms. Dee Dupree, you are locked in with childproof locks. I even had your door set up to lock with the back ones. Don't bother trying to get out on your own."

Dee knew where she had heard that voice and seen that sneer. They were in her visions of Mollie.

"I understand you are the one who got me into this mess with ole Rotten Tamale. You even remind me of her." He started the car and drove down a dirt road to the left of the stores and past a granite company. A few yards down the road, he took another left.

"You made it easy for me driving in this direction. I thought I was going to have to visit you in your apartment and bring you out this way. Miss Know It All, have you seen the inside of a quarry?" He looked at Dee for an answer and she shook her head with a negative answer.

"I thought you were dead," she said.

"Think of me as your savior. Tonight I am going to save you the trouble of growing old. By the way, how did you link me with Rotten Tamale?"

"I purchased her glasses from your family's estate sale and wondered how they got in your family's stuff. After that, I saw a vision where you put those same glasses in the glove compartment of your car. You or someone else emptied the glove compartment when you got your new car a few weeks later. I also saw what you did to Mollie. She was alive when you left her in that car." The look she gave him only made him laugh.

"Well look at you, bitch. You think I left ole Rotten Tamale in a car? Maybe her old man did her in after I got through with her and he found out she wasn't Little Miss Perfect. Maybe she had a boyfriend who didn't like her two-timing him. If Mollie could be so helpful why didn't she warn you about me coming after you?"

"I think she was trying to warn me about you." Dee was shaking all over. She looked at her phone and it had gone back to the home view. The 911 call had disconnected.

He reached over and grabbed the phone and threw it in the back seat. He came to a stop in front of a hole the size of a large pond. Granite boulders of different sizes were scattered near the edge of the hole with a few larger ones off to the sides.

"Don't you want to know about my resurrection?"

She nodded her head, hoping to gain time. If the call went through she might have help coming. If not, she was on her own with Dun Dunsman. It was like *déjà vu*. Mollie had thought the same thing as she and Dun passed her house and neither her mother nor Frankie were in the yard.

She could stall, but for how long? She felt fortunate he was narcissistic, wanting to tell how smart he had been. "It was easy. I got my lawyer to talk the judge into letting me out on bail. It's certainly not the norm to get bail in a murder case. Me and my lawyer are as smart as they come — but he's not as smart as I am. All I needed was a few days to put a plan in place. There are so many homeless good-for-nothings around, all I had to do was find one who looked like me and dress him in my clothes and leave my identification on him. The train messed him up so much they couldn't tell the difference. Besides I left a note saying I just couldn't face a life in prison. My lawyer identified the body. Sucker." He laughed at his own cleverness.

He unlocked all the doors and got out. Dee opened her door immediately and was ready to run. Again, she was surprised at how fast he was in getting to her side of the car.

"Now, Miss Know It All, it's your turn to play Miss Rotten Tamale. Only this time we do it differently. After you and I have a little fun you get to see the bottom of the quarry. They will never find you and I'll be free to live wherever I want to."

As she kicked at him and pulled backwards with all her strength, he placed his right arm around her chest and his left hand pulled her hair back in such a way she couldn't keep fighting. The only thing she could do was pull on his arms, trying to get him to loosen his hold. He pulled her toward the edge of the quarry, dragging her with him over the rough, dry ground and loose gravel. The car's headlights cast long shadows toward the biggest, blackest hole she had ever seen. It was more terrifying up close.

Huge chunks of granite had been removed, leaving a gigantic hole with walls of jagged rock. The light from the car continued to create elongated and distorted shadows that moved like evil spirits on the far side of the rock wall and took on a gruesome effect that frightened Dee even more.

Pieces of granite in various sizes had been left around the hole with fencing on the far side. An outline of trees could be seen beyond the fencing. She pulled backwards, hoping she didn't have to look into the hole before he threw her in. He moved her forward, holding her body with one arm and placing his big hand on the lower portion of her face, forcing her to peer past the rock on which they were leaning . . . and into the quarry. All she saw were dark shadows. She couldn't see the bottom. She turned her head into the palm of his hand and tried to bite him. He laughed and slapped her hard.

The car lights added an eerie pale outline to her evil attacker. She was shaking more than ever. He pulled her away from the edge and threw her to the ground in front of the rock as her cheek hit the edge. "By the time I finish with you, you'll be begging me for it. You'll want me just like all the other bitches." She wondered how many women he had beaten into submission.

He kicked her in the side. As he pulled his right leg back to get in a better position to kick her again the upper part of his body leaned slightly forward, she heard a voice. *"Now, Dee, now. Roll toward him and grab his straight leg and then roll backward toward the hole. Do it now before he leans backward!"*

"I'll teach you a lesson about minding your own business, you little piece of . . ." He lost his balance as Dee grabbed his left leg while his right leg was in the air behind him. Rolling toward him had given her the edge of surprise. As soon as she had a good hold on his leg she rolled backwards toward the edge of the quarry, furiously holding onto the leg. She felt his weight go forward and released his leg. He screamed as his leg snapped when it hit the edge of the granite rock. He went over into the blackness. The same rock that broke his leg stopped her from rolling into the quarry. She heard him scream again as he hit the jagged rock on the side of the quarry. Shortly after, she heard the distant sound of a splash in the water.

She lay on the ground for a few seconds listening to the silence. She hoped he was dead and wondered if he could swim to the edge. She didn't know how deep the quarry was or how much water was at the bottom. She wondered if he could climb out. She listened. Silence. After several agonizing minutes, she rolled away from the rock and crawled toward the car, moving to her left, trying to avoid the bright lights. She could smell the dust her crawling was creating. She was making every effort to be quiet as her nostrils filled with dust particles making her want to sneeze. Fear permeated every inch of her being.

The passenger door was opened and she pulled herself up by holding on to the door and the floorboard. She stood there long enough to get her balance. She opened the back door and with the light from overhead she found her cell phone. She pressed 911 and waited.

"Nine-one-one. May I help you?"

"Yes. I need to talk with Sheriff Dalton. Please. Please," she whispered.

"Where are you?"

"At a quarry several miles down the Athens highway. Tell him to turn at the hardware and tire stores. My car is there. I'm at a quarry. It's a dirt road. I don't know if it's a working quarry. I don't see trucks and equipment around. Just lots of rock. Tell him I need him."

"Who is this?"

"Dee. Dee Dupree."

"Stay on the line. I have a call in to Sheriff Dalton. Are you all right?"

"No. Yes."

"What happened?"

"He tried to kill me." She started to cry.

"It's okay. Sheriff Dalton is on his way. Where is he now — the one trying to kill you?"

"He's in the quarry."

"Are you still in danger?"

"I don't think so. I don't know."

The 911 operator continued to talk with her. Dee had moved away from the car and was sitting out of the light in the shadow of a huge granite boulder with her back against the cold stone. She told the operator she was on a dirt road somewhere behind some stores. She had started to repeat herself.

"Shhhhh," Dee said to the operator in a hushed voice. "I don't want him to find me if he gets out."

"Okay, Honey. I'll talk quietly to you as you wait for the sheriff. Don't hang up. The sheriff was on his way out there already. He won't be long. Someone saw a car being run off the road and called us."

Dee was sitting with her knees up to her chest, her left arm around her legs and her cell phone in her right hand, held near her ear when she saw the blue strobe lights flashing as a sheriff's car drove up behind the rental car. The lights of the cruiser went off and Sheriff Dalton got out. He used his flashlight to look at the tag on the car in front of him.

He looked ahead as he walked to the side of the car and looked inside. Dee saw him and she felt everything was happening in slow motion.

The operator continued, "Dee, the sheriff reported he has arrived. Do you see him?"

Dee nodded affirmatively, not realizing the operator couldn't see her answer.

"Dee. The sheriff is there. You can answer now. Are you okay?"

"I'm okay."

The sheriff heard her and walked over to the large gray rock. He found her sitting in the same position in which she had been for some time in the shadow of the granite boulder.

He held out his hand to help her up. She didn't respond.

"Dee, I'm here. You're safe now. I understand from the 911 operator that he's in the quarry. I assume the bottom of the quarry."

"Yes."

She took his hand and with his help stood up. Her legs were weak and she was shaking. She closed the cell phone and held it tightly against her chest. He pulled off his light jacket and placed it around her shoulders.

"You're safe with me. We've got all the time in the world for you to tell me what happened here. I found your car."

He helped her to his cruiser and placed her in the passenger seat. He walked around to the driver's side and slipped behind the wheel. He had radioed for help earlier and called again to request battery-operated lights and a search party.

He sat in the car with Dee, waiting for her to calm down and talk.

"I see a bruise on your face. Should I take you to the hospital?"

"No. No hospital. He hurt me. He threw me down. I got the bruise when my face hit a rock; he kicked me and would have kicked me again if I hadn't grabbed his leg and rolled over forcing him to fall into the quarry. I probably killed him. He was going to rape me. He said he was going to do to me what he did to Mollie, only I would end up in the quarry."

Sheriff Dalton looked puzzled. Dun Dunsman was dead. He had worked with the GBI and FBI confirming the match with the DNA. He had talked with the authorities in San Francisco about Dun's suicide.

"Are you saying Dun Dunsman was here tonight?"

"Yes. You don't believe me?"

"Why do you think it was him?"

"Because he said so. He said he faked his death by placing his identification on a homeless person who looked like him in a car in front of a train. He said it was all my fault he was in trouble and I would pay for it."

The sheriff absorbed Dee's information and it began to make sense. He was certain the car was a rental but he wasn't certain Dun Dunsman had come back to Elberton for revenge. It was possible he came back to prevent her from telling anyone that he was alive. If she could have visions of him killing Mollie, she could have visions of him being alive. He hoped they recovered the body — and this time there would be DNA tests conducted on the body to ensure the serial rapist and murderer was out of the picture.

He knew he would have to get divers to start looking for the body first thing in the morning. A squad car drove up with two deputies. The sheriff reached over to Dee and patted her on the shoulder, "I'll be right back. I need to get these fellas started on roping off this whole area. They'll stay here tonight to be sure no one gets in or out. You think you'll be okay for a few minutes?"

Dee nodded affirmatively and the sheriff got out to talk with the deputies. He told them he thought the attacker was dead but to not assume it and to stay alert to the fact he may still be out there and dangerous. When he returned to the car she was still shaking and he decided he had better take her to the hospital. She might be going into shock. The cell phone she was clutching rang as he started the car. He looked over and saw she was unable to open the phone she was shaking so much. He took the phone, opened it and said, "Yes."

There was hesitation and then a female voice asked, "Dee where are you?"

Sheriff Dalton said, "Who is this?"

"This is Emmy. Who's this?"

"This is Sheriff Dalton. Dee's with me."

"Why. What's she done?"

"She took care of some unfinished business tonight. It's been a rough night for her. I'm taking her to the emergency room now. Would you call your mom and have her meet us there?"

"Sure. But first may I speak to Dee?"

"Not right now. She appears to be going into shock. Young lady, hang up and call your mom!"

"Okay," Emmy replied and hung up. She immediately called her mom and told her about the sheriff's request.

The sheriff called the hospital and told them he was on his way with a young woman who may need treatment from a beating as well as shock.

Shortly after the call, the sheriff pulled into the emergency entrance to the hospital. The hospital personnel placed Dee on a stretcher and wheeled her into a room.

The sheriff waited outside until Mrs. Jackson arrived. He filled her in about Dun Dunsman's attack on Dee. He told her he didn't have a lot of information. He hoped Dee would be able to give him a more complete story the next day. He didn't know if she would be staying in the hospital and asked Mrs. Jackson to stay with her or to be sure someone was with her until he got back. She assured him she would.

The sheriff stopped and talked with the security guard on his way out of the hospital and explained what had happened. He asked him to check out anyone trying to see Dee until he could get back.

Emmy came in during the night to relieve her mother while Dee slept. Once she knew the story of the night's events, she called Fred and Janet to let them know.

Chapter Twenty Two

"Another Black Hole"

Early the next morning Dee woke up in pain from a broken rib. It hurt to breathe. She tried to move her right hand and realized she could not. She opened her eyes and saw Dan holding her hand with his forehead resting on his arm. He looked as if he had been asleep for a while. He awoke and looked up at her as she moved her arm. Every move she made caused her pain. Her lips were pressed tightly together and her forehead was wrinkled in pain when she made eye contact with Dan. Her upper arms were bruised black-and-blue from being grabbed and pulled the night before. Her cheek had turned an ugly purple-red around a small cut that had been cleaned and treated with antiseptic cream.

He said, "Dee, do you need something for pain?"

"Yes. How long have you been here?"

He pushed the nurse's button on the side of the bed and a nurse answered from an intercom on the wall to the right of the bed. Dan asked for a pain pill for Dee. "You don't have to talk now. Just know I'm sorry I've been such a dunce. We can talk later. I didn't stay all night. Mom stayed the first part of the night and Emmy stayed until I arrived. I've been here for at least two hours."

The nurse came in to give Dee her pill. As the nurse was leaving the room, the sheriff came in. He acknowledged Dan with a nod and asked Dee, "How's the patient this morning?"

"Sore."

"Feel like answering a few questions?"

"Okay."

"As soon as I leave here, I'll go out to the quarry. The divers are there now. Hopefully, they will have found Dunsman by the time I get there."

"What if they don't?" Dee asked.

"We'll handle that if it happens. Right now I need to know if he had a knife or gun when he attacked you."

"No. He didn't have either one."

"Seems to me if he meant to rape or kill he would have had a weapon. That's the norm."

"He's not, or wasn't, normal. For a man over sixty he was strong. Fast, too. He started out with a tire tool. I can't remember what he did with it. Several times I wondered how he got to me so quickly. He told me something that made me believe he often beat women into submission. He said I would be begging for him before it was over — just like all the other bitches. He didn't need a weapon."

Dan interjected, "Sheriff, Dee just took a pill for pain. You may not realize just how much she's injured. Along with the bruises on her face and arms, she has a fractured rib. Mom said they did an x-ray last night."

"I'm not surprised. She was one tough little girl. I think she was so scared she didn't feel the pain just after he attacked her. She didn't let him get the best of her."

Dee said, "Sheriff, I can't take credit for that. I believe Mollie told me what to do. A voice told me specifically how and when to grab his straight leg while he was preparing to kick me with his other leg. Seconds later he would have been leaning backwards instead of forward and wouldn't have gone into the quarry. He would have thrown me into the quarry." She shivered as her mind went back to the black hole. She tried to tell him everything she knew but felt she was forgetting something.

"Well that's all for now. I'll get in touch with you as soon as we know something." The sheriff left the room.

Dee and Dan were quiet for a while. Dee broke the silence, "Dan, did your mom call and ask you to come?"

"She called and told me what happened last night. She didn't ask me to come."

"I'm okay. You don't have to stay. They'll probably let me go home soon. It's not like I have any life threatening injuries."

"I wanted to come. Dee, I know I've been a real coward lately and I have been busy at work. But work is no excuse. I don't know what happened. I've always considered myself a strong person, but I had never seen a skeleton and I don't understand visions.

"I suppose you could say I had my own vision last night. Just before Mom called and woke me up, I was sure I saw you looking into a big black hole. You know, like one of those space movies showing a big black hole in the universe."

Dee was fading fast but tried to hear all Dan was saying.

"While waiting for you to wake up, I realized if it was hard for me to deal with all this how much harder it's been for you. I still don't know what the future holds for us, but I hope you will give us a chance to find out. I've missed you. I've *really* missed you. I think I was hoping you missed me so much you would call me back. I'm not using that as an excuse. I should never have waited so long to let you know how I feel."

She smiled, knowing Mollie had somehow shown Dan the hole and that he must love her a lot to have been open to a picture message from Mollie. She closed her eyes. The pain medicine was beginning to take effect. She remembered the emotional pain and hurt of the last few months. Her smile was replaced by a frown and her forehead wrinkled. "It's too late."

Dan thought he heard her add, *"There was a hole – a big black hole."*

Dan sat by her bed. He'd heard her say, "It's too late," but he couldn't make the steps required to leave her room. He stood up and held both her hands while she slept.

She dozed until mid-morning. Just before waking she dreamed she had fallen into a deep, dark hole. *She hung there with her hands stretched above her head. The black hole was pulling her down. Someone was holding her hands, preventing her from falling down into the blackness. She slowly raised her head and saw Dan risking his life to hang on to her. She said, "It's too late." He refused to let her go. A voice she recognized said, "Dee. Don't be so stubborn. You used your stubbornness to save your life last night. Don't use it now to ruin your future. Your stubbornness can be a blessing or a curse. Use it wisely."*

She woke up and was surprised and happy to see Dan holding both her hands. He had not left, her "it's-too-late" comment notwithstanding. Her parents were there too; they were talking quietly about how pale she looked.

Dan stepped back from the bed, and her father took his place. Her mother was on the other side, rubbing Dee's arm below the bruises when Dee awoke. Tears came to her eyes when she first saw her parents. She saw the anguish in their faces. She hated worrying them.

"I'm really all right," she said as she looked from one to the other. She was careful about moving around. She didn't want to show just how much pain the broken rib caused.

Her mother said, "Dee, I've worried about your stubborn streak all your life. Now I realize you would not have survived last night if you hadn't been strong *and* stubborn."

"Mom, I admit I'm stubborn, but Mollie helped me know what to do to save myself." She didn't tell her mother about Mollie's words regarding her relationship with Dan and how and when to use her stubborn trait. She was sure her mother wouldn't understand.

The nurse came in and said the doctor had agreed it was okay for her to go home. She gave Dee's mom a prescription for a pain medication with instructions.

Her parents insisted on taking her to the apartment. They suggested Dan go to his parents' house and get a nap. He looked exhausted and agreed to the nap as long as Dee agreed to see him later in the day before he headed back to Atlanta.

After a short nap at his parents' home, Dan spent the remainder of the day with Dee. She told him about the dream in the hospital and Mollie's words about her future — their future. She thanked him for not leaving, even after she had essentially told him to go by saying, "It's too late." It was three o'clock in the afternoon when the sheriff called to tell them the divers had found Dun Dunsman's body.

Dan and Dee talked about Mollie and how she had impacted their relationship. Dan told Dee he had learned a lot about himself and never realized he was so closed to things he didn't understand. They were back on good terms when he left on Sunday evening.

Sam left shortly after Dan did. Emmy spent the weeknights at her parents' home, freeing up her bedroom for Anna Marie. Emmy went to work the next day and the school found a substitute teacher for Dee.

Nancy Tremane called on Monday to let Dee know they heard from Sheriff Dalton about the attack and asked Dee if she and Frank could visit later in the week. Frank was finishing up a job on Thursday and they hoped to come for a visit with her sister and to see Dee on Friday. Dee told them that would be great and they agreed on a time after lunch.

As soon as she got off the phone she found her mom in the kitchen and said, "The Tremanes want to come Friday. I'm sure they want to hear the details about how Dun Dunsman actually died." She explained to her mother that Nancy also had family in Elberton and wasn't coming just to get the gory details.

"But your father is coming on Friday."

Dee sighed inwardly. "You and Dad do not have to meet them. If you want to leave before lunch, you will miss them altogether."

"I'll have to talk with Sam." Anna Marie went to Emmy's room to use the phone to call her husband. Dee would have liked to have heard the conversation; however, she resisted following her mom and was relieved when her mom returned within a few minutes.

"I can't believe it, but your dad wants to meet the Tremanes. He said we could stay until they arrive on Friday."

"That's great, Mom."

"I hope you know what you're doing. What if it's obvious they aren't kin? Then Sam will be disappointed. And, if it's obvious they are brothers . . . then what?"

"Mom, don't worry. They both are grown men and can decide if they would like to spend time together — or not."

"Are you going to tell the Tremanes or just put them in shock? They may not like the idea of having a long lost brother found."

"I hadn't thought that far. I suppose I'll have to at least tell Nancy, then she can decide what she will tell Frank. I'll call Nancy before Friday."

Dee was happy to be mothered and her mom did not let the Tremanes' upcoming visit take away from their time together. Dee had no idea how painful a broken rib could be and was glad her mother treated her like a little girl again. Her mother did her grocery shopping and cleaned the apartment. Dee made it a point to steer away from the Dad-and-Frank-are-brothers issue.

Nancy Tremane took the news well when Dee called and told her there was a chance Frank and her dad were brothers. In fact, she could hear excitement in Nancy's voice.

"Dee, I hope that's true. I don't know for sure how Frank will handle such, but I believe he will be pleased."

"What will you tell him?" Dee asked.

"As little as possible until we arrive at your place. I don't know enough of the background to give him a lot of hope. We'll see."

After saying goodbye, Dee started worrying. What if Frank took the information as her mother had? Her mom seemed to be resigned to the possibility now, but Dee remembered how disappointed she was with her parents' initial responses.

Chapter Twenty-Three

"The Spittin' Image"

Sam returned to Elberton on Friday morning with a photo album and his birth certificate, both requested by Dee. He helped do a few maintenance chores around the apartment and both parents did all they could to make her comfortable. Staying busy also kept their minds off the Tremanes' visit after lunch.

When the doorbell rang, Dee told her parents, "Stay here and let me bring them in. We might scare them to death if we all run to the door at the same time." She walked slowly and purposefully to the front door, the broken rib still obviously painful.

Her parents stood off to the side near the kitchen as Dee ushered the Tremanes into the living room. She watched Frank's face as he looked at her father. "Frank Tremane, this is my father, Sam Dupree, and my mother, Anna Marie." Dee was surprised that Frank's face showed no emotion whatsoever.

Sam stuck his hand out for a shake and said, "Proud to meet you, Frank."

Frank and Sam shook hands as they looked guardedly at each other. Dee broke in, "Mom, Dad, this is Frank's wife, Nancy."

Frank was first to break away from Sam's eyes and shook hands with Anna Marie. His expression was serious. He had not said a word.

Nancy came to the rescue. "Anna Marie, we can't tell you enough how much we appreciate Dee." Nancy was holding Mrs. Tremane's Bible and a photo album.

After shaking hands with Anna Marie, Frank walked to Dee and said, "Hey." He started to give her a hug when he saw her arms go up to prevent it. "Oops. I forgot. How's the rib doing?"

"Better, but it still can hurt like crazy if I make the wrong move. Let's go to the kitchen and spread out some of the things I've asked each of you to bring."

They sat around the table as Dee placed the items on the table. Frank had pushed his chair away from the table as though he was not going to participate. Dee looked at him and asked, "Did Nancy tell you what I suspect?"

"She said your family might be kin to us. That's all."

"I'll show you why, then, if you and Dad want to, you can get DNA tests done to confirm or deny the connection."

"I don't need no DNA. He's the spittin' image of Pa." Frank got up and took a couple of steps to the table, opened the album Nancy brought and flipped through several pages before stopping.

"See this?" He pointed to a picture of a tall, thin man wearing a hat and dressed in a suit, standing almost behind a woman. "This is Pa. He was about forty or fifty when this was taken. See the favor? If he didn't have on a hat, you'd see his hair would look just like Sam's."

Dee had never heard him talk that much. She had not seen the likeness when she looked through the album last summer because Frank's father had on a hat. "Was he bald or did his hair recede like Dad's."

"He didn't go bald. It was like that." Frank pointed to Sam. "He also had Sam's handshake. Just like Pa's. He even sounds like Pa." Frank's chin trembled; he quit talking, pulled his chair up to the table and sat down. Nancy reached for his hand and held it tightly.

Dee laid out her dad's birth certificate beside that of the Tremane stillborn baby. The only differences came in times and parents' names. The Tremane baby's time of birth was listed as 1:20 a.m. with Sam's birth at 1:30 a.m., same day, weight, height. Sam's name was listed as Jack Gibbs with the mother, Ginny Gibbs, seventeen years old. The space for the paternal name was left blank.

Dee was the first to comment. "Think about it. It was a small hospital. It was in the middle of the night and possibly during a shift change. The doctor probably delivered the two babies and then left. More than likely they didn't have a full staff due to the late hour. Dad's parents gave him their name when they adopted him at two days old. I believe two babies were born that night or early morning and one didn't survive and the paperwork got screwed up. Obviously, one child didn't get documented correctly. There is no way both babies would weigh the same and have the same height. Maybe one person started the paperwork and another finished it. What do you think Dad?"

"I don't know." Sam sat quietly and appeared to be in deep thought.

Dee looked at Nancy, "Did you bring pictures of your boys?"

Nancy reached in her purse and pulled out an envelope. "Here they are."

Dee took the envelope, took out five pictures and placed them in front of her father and mother. "Mom, Dad, look at this one." She pointed to a close-up of Jake. "And this one." She pointed to a picture with all three boys. She reached for the album her father had brought with him and found the picture of him when he was about thirty. She took it out of the album and placed it beside Jake's picture.

Anna Marie leaned forward to get a better look. Her right hand went to her chest as she said, "That's uncanny. He could be Sam's twin when Sam was younger."

Dee hoped the pictures would bring her mother around to her way of thinking.

Frank's eyes were drawn to Sam; he finally said, "Want to get some fresh air?"

"Sure." Sam left the table and walked ahead of Frank to the door, opened it for him and followed him out. The three women watched as the men left the room. They each wondered just how talkative the guys would be together since being short on words was a characteristic they apparently had both inherited.

"Nancy, what do you think?" Dee asked.

"I believe Frank said it all when he said he didn't need any DNA tests run. Sam is more like Mr. Tremane than Frank. Frank is a mixture of his mother and daddy. Sam is Frank James Tremane made over. But we could have the DNA test done anyway. Then there would be no doubt."

Dee fixed sweet iced tea for Nancy and her mom. She went to the door and asked her dad and Mr. Tremane if they wanted something to drink and received negative answers. She tried to read their body language to figure out how they were getting along. They were leaning against Nancy's car, facing each other. Other than the shake of their heads to say no to the drinks, they didn't acknowledge the interruption. Quietly, they continued their conversation.

After a while Nancy said, "I hate to end this for them, but I promised Susan we would stop by before driving back to Easley." She looked at Anna Marie. "We would love to have you visit us and meet our boys and their families. Dee has met them and she's been a little detective through this whole thing. Frank acts like a huge burden has been lifted off his shoulders and he gives Dee the credit — where it belongs." She got up from the table and the others followed her to the door.

Outside, they all exchanged hugs, except for Dee. Frank quietly got Dee off to the side and said, "Dee, you're a special girl. Thanks."

"You're welcome, Uncle Frank."

Frank beamed and started to say something when Dee interrupted, "Oh, wait. I have something for you."

As much as her sore ribs would let her, Dee hurried back inside. Within a few minutes she came out and offered something to Frank. "Here, I want you to have these. You can place them with your mother's notes and Mollie's stuff. I think Mollie's stuff should be kept together." She handed Mollie's glasses to Frank.

Frank gave Dee a guarded hug. He said his goodbyes to the Duprees and joined Nancy in her car. The Duprees all waved as the Tremanes backed out of the drive; they walked back to the front door hand in hand.

"Well, Deedle Bug. You really did it this time." Sam said. "What you don't get in visions, you pursue relentlessly to the end, whatever that is."

Dee took it as a compliment and wondered what her mother thought. She didn't have long to wait.

"You and Dee need to understand, the more people we bring into our lives, the more complicated life can be. For instance, if we invite them for Thanksgiving, do we invite their children and their families? And, if we do that we'll have to rent a social hall or something."

Dee and Sam both laughed. Sam said, "Don't worry, Hon, they might have their own Thanksgiving plans. We have to remember they had a life before they knew we existed. I hope to learn a lot from Frank. He said Jake is quite a golfer."

"That puts it in the right perspective, Dad."

Dee could see her dad was pleased. Evidently he and Frank had had the first of many conversations to come. Her parents left before dinner and Emmy came back from her parents' house.

Dan visited on Sunday and they talked about taking a trip. He asked Dee to decide where she wanted to go. He would try and make it work. She didn't tell him that her first choice, for a long time, had been San Francisco. She just wasn't sure she could handle Dun Dunman's San Francisco. She told him she would think about it.

Dee went back to work the following Wednesday to students who could hardly wait to ask her questions about the body found in the quarry and what kind of moves she used to protect herself when he attacked her. They seemed more interested in the physical aspects than the visionary parts. She explained both as truthfully as she could without being too graphic. They were far too young for her to disclose the gruesome details of Mollie's death and her attack.

Miss Wilma called on Thursday afternoon. Dee had come in from work and had just begun to rest on the sofa when the phone rang.

"Is this Dee Dupree?" Miss Wilma asked.

"Yes, this is Dee."

"Hi. This is Miss Wilma Jones. I called to see how you-ah doing, Sweetie."

"Miss Wilma. Thank you so much for calling. I owe you an apology for not calling you or visiting since our last visit."

"No, no, you don't owe me an apology. It sounds as if you've had you-ah hands full. I actually called you to thank you for pursuing the Dun Dunsman affai-ah to the end. I know Bea and my moth-ah are in Heaven today thanking you for stopping him from hurtin' more people. My goodness, he was such a wretched person. Sorry, I didn't mean to go on and on. So, are you hurt badly?" Miss Wilma's southern accent was heavy.

"Not too much. My broken rib is better. The bruises look a lot worse than they feel. Yesterday was my first day back at work and I'm exhausted at the end of the day; however, my students are so understanding. I can't complain."

"When you feel bett-ah, Honey, I hope you will stop by for a visit. I also wanted to ask you one mo-ah thing. Does Bea's husband know he might have the wrong ashes?"

"Yes. He called me just this week to tell me he had not received the ashes from the California man's death. He also said he had gotten a call from someone with the GBI and they assured him he would have to make arrangements for the disposal of the real Dun Dunsman's body. Dr. Spence plans to go through with the plans he and I made earlier. Those ashes will be flushed."

"That's a good thing. I should'ave known you two wouldn't let that get lost in the shuffle. You take ca-ah, now."

"I will. And, thank you for thinking of me."

"I'm delighted you-ah okay, Sweetie. Bye bye."

"Bye, Miss Wilma." Dee hung up realizing she must make a visit to Miss Wilma's in the near future. She had been so helpful in her pursuit of justice for Mollie. Somehow a shadow lingered over the whole affair and Dee couldn't quite put her finger on what was not right.

Chapter Twenty-Four

"The Silver Lining"

Dee finally got up the nerve to tell Dan that she had always wanted to go to San Francisco, but questioned if she should go since Dun Dunsman had lived there. Somehow she had not completely gotten past the fear he instilled inside her. Just thinking about him made her shake. In a late night phone conversation with Dan she said, "I've always wanted to go to San Francisco, but with all that's happened I'm not sure I should. What do you think?"

Dan replied, "I think we should go and face the demons Mr. Dunsman placed in your head. Actually, I think that's the best thing for us to do — face them head on. Between your family and mine, we never get to spend time together, just the two of us. We're going to have to plan it and make it happen."

She loved hearing him say "*for us to do*" and "*time together.*" Just hearing that made her know he was with her now and she wouldn't have to face problems on her own any more. Even so, she couldn't shake the feeling that something was wrong regarding Mollie and her death. It was such a vague feeling she didn't know how to express it, so she kept quiet.

She and Dan made the trip work for the Thanksgiving holiday weekend. She had saved for a vacation in the summer, and the trip would give her a chance to spend time with Dan without the threat of visions and fear. She was hoping to get back what they lost in the summer and maybe make progress toward the future. She felt her life had been on hold long enough. In retrospect, she was glad to have gone through finding Mollie and getting her murderer out of the picture for good. She thought about the saying, "Every cloud has a silver lining." Finding her dad's family was the silver lining as well as finding Mollie. Now she was ready to move forward.

Time had wings for Dee. Thanksgiving and the trip to San Francisco came shortly after a conversation with Dr. Spence. He called her to confirm the culmination of Bea's plan and assured her that he had the real

Dun Dunsman's cremains.

In the beginning she had planned to meet with Dun Dunsman's lawyer in San Francisco and try and find the names of some of Dunsman's victims, the ones he called "the bitches." After talking it over with Dan, she decided to let that part of her life go. The trip would be only for the two of them.

Dee looked on the internet and found more things to do in San Francisco than they could possibly accomplish: cable cars, spending at least one afternoon across the Golden Gate Bridge in Sausalito, Chinatown, Fisherman's Wharf, Alcatraz . . . the sight-seeing possibilities seemed endless. The words *"San Francisco, here I come"* kept running through her mind.

They met their family obligations for Thanksgiving Day by having breakfast with the Jackson family and lunch with her parents and The Girls and their families at Aunt Becky's house in Alpharetta. Their flight left late in the afternoon.

While on the plane, Dee insisted Dan make a list of the things he wanted to see while she did the same. She suggested they prioritize the list and alternate, choosing one from his list and then one from hers. Since it was her idea she insisted taking his number-one choice first. He chose the prison on Alcatraz Island. It was on her list, but far from the top.

The plane arrived in San Francisco late on Thursday evening. The rental-car drive to the hotel added to a very long day. Tired and exhausted they checked into the quaint hotel a few blocks from the wharf and halfway up a hill. Their room had a king-sized bed and they both fell into it, exhausted. The exhaustion didn't last long. As soon as their eyes made contact, they started undressing each other. Their clothes came off faster than they felt possible just ten minutes before. He pulled her to him with an intensity that surprised her and she responded to his body with the same heat.

When Dan reached over to turn off the lamp beside the bed, Dee asked him to leave it on and told him she wanted to see and feel everything about him. He smiled up at her as she became aggressive, exploring his body with an abandon he had not expected. He let her explore until he could no longer hold back and he quickly changed places with her. As she gazed up at him, tears slipped from the corner of her eyes. His look of concern, as he held himself slightly away from her made her cry out for him not to stop. Her smile let him know the tears were tears of joy. She wanted to tell him she loved him but she didn't want the physical act of love to overshadow the deep abiding love she felt for him on so many levels.

Even though she was certain of her love for him she didn't want to force him to profess his love for her. Afterwards, they went to sleep entwined in each other's arms. When she woke up, her back was pressed against Dan's chest and his arm was resting comfortably around her waist. It hadn't been long ago that she felt she would never be safe again and marveled at how safe she felt in his arms. She stayed still for a long time, savoring his closeness.

The time change from Eastern to Pacific gave them a few hours to catch up on sleep. It was early in San Francisco the next day when they took a boat to the island and toured the Alcatraz facility. Being a history buff, Dee was delighted to learn so much. She didn't know that, after the prison was closed, Indians lived on the island for a few years. It was eerie walking through and seeing the small cubicles that housed some of the most notorious criminals in American history. Some of the cells had the names identifying the homes of the most famous. A posted menu showed how the prisoners fared with their meals. She was impressed with the menu. It never occurred to her that prisoners ate so well. They saw the wall with windows where visitors could sit and talk with prisoners as well as the view from the prisoners' side of the wall. She took a picture of Dan behind bars.

At the back of the prison was a small yard where the prisoners spent limited time outside. The waters around the island were choppy, cold and uninviting — a natural deterrent to the prisoners planning a breakout. Normally the weather was cold or at least cool in the area. Today, however, was unusually warm. Dee said, "It must have been difficult to see the city of San Francisco so close, yet for the prisoners it was completely unattainable."

"Don't feel too sad for them. Remember, except for one or two cases, they weren't in Alcatraz for a simple burglary. They were murderers."

They were holding hands and looking back on the city when Dee tried to explain how she felt about the scenery. "San Francisco reminds me of Europe. My parents and I traveled to Italy several years ago. Dad had a friend from college who lived there and we stayed with him and his family. It's hard to believe we are still in the United States. Just the way the houses are built into the hills is reminiscent of Europe. It's so different from the east."

"It does feel foreign," Dan agreed.

They arrived back at the wharf area just in time for a quick lunch. The afternoon was spent at Dee's first choice, the Legion of Honor, San

Francisco's most beautiful museum. The columned entrance created the feeling of the old country again. Dee had to dig back to her college art history class to remember that Auguste Rodin created *The Thinker*, a statue located in the open area near the front of the museum building. They smiled at a young boy sitting in front of it with his bent head resting on his fisted hand and his elbow on his leg, mimicking the statue. It took them longer than expected to see all the paintings and exhibits in the museum. They had dinner near the museum at the famous Cliffs Restaurant at the water's edge.

Originally they planned to go out on the town for the evening but were both happy to turn in as soon as they returned to the hotel. Whatever energy left from the day's touring was used up quickly as they explored more about each other — physically and emotionally. Dee felt like the luckiest girl in the world when she fell asleep in his arms again that night.

Early the next morning they made it just in time to take the first ferry to Sausalito. The chill was still in the morning air and the sweater unwanted on Friday was welcomed on Saturday. They saw the Golden Gate Bridge as they crossed the bay with Sausalito to the right and Marin Headlands to the left. Sausalito sat at the water's edge and was heavily populated. The Marin Headlands, in direct contrast, offered walking trails, trees and wildlife. Dee and Dan spent the entire morning looking at the spectacular scenery of both locations and enjoying the myriad of sailboats in the bay between them and San Francisco.

They made it across the bay for lunch, which was fun and different in Chinatown at a Dim Sum — a Chinese rolling buffet normally served around noon. Dan told Dee that Dim Sum buffets were becoming more and more popular even though the practice had been around for a while in the big Chinatowns of the world. The waiters came by the table with carts of things she did not recognize. Dan had eaten Dim Sum once before.

Dan expected an important business call and purposely left his cell phone on. The call was a deciding factor as to where he would be working come Monday morning. When the call came, he left the table in order to talk outside as a courtesy to Dee and the other customers in the restaurant and before he and Dee made any choices.

Four carts came by while he was gone and Dee chose several platters of different foods to ensure having choices of vegetables, meats and sweets. When Dan came back to the table he stood, eyeing Dee's multitude of platters. "You must be really hungry."

"I just wanted to try several things. That one has pork inside it." She pointed to a platter containing pastry pieces. "The one beside it with the green leafy stuff is good but I don't know what it is. It looks kind of like big thick spinach leaves, but isn't. Oh, yes, that one, I think, has seafood." She pointed to a large platter near his plate.

Dee didn't know that the buffet price was charged on a per-platter basis, and Dan did not enlighten her to the contrary, apparently deciding to let it go and enjoy the choices she made. She encouraged him to choose something when the next cart came by their table. To her surprise, he declined. When the bill came he took it quickly and said, "This is on me."

"No way. It's my turn. It's on me."

"No. I insist."

"Daniel, let's go Dutch. I'll pay half."

"Because you called me 'Daniel' for the first time since just after our trip to Abbeville, I'll call it a celebration and I will pay." Dee looked surprised and wondered for an instant if he was keeping score on other things, whatever they might be. He quickly changed the subject. "Let's hop a ride on the cable cars, just for the fun of it."

"That sounds good."

Dan parked the rental car at the hotel. They asked the concierge about the cable cars. He explained the routes and gave them a map. They had to walk a block over to get to the tracks and wait at the corner for the cable car. The operator didn't wait long for the passengers to get on. The car was loaded. With no seats available, they held onto poles until, two stops later, seats opened up as passengers disembarked. The steep inclines combined with being in a moving object forced them to hold on tight even though the car traveled at a rather slow speed. At one time, they could see several blocks down from where they came. It was amazing how the people in San Francisco were so accustomed to walking up and down the hills. Dee and Dan had to do some walking to get to and from the hotel and were left with sore calf muscles at the end of each day.

After the cable-car ride they took the city bus to the botanical gardens and entered the gates that appeared to be the back entrance. Several times Dee asked to sit on a bench as they toured from one section to another so she could enjoy the wonderful plants and rest her sore legs. Several plants had familiar names; however, they grew larger in the California climate. The rhododendrons were twice as tall as Dan. The gardens were beautiful and interesting with an Asian influence. Each section of the garden was unique and they talked about coming back in the spring or summer when more plants were in bloom. They exited through the stalls on the opposite side of the garden from where they entered.

By the time they got back to the hotel, Dee's calf muscles were so tight they hurt. She wasn't sure she wanted to go out for dinner. Dan seconded her reluctance, and they ordered cheese, fruit, crackers and wine from room service. Both were lethargic as they sat at the small table eating and talking. The summer's events had been shuffled to another era, one now past.

Dan took her hand and guided her to the bed. She cuddled against him. They talked about the things on their lists they didn't get to do while in San Francisco. They promised each other that they would visit San Francisco again.

They also talked about the status of his job. His engineering company had gone ahead with the plans to open a branch office in Athens. Dan had applied for a position there and hoped to know something soon.

Dan asked, "After all that's happened, do you still want to live in Elberton?"

"Yes. That crazy Dun Dunsman doesn't live there anymore and has no family in Elberton. I think that makes Elberton safer than most places. Don't forget, I grew up in Atlanta where homicides are on the eleven o'clock news almost every night."

Dee fell asleep in his arms. *She thought she was awake when she heard Dun Dunsman say, "I didn't kill her, bitch." She felt like she was back in one of Mollie's visions and saw Mollie being dragged through the grass. As she was being lifted into the trunk she reached up and removed her attacker's sunglasses and looked into the small dark eyes of an evil old man — Dun Dunsman's grandfather.*

Dee sat straight up in bed shaking.

Dan, half asleep as he sat up beside her, pulled the cover up and around her and held her tight. She was shaking so hard, at first she couldn't speak. She started rocking back and forth. Finally, she told Dan that Dun Dunsman had not murdered Mollie.

He asked, "If he didn't do it, who did?"

"His grandfather."

"Are you sure?"

"Yes. Well, maybe. At the quarry, he asked me if I thought *he* left her in a car. I was so scared; his words didn't really sink in and I thought he was trying to confuse me. He kept calling me Miss Know-It-All and saying things that alluded to the fact that I didn't know something important. I think my subconscious has been working on this for a long time and finally presented the answer to me in this awful nightmare. I just couldn't put it all together until now. What am I going to do? The Sheriff really will think I've lost my mind."

"What does it matter? It sounds like you had a nightmare, not a vision. Besides, he was going to kill you and that makes him a killer. I find it ironic that he got blamed for something his grandfather did. Dun finally had to answer for his actions and his grandfather's actions. Seems fair to me."

"His grandfather did cover for him when he was in trouble. I believe he saw Dun rape Mollie, and he killed her rather than have her tell anyone. Miss Wilma said he never blamed Dun for anything. It was *always* someone else's fault. It wasn't like a vision. But it seemed real. I wonder if Mollie knew. Oh, Daniel. What if Mollie misled me on purpose?"

They talked for more than an hour before she agreed with him that it wouldn't change anything if she revealed what might be the truth of Mollie's murder. She told him about the vision at the pond and how something had changed just before Mollie was hit with a shovel. The nightmare had created more questions than answers. Did Mollie know Dun's grandfather had placed her in the car to die? And, did Dun know his grandfather did it?

Dan finally convinced her that both the Dunsman men were ruthless and she had no proof about the grandfather to offer the sheriff. She made the decision to leave it alone after she and Dan talked about how upsetting it would be for all the family to have to go through the entire process again. Her father and Uncle Frank had become close. She didn't want anything to endanger their newfound family ties.

She felt Mollie's presence and approval as she dozed off and managed a couple of hours sleep before having to wake to leave San Francisco.

On the flight back to Atlanta, Dan teased Dee about whether or not her toes curled while they were in San Francisco. They laughed and agreed to have future explorations on the matter, as often as possible. As always they were careful about using those three little words. Dee didn't want to be the first to say, "I love you" and wondered if he was thinking the same thing. She wanted his commitment to be as sincere as hers . . . *when* it happened. She was sure that it would.

The trip to San Francisco with Dan had replaced the negativity and fear that Dun Dunsman had planted in Dee's mind. She had made peace with Mollie and knew she could face the future without looking over her shoulder. Dan had been right about going to San Francisco; he'd also been right about not telling anyone about the rest of the story of Mollie's rape and murder. He had shown her that beautiful loving memories could make the ugly evil memories fade. No man had ever come close to touching her heart — until Dan. She knew she loved him with all her heart and she was determined to tell him when the time was just right.

The remainder of the year was spent in a whirlwind. Emmy and Fred were busy getting ready for their wedding planned for New Year's Day. Sam and Frank had DNA samples sent off for testing and the final outcome confirmed they were brothers. Dee reserved a dining room at a restaurant in Anderson where both families got together to celebrate. Dee was concerned how her mother would handle meeting Frank's and Nancy's children and grandchildren and was pleasantly surprised to hear her mother talking with Nancy about how some of the children favored Sam. Her mother sounded proud to have found Sam's biological family.

Fred and Dan were in Elberton almost every weekend for pre-wedding festivities as well as the high school football games. Dee and Dan managed to see a couple of UGA football games and enjoyed tailgating in Athens with their friends. Christmas was hectic and fun.

Chapter Twenty Five

"A Dream Come True"

Emmy and Fred got married as planned on January 1st in the Methodist Church Emmy attended as a youth. She and her mother compromised on many issues and pulled it off with only minor misunderstandings. It was especially difficult to do with Emmy's moods swinging in all directions. She thought it was wedding jitters; however, by mid January she knew she was pregnant with the Jacksons' first grandchild.

Dan asked Dee to meet him at DePalma's Italian Restaurant in East Athens for dinner on Valentine's Day. They had spent most of the weekend together; therefore, she was surprised by the invitation — even if it was Valentine's Day. She drove from Elberton, using a shortcut though Winterville, and arrived first at DePalma's. She placed their names on the list for seating and waited outside for Dan. When he arrived, she greeted him with a quick kiss followed by, "I love you, Daniel."

He took a second look at her and said, "That's a first. You've never said that before."

"I know. I just wanted you to know tonight." She gave him a valentine card as they walked inside. While they were waiting to be seated, he looked at the envelope, which had the day's date rather than Dan's name on it. He opened the envelope and read the card and gave her a quick kiss.

He winked as he said, "You're my valentine too."

They were seated shortly thereafter. Dee was delighted with the menu and ordered the day's special: vegetarian lasagna filled with her favorites, artichoke hearts, red and yellow peppers, mushrooms and onion. Dan chose grouper covered in a sauce with capers. After dinner Dan said, "I love you," and gave her a small heart-shaped box filled with chocolate.

"Thank you," Dee said. "And thanks, too, for the 'I love you.' That means the world to me."

She made no attempt to open the box and placed it near her purse.

Dan said, "Aren't you going to open it?"

"I'm so stuffed. I thought I would enjoy the chocolate later."

"I would like a piece now."

"Oh, I'm sorry. It didn't occur to me you wanted some. You very seldom eat chocolate." With a questioning look she opened the box and was handing it to him when she realized there was no candy in the middle slot. There was a ring with a rather large diamond.

"Will you marry me?"

Her eyes were bright with tears as she said, "I do. No. I mean I will." An engagement ring and those three little words left her flustered.

"'I will' works. 'I do' comes later in the church." He laughed and was quite pleased with himself for surprising her.

"Then you won't mind a church wedding? In Elberton, of course."

He laughed and said, "I take it you don't want to take the easy way out and elope?"

"My mom and her sisters would never forgive me."

"Oh, no. I expected to have to jump through a few hoops, but I don't think any man could make that many women happy."

Dee laughed, "I'll let them know up front that you and I will be making the decisions. Maybe we can actually have some fun with it."

"Always the optimist," Dan said as he squeezed her hand.

The wedding took place in Elberton on June 12 at the Presbyterian church Dee had been attending since moving to Elberton. Before the wedding, Dee was in the room with her bridesmaids when she walked up to her Matron of Honor, dressed in an off-the-shoulder sea-green dress that hung several inches below her knees. "Emmy, you've been my friend for years. You've been like a sister to me. In one hour, you and I will truly be sisters. I want to thank you for being there for me. Through you I met the man of my dreams." Dee gave her a hug, leaving space to ensure Emmy's growing tummy wasn't squeezed too tightly.

"Wait, considering your history with dreams, I'm not sure Dan would like being the man of *your* dreams," she teased.

"Be serious."

"I know what you mean. I love you, too," Emmy said as she gave her a big hug. "I'm going to miss you. You know I expect you and Dan to come to Sun City often."

Dee laughed. Emmy's mischievousness was endearing. Fred had finished at UGA and accepted a job with a landscape architect/management company on the coast near Hilton Head Island,

South Carolina. She knew she would never be bored with Emmy around and she would always be loved with Dan in her life. He had worked it out to move to the new branch office in Athens. Her dreams of raising a family in Elberton could come true.

Emmy and Anna Marie assisted Dee with dressing in her simple-but-elegant white wedding gown that exposed her shoulders and highlighted the simple-lace sea-green ribbon around her neck. The same ribbon curled amongst the white orchids of her bouquet and flowed down the front of her wedding gown, complementing the white. Emmy had helped Dee choose her wedding dress and suggested she bring in the color of her bridesmaid's dresses into her outfit. Dee loved the combination.

Tears flowed from Anna Marie's eyes as she placed the veil on Dee's head of curls. For once, she seemed to be at a loss for words. She started to say something to Dee and finally shook her head, trying to stop the tears. Dee hugged her mom and said, "You don't have to say anything. I love you and Dad so much. Thank you for everything."

Dee had many pictures in her head and in her photo album to remind her of the special day. Janet sang Mariah Carey's version of *I'll Be There* before the ceremony and Dee walked down the aisle with her father, who sat down beside her mom after giving Dee's hand to Dan. Janet sounded very much like Shania Twain as she sang *From This Moment On* after Dee and Dan exchanged rings. Behind Dee's parents were The Girls, their families and the entire family of Tremanes. It reminded Dee of lines like "the tie that binds." Their families were bound together forever — beyond time.

At the reception across town at the Civic Center, Miss Wilma visited with what seemed like everyone from Elberton and Dee was happy to introduce her to the out-of-town guests including her parents, The Girls, the Tremanes, Janet and Judd.

Janet had learned a lot about her handsome Judd. The night they met, her gaydar had not been working. He was funny, talented and gay to the bone. He had become friends with them all; however, he had become Janet's best friend. They had spent a great deal of time together since the karaoke night at the Beef Baron. Janet often introduced him as the other black-eyed pea. She would laugh and say, "We're two black-eyed peas in the same pod." No one could argue with her. They often finished each other's sentences and could communicate with a look. When Janet found out he was gay she told Dee and Emmy, "It doesn't matter. Lovers come and go. Friends last forever."

Granny Nida had taken a liking to Sam the first time she'd been introduced to him at a family gathering a few months before the wedding. She stopped to talk with him at the reception, addressing him with a nickname she had created just for him and changing his wife's name while she was at it, "Sambo, I sure hope to see more of you and Anna Maria now that those two children are married."

"I hope so too, Miss Nida."

"I hope they live as long as old Mr. Smythe," Granny Nida said.

"How old was Mr. Smythe?"

"Oh, he's still alive. I was thinkin' about his nine-tieth birthday. He decided to celebrate in Atlanta at one of those rit-zy hotels. After havin' a par-ty with friends, he went up to his room to go to bed. Shortly after arrivin', someone knocked on the door. When he opened the door he was sue-prised to see a young woman with large breasts dressed in a tight dress with plenty of cleavage showin'. Everything she had on or I should say didn't have on showed off her voluptuous tall figure. She said, 'Mr. Smythe, I have a sue-prise for you.' He said, 'What?' She said, 'Sup-er sex.' He cupped his hand behind his left ear and said, 'What? Soup or sex? I'll take the soup, thank you.'"

Sam and Granny Nida had a good laugh and Granny Nida went off to find another unsuspecting person to sue-prise. As she walked away, Dan grabbed her elbow and said, "Here's my favorite octogenarian."

"Yore what?" Granny Nida asked with a frown on her face.

"You know. A person in her eighties."

"Well, octo... octo... whatever that word was sounded like the name of a dinosaur, Danny Boy. Maybe that's supposed to be a nice way of saying I'm a dinosaur," she said with her thin lips pressed together.

"No Granny Nida. I apologize. It was a reference to age, but you'll always be my young granny. You don't look over eighty today. Dance with me, Granny Nida." He guided her to the dance floor. He said, "Granny Nida, you do look different today — younger I think."

"I know. That's why I can't believe you called me that name."

"Do you have a secret youth potion you've been hiding from us mere mortals?" He bent way over to hear her answer.

"No. It's makeup. Yore mama took me to a spa thing this mornin' and they did a complete makeover. Looks good, too."

"It does," Dan agreed.

She had him bend even closer. "All I have to do is make yore mama think I'm gonna use Preparation H on my face and she'll take me any where I want to go and git me anything I want."

"That may be true, Granny Nida. However, she wants you to be happy, so she would probably do it any way."

Granny Nida looked serious for just a few seconds before looking up at Dan with a crooked little grin. Dan wasn't sure if she agreed with what he said or if she was already planning her next mischief.

When the song was over, Dan walked with Granny Nida to the edge of the dance floor and left her talking with Miss Wilma.

Dan sneaked up behind Dee, pushed her veil to one side and kissed her on the nape of her neck. He couldn't resist a second kiss and the urge to wrap his arms around her. She turned into his arms and they both knew she belonged there. He reminded her it was time to start saying their goodbyes to everyone before starting their trip to the Belmont Inn in Abbeville for the first night of their honeymoon. They planned to drive to Atlanta the following day and fly to Hawaii for the remainder of their honeymoon. As Dee left the Civic Center with her red-headed husband she knew all her dreams would come true.

Dee's and Dan's wedding night reflected the strong love that had grown in the past months on all levels. They were physically, emotionally and spiritually bound to each other long before the exchange of rings.

On their wedding night Dee's toes curled so many times she quit counting. Her heart raced, but it wasn't from fearful visions. When she slept she dreamed of the future. The dream came into focus like a home movie with the edges blurred.

On a sunny summer day she and Dan were on the patio of their home with a three year-old red-headed daughter. She had a few freckles scattered across the bridge of her nose and cheeks. Little Sara was holding her very first "big girl" doll. Dee and Sara were sitting on the top step leading to the backyard and were having a conversation while Dan listened from a wrought-iron chair a few feet away.

Dee said, "Sara, what do you want to name your doll?"

Sara immediately replied, "Mollie." She looked up at Dee with the same deep crystal-blue eyes that reminded Dee of her Aunt Connie.

Dee and Dan looked at each other.

Dee asked, "Why Mollie?"

" 'Cause Mollie is my friend."

"Where does Mollie live?"

"Oh, Mommy, Mollie lives with the angels. She is my guard on the angels."

"How do you know that?" Dee knew Sara was trying to say Mollie was her guardian angel.

"She said she lives with the angels." She added, "She loves me and

will take care of me."

"When did you see Mollie?" asked Dee. Her concern was growing.

"In my room. She was at the end of my bed singing me songs."

"What kind of songs?"

"Happy songs. Mollie's happy."

"How do you know she's happy?" Dee was worried as to where this was leading.

"'Cause happy angels sing. They can't sing if they not happy. Mollie said she 'pose to sing," Sara stated in her matter-of-fact tone.

"Did she say why?" Dee asked.

Sara held her doll close to her chest with her right arm and lifted her small left hand. Her tiny index finger went into the air and she moved it up, down and around as though she were writing in the sky. "'Cause it's wrote on a rock," Sara said in her three year old language.

Dee's mind immediately brought up the image of the monument at the head of Mollie's grave with the engraving, "Singing With The Angels." She added, "Sara, you are so right. Mollie is supposed to sing. It is written on a rock."

Dee woke up, looked at Dan sleeping quietly beside her and snuggled up to him. She smiled and closed her eyes.

Almost four years later Dee and Sara placed flowers on Mollie's grave. Little Sara placed a small batch of daisies just below the words, "Singing With The Angels." Dee placed a colorful mixed bouquet on the other side below the words, "She came back to us." Dee took Sara's hand and walked away with the happy knowledge that her little Sara was not a vision . . . just a dream come true.

If you enjoyed *Written On A Rock,* you might enjoy some other great fiction from ThomasMax authors.

The Resemblance by Randall Arnold

Jim Greyson is the last of a rich family line. He lives in rural Georgia with an old black brother-and-sister couple, the only "family" he has had since his grandfather died. Jim loves the forest, and he also loves reading and updating his family journals, books kept for generations that document everything from love to angels to deer hunting. When he falls in love with Mary from Atlanta, his world is turned upside down when his solitary life meets urbanity. Mary's son, also named Jim, has had a problem with alcohol since the death of his own father. Can a city woman find happiness with man of her dreams far from her city pleasures? And somewhere in that simple country life, could there be hope for her addicted son? **$14.95**

Includes "Incrediglossary" to help young readers to build their vocabularies.

IncrediBoy: Be Careful What You Wish by Lee Clevenger

To Christian Savage, 11, life is a cruel joke. He's the smallest kid in his class, a target for bullies, and, thanks to a "perfect" older brother, has world's greatest inferiority complex. In his daydreams, Christian is a superhero he calls IncrediBoy, and his life changes when he finds two rings lost by Yoqe, an evil alien, during a brief stop on Earth. Through the magic of the rings, Christian becomes IncrediBoy in real life and does good deeds just like the comic-book heroes. But Christian finds being a superhero isn't all it's cracked up to be. And Christian doesn't know it, but Yoqe is headed back to Earth to reclaim his rings. Before it's over, Christian vs. Yoqe will determine the ultimate fate of the entire universe! For ages 9 & up. **$ 12.95**

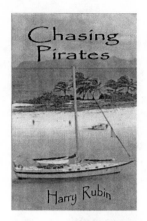

Chasing Pirates by Harry Rubin

Modern-day pirates are attacking vessels off the coasts of Yemen and Somalia, and holding crew members for ransom. The United States Navy is given the mission to combat the piracy. It initiates Operation Chameleon that sends a small vessel and its crew of six into harm's way.

$15.95

The Counterfeit War by Harry Rubin

In this sequel to *Chasing Pirates*, the president of Venezuela has initiated a plan to flood the nations of the Caribbean with counterfeit $100 bills to destroy their economies. He plans to use his petro-dollars to bail the small nations out and control the Caribbean basin. The U.S. Office of Naval Intelligence initiates Operation Venback to combat the plan with a small vessel and a crew of eight. **$15.95**

Crackajack Love by Bill Jackson

Brokeback Mountain meets the U.S. Army and Tinseltown in this tale of romance and intrigue. While serving Uncle Sam in 1960, Alexander Price dreams of becoming Hollywood's next great leading man while juggling his love life. He falls in love twice, first with a fellow soldier, then with the daughter of a TV star. Alex's journey is complex and sometimes tragic, but he discovers the power and determination of love in a story told with Southern frankness, compassion and humor against backdrops of Seoul, New York, Hollywood and others in the early 1960's. Adult content. **$18.95**

Bubba Goes To Alabama (hardcover)
by Kenneth David Mobley

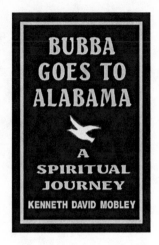

On the eighth day, God created Bubba, who makes friends with animals and wonders why he's the only one of his kind. When he realizes he was created by God, his prayers are answered, when on the ninth day, God creates Lucy, and they raise a family and all is well until a scout from another race, the Canites, comes to call. Eventually the Canites colonize near Bubba's home, and his children marry into the Canite tribe. But there's a secret Bubba and Lucy haven't told their children, a horrible secret that brings tragic results. Throughout it all, Bubba prays, has dialogues with God and is ultimately fast-forwarded into the future to Alabama, where he's befuddled by modern man. A spiritual journey with a lesson in faith no one should miss.   For all ages.   **$26.95**

The Moulin Huge by Robert Preston Ward

A hilarious and poignant tale of Evan and his two friends, Loyd and Diva . . . longtime friends who have gone their separate ways but who keep in touch by phone daily . . . who reunite in (of all places) a trailer park in Niceville, Florida, where Evan will make his performance debut in a drag show/talent contest. Evan lives in a fantasy world fueled by marijuana and wine. Family-rich Lloyd stars in his own melodramas. And Diva is never quite sure which reflection is hers and which is the mirror's. Divacity Press.   Adult content.   **$13.95**

All ThomasMax books are available through almost all booksellers, both retail stores and internet marketers. If your favorite store doesn't have the selection you want, ask the store to order it for you!

Printed in the United States
119832LV00002B/1-99/P